USA TODAY BESTSELLING AUTHOR

Dale Mayer

BARRET 04

SHADOW RECON

Books in This Series

Magnus, Book 1

Rogan, Book 2

Egan, Book 3

Barret, Book 4

Whalen, Book 5

Nikolai, Book 6

About This Book

Deep in the permafrost of the Arctic, a joint task force, comprised of over one dozen countries, comes together to level up their winter skills. A mix of personalities, nationalities, and egos bring out the best—and the worst—as these globally elite men and women work and play together. They rub elbows with hardy locals and a group of scientists gathered close by …

One fatality is almost expected with this training. A second is tough but not a surprise. However, when a third goes missing? It's hard to not be suspicious. When the missing man is connected to one of the elite Maverick team members and is a special friend of Lieutenant Commander Mason Callister? All hell breaks loose …

A teammate goes missing right as Barret arrives at the camp of horrors. Immediately he heads out to help in the search for the missing man – to no avail. And once again the numbers go down by one. No explanation, no body… nothing. Are drugs involved? Blackmail? Or stupid bets? There's too many options and none of them make any sense.

At least Avalon is there, a woman who caught his interest on the first day. Although she's just as confused and worried about what's going on in the arctic camp, she's level headed and with a great sense of humor.

Subbed in for someone who couldn't make it, Avalon ends up helping out in the kitchen. At least there she's warm and can keep busy. Until someone falls ill from suspected food poisoning and all eyes turn on her. She knows she hasn't done anything wrong, but tempers are short and she's an easy scape goat.

It's going to take both of them to keep her safe and get her out from under the cloud of suspicion. Thankfully Barret has no problem helping a damsel in distress…

Sign up to be notified of all Dale's releases here!
https://geni.us/DaleNews

PROLOGUE

A T DINNERTIME BARRET Dillinger walked into the dining area of the Arctic military base and stopped, surveying his surroundings. He understood from Mason some of what had just gone down. Sure enough, off in a corner, he saw four heads, two males and two females, huddled together at a table. Smiling, Barret walked over and sat down beside them, without any warning. Immediately the nearest woman stiffened, but he gave her a reassuring smile. "The name is Barret," he greeted her gently, then turned and looked at the men.

Magnus smiled at him. "You're here to help, aren't you?"

"If that's what you call it," he replied, with a casual glance around. "Not that anybody is supposed to know that," he added, with a warning.

Magnus nodded. "However, you'll find out very quickly that nothing stays quiet in this scenario."

"Of course not." Barret looked back at the women. "Which one of you is Berry?" Immediately the smaller of the two held up her hand.

"I'm Berry. This is Sydney. She's the doctor here."

"Honored," he said, "to meet you both." He looked around and added, "Sounds as if you guys have been having fun. You should share all those good times."

"Now you can take over. I've had all the fun I want,"

Berry declared, with a shudder. "Personally I'm okay to just have some peace and quiet for a while."

"And yet you're staying." Barret frowned, his gaze intent as he studied her.

She took a deep breath. "Yes, I am."

He nodded, not arguing with her at all. People had all kinds of reasons for staying after trying times such as this, and maybe she was in the right of it after all.

As another woman walked in and headed to the table, the woman grew nervous, her steps choppy. She looked over at Magnus. "May I speak to you for a minute?"

Magnus immediately stood. "Of course."

She pointed him toward the hallway.

At that, Barret joined him. "I'll come too, if that's okay."

She hesitated and frowned. "Sorry, but you're new."

"I am, indeed," he confirmed. "Therefore, I'm not connected to anything already going on." He watched as that worked its way through her thoughts, then she ignored him.

"Fine, as long as he says it's okay." She pointed to Magnus, who nodded.

"It's fine," Magnus murmured. "What's going on?"

She shook her head. "I haven't been able to find Scott anywhere."

Magnus stared at her. "Scott, as in kitchen assistant Scott?"

She nodded. "We're both new here, having come in a few days ago as replacements. Scott was here to help Chef, and I'm mostly doing reports and supplies for the compound. The base isn't very welcoming, so Scott and I just stuck together. Scott wasn't expecting this weather or the isolation. It's really bothering him, so I check on him throughout the day," she shared, with a side glance at Barret.

"I step into the kitchen sometimes to give him a hand, but, when I went there a couple times already today, I saw no sign of him. Now I just talked to Chef, and he hasn't seen Scott all day."

"All day?" Magnus repeated.

She nodded. "Chef told me Scott wasn't feeling well and went to lie down. I talked to him this morning, and he said he just needed some fresh air. This place, the isolation, being stuck inside, … he found it very claustrophobic."

"Ah, shit," Magnus said, as he turned toward Barret. "Nothing like jumping into the deep end."

"I'm all for it," Barret replied, still studying the woman. "What's your name?"

"Avalon Pritchard," she said, with a smile. "Please help Scott. He's a nice guy, and honestly he's not like a lot of the men here."

"When you say that, what do you mean?" Magnus asked.

She shrugged. "He's definitely not the alpha type. He's quiet, studious, shy, and a really nice guy. I'd hate for something bad to happen to him. Since arriving, we'd heard all kinds of horror stories. With all the shit that's been going on around this place," she explained, "when somebody goes missing …"

"*If* anybody goes missing," Barret corrected her immediately, then turned to look at Magnus. "I suggest we do a full-scale internal search and then head outside."

"Yeah, already on it," Magnus noted, holding up his phone. "We'll set up the sirens and send out a full search party," Magnus added for Avalon's benefit, with a smile.

Barnett turned to face Avalon. "Thanks for letting us know."

"Just find him please. I'd really hate to think of something else happening here." And, with that, her arms wrapped around her chest, she walked slowly back to the kitchen.

Barret turned to Magnus. "I guess you weren't expecting that, *huh?*"

"No, but we also don't know that it isn't a false alarm. Scott could just be out with the dogs or something."

"Ah, maybe I'll start there," Barret offered.

"Sure, you do that, but we can't waste time. If he's there, that's great. If he's not there, we'll be hitting the road real fast, before we lose out on any sunlight hours. In these temperatures, without proper outerwear and supplies, in twenty minutes you're done."

"Got it," Barret noted. "Considering that Scott might have been missing since sunup today, he's already well past that point."

"I know," Magnus replied, his voice dark. "Yet we can't assume anything, not yet."

DAY 1 LATE AFTERNOON

Hell of a deal up here, Mason. Fear is an undercurrent. Suspicion the overcurrent. Already out here to search for the newest missing person. No one can survive in these temperatures for long. Heard Teegan Rode has been missing, and still is, for weeks now. Doesn't bode well.

To say *jumping in with both feet* was to put it mildly. When Barret finally made it back inside too many hours later, he was cold and tired. His toes were thankfully numb for the moment, and his cheeks were burning red, as he quickly attempted to warm up. He'd been in cold environments before, and in ugly weather too, but both of them together, up here, was something else entirely. The dogs though, … they were loving it.

He loved working with dog teams, and it hadn't taken Barret long to get them onboard with the day's search. Joe had helped Barret harness the selected dogsled team, and he'd taken off. But to no avail. Not quite whiteout conditions but still very limited visibility, so he'd had to rely on the dogs' innate navigation abilities a time or two. Now back, with Joe's help, Barret had given the dogs a good rub behind the ears, and they were all happy and spread out, ready for a good nap. Barret was looking for some hot food and drink. "Joe, do you want me to bring you back something from the kitchen?"

Silent as ever, Joe shook his head, muttered something under his breath that Barret couldn't hear properly and probably didn't want to. In fact, Joe hadn't had a whole lot to say, but his expression had been pretty ugly when they'd come back in empty-handed. Barret had the same attitude himself.

Leaving Joe to his solitude and his canine companions, Barret felt a little jealous that he couldn't have a couple dogs in the main building with him. Barret headed to the kitchen area. When he walked in, many other people milled around, and the news had already filtered inside. An ugly rumbling murmured throughout the main dining room. Barret hadn't had a chance to get to his room yet or to get anything else accomplished, but, hey, he was here. So far, the suddenly missing person, Scott, was not.

It blew Barret's mind that somebody could just go out for a walk and disappear into thin air like that. It didn't make any sense to him, so, of course it made him suspicious as hell. Yet the entire camp had been turned inside out, and there was no sign of Scott. As Barret walked into the dining room looking for the nearest hot drink, he saw several of the men he had already met.

Magnus stood and waved at him. "Come on over here," he said, motioning to the group.

Barret nodded and pointed toward the front. "I'll just get a hot drink."

As soon as he grabbed a hot coffee, he moved slowly toward the group. The table was full with heated discussions regarding the situation. As he sat down, several of them looked at him, a question in their eyes, and he shook his head.

Shoulders sagged and Avalon, who he remembered from

earlier, cried out in frustration, her voice shaking. "I don't understand. How could he have just disappeared?"

"If he didn't hook on to a lifeline," Magnus pointed out, "it would be way too easy to get lost in the present near-whiteout conditions here."

If he hadn't hooked on the safety line as soon as he stepped out, and only held on with a hand, it was easy to release the rope to wipe the blowing snow from your face, to pull your hood in closer, or to do any other number of hand gestures people made without thinking. After that? Then trying to find the safety rope—probably still within arm's reach but now completely invisible—well, without that guiding rope, it would be almost impossible to find his way back.

In a storm such as this, as soon as you go out more than a couple feet, you couldn't find where you belonged. And the heavy snowfall would cover your body in very short order.

"Damn it, that's exactly why those ropes are there," Barret snapped. He glared around at the group, trying to get his temper under control. "I know he was well trained in these dangers, so I'm not sure what the hell went on."

"He had a fight with somebody this morning," Avalon noted in a clipped tone. "I know that he stormed off, pretty upset. It's possible that he just didn't think about it."

"That temper may have just gotten him killed." Magnus looked over at Barret in agreement.

She hesitated and then whispered in a lower voice, "But wouldn't you have found his body?"

"Not yet," Barret replied. "We can't find anything out there in these conditions. We'd have to trip over it, and believe me. Right now you can't tell a lump in front of you from a dip. Therefore, until this weather calms down—"

At that, somebody at a nearby table snorted and called out, "Mother Nature's a bitch."

Barret looked over at him and nodded. "Yeah, it seems as if we're in for a spat of ugly weather again."

At that, the other people in the dining room slowly dispersed. In silence. The crowd too depressed to grumble. Or too afraid.

As he sat there pondering what Magnus had just said, Barret faced Avalon. "Do you know who he had the fight with?"

She shook her head. "No, I don't. I just heard somebody mention that there had been some yelling and grumbling, so I presume Scott just headed off in a temper."

"Could be a bunch of reasons for that too," Barret pointed out. "What we have to do at the moment is make sure we stick to facts."

She glared at him. "If I had any more facts, I would have found him myself."

"Did you go out looking?"

"I did right away," she stated, "but I didn't go outside the building. I just stood in the open doorway looking for him, and, of course, I couldn't do that for long either," she muttered, wrapping her arms around her shoulders. "God, this place is just ... it'll take us all out, won't it?"

"No, it won't," Barret snapped. "It never has before. I don't know why this particular training session is so jinxed."

"I hear a lot of the gossip," Avalon replied. "An awful lot of people on base think that the curse is powerful enough that the survival camp should be shut down before anyone else dies. I know a lot of the guys are rumored to be contacting their bosses and asking for a way out."

"Sure they are," Magnus agreed in a quiet tone. "They've

been doing that since the first guy went missing, yet the same reasons for denying those requests still apply. We could have a murderer in this group," he pointed out, his voice low. "So nobody leaves."

"*Yeah*, but," Avalon argued, "I also heard that nobody else was entitled to come either, and you guys keep breaking that rule."

Magnus smiled at her. "Different rules for different folks."

"*Sure.*" She raised both hands in frustration. "Doesn't that just confuse the issue?"

"I don't see how," Magnus noted calmly. "We must have some men to replace the ones who died or went missing."

She shot a look at Barret. "So, how do you feel about being a replacement for a dead man?"

He gave her a flat look and shrugged. "It's not as if it's the first time."

She winced. "Great, as if I needed *that* in my thoughts." She got up and added, "I'll lie down for a little bit before dinner."

"Maybe you should stay here and get warm," Barret suggested to her. "I noticed that you haven't stopped shivering."

"That's why I wanted to go lie down," she muttered. "I know I wasn't out there all that long, but the cold has been with me all day now, and I still can't get warm."

He moved a chair into the corner and pointed. "Sit here."

"Why?" she asked, staring at him as if he were off his rocker.

"Because my body heat will help warm you up," he stated. "And this isn't the time to think that I'm coming on to you. I'm not." His tone sounded harsher than he intended.

"You're obviously freezing, which isn't something to fool around with."

She hesitated and then slipped between him and the wall. She gasped almost immediately. "You're a bloody furnace," she blurted out, twisting to look at him. He shifted over a little more, and she ended up almost too tightly up against the wall.

"Now, just stay where you are, and let's see if we can get that body temperature back up."

"I hate to admit it, but I was wondering if I should see Sydney."

Barret raised an eyebrow. "The doctor?"

"Yes, although why she's still here, I don't know. Especially after what she's been through."

"She's here because she wants to see this thing to the end," Magnus stated from the other side of the table.

Avalon nodded. "Believe me. It's nothing against her. It's just, if there were a way to get out of here …" Avalon groaned. "I shouldn't whine, but sometimes you just wonder if there is some reason, something voodoo that you don't know about going on here. Then, because you didn't know, it's coming around to get you."

Magnus's lips quirked. "I do know what you mean, but I'm pretty sure that all the problems here are man-made."

She hunched into a smaller ball. "If you're trying to make me feel better," she said in a hoarse whisper, "that's not working."

He nodded. "You haven't seen too much action, have you?" She glared at him, and he held up a hand. "Hey, I'm just asking."

"No, I haven't," she admitted. "And honestly after this? … I'm seriously wondering if I want to just find something else to do with my life."

"You still have to serve out your time," he pointed out.

"Yeah, but that doesn't mean I have to do it up here."

"Did you not ask to come?"

"I was subbed in for somebody," she explained, rolling her eyes. "I didn't really think about it. I just thought, *Yeah, why not.* I mean, what a great experience, right?" She shuddered. "Talk about the mother of all bad ideas."

Magnus chuckled. "Oh, I don't think it's so much a bad idea as much as potentially bad people are involved in this."

"Oh, it's always bad people," she muttered. "At least that's my take on it. I don't think Mother Nature is bad. I think she can be a bitch, but I'm not sure she does it out of maliciousness. But people? Now that's a different story." She continued to explain. "I mean, look at what's happened so far and at the people found to be involved. What the hell were they doing?" she cried out. "Using drugs of all things."

Barret just nodded. He'd been brought somewhat up to speed with a quick overview of some of these issues, and it was shocking that it would have happened up here at a military base under these circumstances, since this was not a location to fool around with. Conditions here were far too unforgiving. Yet, at the same time, people will be people and, as such, could do the dumbest things for all kinds of reasons.

"And yet you know that Cherry only took the drugs to try to get through being so isolated up here," Magnus pointed out. "Same goes for Yegorahn at the core of it."

"Yeah, really? Yet Raffi was using drugs too, but that was all about blackmail, trying to get Berry out of the way. Permanently even. And he wanted more drugs to control his operation to win over Cherry."

Barret shook his head. "Whoever was involved and

found out about so far, they've paid a high price. Some have paid the ultimate price."

She groaned. "I know. I know. Both Yegorahn with his life and Raffi forfeiting his freedom and his military career. God, this place though." Avalon looked around, as if a deer caught in headlights. "It's starting to be too much, ... even the wind howling."

"That's when you need to stop the complaining because you can't control Mother Nature," Barret declared, "and just keep your focus on feeling warm."

She let out her breath with a harsh sigh and nodded. The discussion continued for a little longer, but, about ten minutes later, Barret turned to Avalon and noted, "You're not shivering anymore."

She nodded and gave him a hesitant smile. "Thank you for that. I didn't realize someone could produce that amount of heat."

He chuckled. "Some of us are just hot bodies," he noted.

"Yeah, but you were out all day, so you should be freezing."

He shrugged. "I was cold, but my body's returned to normal."

Just then Chef came out and told them that dinner would be a little late.

She winced and nodded. "That's because he doesn't have any help."

Magnus snorted and turned around to frown at Chef. "That bad, *huh*?"

"That'll have to change," Barret said.

"Yeah, good luck with that," somebody replied from behind him. "You go talk to the boss. I'm not doing it anytime soon."

Magnus nodded. "I have somebody who can talk to the CO." And, with a fat grin, he pulled out his phone and texted someone.

Barret wasn't sure who Magnus had contacted but noted, "That should have been done earlier today."

"Hopefully it was addressed by Chef," Magnus replied, "but he's still got nobody here full-time and hasn't had someone permanently assigned to the kitchen for quite a while. That'll be a problem."

"At least until he adapts," said the disgruntled guy at the next table.

"Sure," Magnus agreed, "but it's not the easiest thing running a camp for this many and with short rations."

"No, but I've seen it done all the time," the argumentative guy pointed out and got an eye roll and some grumbling from the present company.

"Sure, and Chef is great, but the circumstances here are not the easiest to work under."

"No, I'll give you that," he muttered.

Not too long afterward they were headed back to their table with plates full of food. When they sat back down again, Barret wasn't surprised that Avalon sat down beside him.

She smiled. "Hey, I won't turn down free heat," she muttered.

"No, and you don't have to," he said, with a chuckle. "Glad you're smart enough to make good use of it."

At that, somebody nearby looked over at them and offered, "Hey, if you want a warm blanket for the night, I'm pretty happy to be there for you." The comment was made in good humor thankfully.

She laughed it off. "No, I'm good, thanks."

"You are sharing a room, right?" one of the guys asked. "It would certainly be warmer if you were."

"I am," she replied easily, but Barret picked up a hitch in her voice and realized she was lying through her teeth. Was that a safety thing? Maybe, considering all the problems that they'd had here at this camp in recent weeks.

When the pushy guy left, and the numbers in the dining room dwindled down, Avalon started to get up.

Barret quickly grabbed her hand and gently tugged her back down again for a moment. Surprised, she looked at him. He leaned over and, under his breath, whispered, "Are you worried about somebody showing up at your room overnight?"

She hesitated and looked around and then shrugged. "Some of the problems lately sure make you consider that. I'm feeling way more cautious than I was before."

"Did you want to change your room reassignment so you do have someone else nearby?" He studied her face, looking for the truth. "Surely there aren't that many bunks here."

"No, I understand, but I honestly didn't want to make a fuss about it."

He nodded, then pulled out his phone and said, "Grab my number, and, if you have a problem in the night, you call me." She frowned at him, and he shrugged. "Hey, you've already trusted me enough to grab some body heat, now don't hesitate to grab a little protection if you need it."

"I'm not supposed to need it, you know?" she muttered.

"At times we all need it," he declared. "And, in the middle of the night, if somebody is encroaching boundaries, having an edge can make all the difference."

"I do know basic self-defense techniques. You know

that, right?" she muttered. He just stared at her steadily. She frowned and then snatched his phone and typed her number in a text box for him. "That's mine."

She hit Send, and her phone buzzed with his response. She looked down at it and put his name in. "Thanks. Let's hope I never need it."

"I hope so too," he agreed. "However, there have been enough issues here that this could help."

"Yeah, that's true enough," she muttered.

"Speaking of drugs, were they all found?" Barret asked, looking over at Magnus, who'd been watching the byplay.

"We're not sure," Magnus admitted. "It depends on how much each person was given, and we don't have any way to calculate that. And that's just counting the people we know were drugged, not others who may have been as well. So it's entirely possible there are more drugs still floating around."

"Damn." Barret frowned at that and shook his head. "That means nobody's safe, male or female."

"Yeah, don't worry. We've all thought of that," Avalon noted, still seated beside him. "Maybe you want my number for protection?" she teased, batting her eyes at him.

"I already got it," he declared, flashing her a quick grin and appreciating the sense of humor. "Don't worry. I'll call if I need help."

She burst out laughing, got up, patted him on the shoulder, and said, "Do that."

AVALON WAS STILL chuckling to herself as she walked down the hallway to her room. She really appreciated Barret's sense of humor. The fact that he was a new guy was fun, someone interesting, and, because he wasn't here when all the other shit went down, safe. So that gave him a completely different appeal than any of the other guys she had been studiously avoiding getting too close to.

She'd had a roommate, up until the woman had moved in with one of the guys. With all the problems lurking inside these walls, Avalon certainly understood the woman's desire to move in with her boyfriend, but it also left Avalon more vulnerable and more alone. Of course she wouldn't do anything to stop romance from happening, even if it was just for the sake of convenience and safety. However, Avalon still made a point of not advertising the fact that she was bunking on her own.

Not that it would take much for anybody to find out, and that was another concern. Yet it was interesting that Barret had seen through her ruse and had picked up on it, providing his number to call, should she run into problems. Yet running into problems was not something that they were supposed to do here. She had all the same training as everybody else, except she didn't have special weapons training, and that was on her bucket list to get, whenever it was on the table.

The trouble was, when it came to armed combat, she was still at a disadvantage just in size. She was five-five and 135 pounds, but everybody around here was way-the-hell bigger, and it wouldn't take very much for somebody to get the jump on her. That was her main concern, even with the training she had. She didn't want to even consider the added factor of drugs on base.

Shaking her head, she knew she was equipped to take on most people with equal skills and no weapons involved. However, those with better skills or guns, not to mention the possibility of their getting the drop on her and she were taken completely unaware, it would be that much harder for her to rebound into a position of power.

That was not a thought she wanted to take to bed with her. Frowning, she quickly went to the bathroom and got ready for bed, then headed back to her room, checking to make sure nobody was looking when she stepped into her room and quickly locked it behind her. Locking it was kind of a foolish thing though, since there wasn't a lock in this place that anybody with decent skills couldn't pick, something she had considered many times.

And yet what was she supposed to do when her roommate asked if Avalon would mind being on her own? It's not as if she wanted to say no, and the woman would have just spent all her time away with her boyfriend anyway, instead of making it official. There wasn't any good to come from saying no, but still, as Avalon lay in bed, listening to the various sounds around her, it bothered her to think that, in the back of her mind, there was always that level of fear that kept her nervous all the time.

She frowned at that.

When she got a text, she looked at her phone and smiled. It was Barret, asking if she was tucked in for the night. She sent back a one-word response. **Yes.**

He gave her a smiley face and a thumbs-up at the same time. She smiled, curled up in bed, and fell into a deep sleep.

DAY 2 WEE HOURS OF THE MORNING

W HEN AVALON WOKE up in the middle of the night, she wasn't sure what had disturbed her. As she sat up in the bed and looked around, she pulled the blankets closer, shivering in the cold. She heard voices and running foot-steps. She hesitated, not sure she wanted to get up and find out what was going on. However, knowing everything else happening around her, turning a blind eye wasn't smart either.

She quickly dressed and headed toward the dining room, which was where everybody gathered. As she stepped in, she looked around and noted Barret talking to Magnus. She slipped over beside them and asked, "What's going on?"

Barret wrapped an arm around her shoulders, pulled her up close, then, against her ear, he whispered, "They found Scott."

She stiffened and looked over at him, mentally preparing herself. "Who? Somebody's been out there searching at this hour?"

He shook his head. "No. I guess Chef heard something and got up, not sure what it was. He got dressed and went out and did a full-on check all around the building itself. Still not liking the scenario, he got Magnus out of bed, and they went out to check the generator and the outer perime-ter. They found Scott bundled up outside. He'd been left close to the rear kitchen door, beside the generator shed."

She stared at him in shock. "Dead?" she asked, her voice in a hoarse whisper. Only it came out more as a squeak.

He nodded. "Yes, he's dead. I'm sorry. Looks as if he froze to death."

She sucked back her breath and slowly nodded. "So …"

"Yeah." Barret glanced at Magnus. "Magnus suggested that somebody named Amelia may have returned him. However, it could have been somebody from the nearby village too."

Avalon stared at Barret and then nodded slowly. "But she's supposed to be missing too. So, if she's not missing, that means she's keeping a close eye on the place." He nodded at that, and she almost shrieked. "Jesus, if that's the case, why haven't we been able to find her?"

Magnus turned to her and, in a low tone, said, "Keep your voice down, please. As to your question, she clearly doesn't want to be found. And we don't know if she did return Scott. Remember. It could have been one of the locals."

Her breath came out in a *whoosh*, and she nodded slowly, obviously feeling stunned. "But still, this was an ugly accident, right?" When there was no response, she looked back and forth between them. "Right?"

Magnus shrugged. "We don't really know at this point. The doc is inspecting his body right now. We won't know the cause of death until an autopsy is done, which obviously can't be done here."

"*Great*," Avalon muttered, "so none of us get any more sleep tonight then, do we?"

"And this will just get the rumors going again too," Magnus stated, looking at her. "So please don't add to them."

She shook her head. "I wasn't planning on it. I just wanted to find out what was going on," she explained. "I heard footsteps up and down the hallway, and I wasn't sure."

"Now that you know, it might be a good idea to go back to bed and see if you can grab some more sleep," Barret suggested. "There'll be another investigation."

She winced. "I feel as if I've been questioned to death already."

He chuckled. "Really no other way to handle it except to keep asking questions. Who saw what, who saw what where, who saw what when."

"And yet most of us don't even realize what we did see, even when we see it," she replied. "So many of us have just been so wrapped up in our own crazy world that we haven't thought about what we're looking at."

He studied her and then nodded. "I get that," he murmured. "I don't suppose you have information by any chance, do you?"

She shook her head. "Not really. I mean, I did see Cherry going into Yegorahn's room, way back when," she shared, "and I realized they were having an affair, but it didn't occur to me that, when he left the room not all that much later, something else was going on."

"It's probably when he wanted to get his drug supply," Barret guessed. "I didn't realize you had seen that."

"And I didn't realize what I'd seen was of any value," she exclaimed, raising both hands. "It's not as if they were the only two visiting each other at night. Even now I'm not sure I told anybody about it. I mean, I saw him, but that doesn't mean much. A lot of people go in and out of various rooms all the time."

"No, it doesn't have any value, not in and of itself, but, because of all this craziness, … it might have been important at the time."

She frowned at that. "I hope not," Avalon grumbled. "I would hate to think I had any knowledge that could have helped somebody."

"I know that," Barret confirmed, with a half smile. "Just keep your eyes and ears open, and, if you see anything now, … I suggest you let us know."

"Right, but Yegorahn's dead," she noted. "A lot of people are dead now, Scott being the latest."

"So, you're the one who alerted us to Scott's disappearance."

"Well, yes, because I'd been looking for him," she stated. "I just … I'd heard something about him having an argument. I didn't pick up on it being a big deal or anything, until he didn't show up again. Then I was talking to Chef, who was pissed because Scott needed time off, and, while Chef understood, he wouldn't approve it because they were short-handed. Instead he gave the kid some time to go out and take a bit of a break, and somehow Scott got into a confrontation with somebody and ended up storming outside to clear his head."

"Only he ended up dead. And dead happens when you go outside not dressed to be out there. And that is one of the things that we did see. Scott wasn't dressed for this weather. He went out there to have a cigarette and basically curled up in a corner, puffing away, and died."

"Only he wasn't there to begin with, was he?"

"No, he wasn't, and somebody wrapped him up so we couldn't miss him."

"So, in theory, we could have found him earlier, when

you went out looking again, right?"

"That's possible, and now we're heading out to see if we can follow the tracks that left his body there."

"But why? I don't understand that. If Amelia wanted to come in, she would have. And if she wanted anything to with us, she would have contacted someone."

"Maybe," Magnus agreed, looking at her intently. "Yet you have to wonder if she's the one calling the shots behind any of this."

Avalon stared at him in shock and then shook her head. "Please don't say that. Jesus, that's the last thing I want to contemplate."

"Why?" Magnus asked. "Because you have built her up as being some sort of independent scientist, sticking it out in the wilderness on her own, all just to avoid dealing with the craziness happening here?"

She stared at him and shook her head. "Wow, that's pretty rough. I was surprised she hasn't gone back to the scientists' camp. Even without the generator, surely it would be warmer than braving Mother Nature outside."

"Not necessarily. If she's got any skills to make a winter protection, she could be doing just fine."

"What about the rest of her team?"

"I don't know. We're not even sure how many scientists are still here. We got conflicting information on that. It's possible that two of them are out there together. It's also possible that the rest of Amelia's team left by another route at another time. We just don't know."

Barret frowned at Magnus. "Has anybody checked in with the village lately? Sounds as if the Inuit settlement has been helpful in that regard."

Magnus shook his head. "Not recently, but maybe I'll

make a trip." Then he frowned and added, "You know what? Mountain might have."

"Right. He was spending some time there, wasn't he?" Barret noted.

Magnus nodded at that. "But I'm not sure how recently that was."

"Are you thinking Amelia's there?" Barret asked.

"Or dropped off some of her team there."

Barret laughed. "The way you guys are talking, it sounds as if, were anybody out there who could handle surviving in these elements, it might be Amelia. And yet why?"

"Why not?" Magnus countered. "What she's doing is not illegal. If she doesn't like anything she's hearing about the base, then that makes sense. She did have at least one of our team members, and, if he lived long enough or told her something about what was going on here, maybe she wouldn't come back here on her own," Magnus suggested. "So, it kind of makes sense, and again she's not doing anything illegal. Plus, so far, she's been a help."

"*If* it's her," Barret pointed out.

At that, Magnus's face thinned, and he nodded. "Exactly."

Barret added, "Who's to say what is going on out there in her mind or what she believes is going on here at the base as well."

"Yeah, as usual, we have more questions than answers," Magnus stated, looking frustrated. "Were you going outside this morning?"

"I'm probably fresher than a lot of people, so yeah," Barret confirmed. "Count me in. Sounds like an opportunity to track her."

"Or whoever it was who dropped Scott off," Magnus

corrected.

"No notes or anything?" Avalon asked both men.

"No, that implies they would have something to write a note with," Magnus noted. "Maybe she thinks we would figure it out anyway. I mean, she had wrapped him up in a blanket."

"Can you identify the blanket?" Avalon asked.

"I can't, but that doesn't mean somebody here can't." Magnus gave her a quick lift of his shoulders. "Anyway, all of that is in Sydney's hands at the moment."

Avalon twisted and looked in the general direction of the medical clinic. "I wonder if I should go see if she needs help."

"I don't know that she does," he replied thoughtfully. "You don't have any nursing training, do you?"

"No, I don't," Avalon admitted. "I'd be better off helping Chef in the kitchen." And then she winced. "God, I really would be better off helping him, wouldn't I?"

"If you can, he definitely needs it. We can round him up some help and run shifts in the kitchen, but right now he could probably use a hand. He's had a really shitty start to the day."

"Right." She nodded. "Let me go see if he's up for it and if he even wants a hand, considering many chefs are territorial. Just for the day though," she added, with an eye roll.

"Yeah, well, we can get Chef to make rotating assignments if we need to," Magnus noted, "even if they're not terribly handy in the kitchen, it's still another body. We'll give Chef some time to figure out what he wants."

"Right." Avalon turned and headed toward the kitchen.

As she walked in, she found Chef sitting on the floor, leaning against one of his coolers, sipping a cup of coffee, his eyes shut. She walked over to him and sat down across from him. He opened his eyes, looking at her with a questioning gaze.

"Look. I know it's Scott out there," she shared, "and I'm really sorry." He just nodded. "I came to see if you needed a hand today, until they can get you some regular help."

"Scott wasn't even regular help," Chef noted, "but, yeah. I could use some help, if you're up for it. You any good in the kitchen?"

She snorted. "Probably about the same as everybody else here. Am I a chef? Hell no. Have I got any formal prep work experience? No. Was I raised with lots of brothers and sisters, and did I have to help my mom? Oh yeah."

He laughed. "I'll take it. Right about now, I don't really have a whole lot of choice."

"That's what I figured," she said. "Obviously this isn't what I want to do for the rest of my life or even while I'm here. However, right now, I know that meals still need to be prepped, so, if you can put me to work until we can get you some proper help, that would be a step forward."

He nodded. "Thanks. Do you want to have a coffee first?"

"Yeah, I really would like a coffee." Then she laughed. "I guess there are perks to being here and helping, aren't there?"

"There absolutely are." Chef gave her a wan smile. "Yet apparently there are also dangers."

"I don't think you're to blame for this one," she replied. "My understanding is Scott got upset about something and headed outside."

"Yeah, sounds as if he had a confrontation with some-body, and I don't even know what it was about. He headed out for a cigarette. I've told him time and time again not to go out without fully gearing up, but he just told me that he was a tough bugger. The trouble is, when the temperatures drop like that, you really don't even get much chance to understand just how cold it is and how quickly that cold hits your lungs. Then, when you're breathing in smoke from a lit cigarette, it can mask how quickly you go down. So, in this case, it looks to be an accidental death, but it was another death we sure didn't need for morale around here."

"I agree with you there," Avalon muttered, as she poured herself a coffee and sat down beside him. "I've only been here a month, and I already want to leave. So, for those who have been here since the beginning of this training session, I totally understand how everybody else requested the opportunity to get out, even though they were all denied."

"Yep." Chef sighed. "Everybody who's been here from the beginning is still here, unless they left in custody or in a body bag."

"*Great*," Avalon huffed. "Given those options, I think I'll stay."

He burst out laughing and nodded. "That's the best attitude to have," he said, with a dry tone. He tossed back the rest of his coffee. "I'll get started with breakfast. You any good at flipping pancakes?"

"I can be," she replied, looking at him with a smile. "I've certainly done a few in my time."

He nodded. "Good. We're getting a late start today with breakfast. So we'll do a fast brunch menu. I'll mix up the batter and get the griddle going for you." And, with that, he headed over into the kitchen area, while she quickly drank her coffee. Feeling better with something to do, she got up and dove in to help.

DAY 2 MORNING AFTER BREAKFAST

AFTER BREAKFAST WAS over for everyone else, Avalon sat down with her meal, tired but happy to have had something occupy her morning and keep all those depressing thoughts at bay. The colonel caught most of the trainees having breakfast and made several announcements, including condolences and a *chin up all around* message, followed by *stay strong* and *hang in there* speeches, that no one particularly appreciated. By the time the colonel had finished speaking, a pall had fallen over the dining room. When he walked away, a dead silence remained, as people just couldn't believe that, once again, somebody was gone.

She hadn't seen any sign of Magnus or Barret and couldn't help but wonder if they'd found anything else. When she looked up next, they bustled in. She smiled. "You know that you guys missed breakfast." They stopped and stared, and she shrugged. "However, I happen to know there's a little bit to spare in the back room."

"Any chance of us getting some of that spare food?" Barret asked, as he walked over with his hands out. She saw how cold they were and bounced to her feet.

"I'll get you some food, as long as you don't touch me with those little slabs of ice," she stated, as she disappeared into the back. As soon as she saw Chef, she told him, "The two men out searching are back, and they missed breakfast."

He peered around the corner and nodded. "Serve them whatever we've got left."

"Yeah, that's what I was thinking," she agreed. "They headed out the first time in the wee hours, so going out again to find the tracks, I know they're cold and tired."

He smiled at her. "And you have a soft spot for one of them."

"Hey, I was pretty cold last night, and he stepped in to warm me up, and that goes a long way."

"It does, indeed," Chef replied. "And there's still coffee for them."

"Yeah, and that's only because you didn't tell anybody you'd made more."

"Nope, I sure didn't." He chuckled.

She came out with two steaming mugs and put them down in front of the guys, then returned with plates of pancakes, scrambled eggs, sausages, and the last of the bacon. When they took one look at the feast in front of them, their eyebrows shot up.

"Hey," she explained, "I've been working in the kitchen all morning, so eat while you can. No guarantee that the next guy helping out will give you the same treatment."

"I'm not arguing," Magnus said, around a mouthful of food. "This is much appreciated. Burned a lot of calories skiing."

"Skis?" she asked, with a shiver. "Did you find anything?"

They looked at each other and shrugged. "Maybe."

She sat down hard and whispered, "Is that a good maybe or a bad maybe?"

In a whisper, Barret replied, "We're not sure yet, so don't pass it on."

She nodded. "Good enough. It sure would be nice if we had an idea of who was behind all this bullshit though."

"It kind of depends on if we've got somebody behind all the bullshit or if we've got somebody behind all the good things," Magnus pointed out.

"I'm voting that Amelia is behind the good things," Avalon shared, "and that we'll find the asshole who's behind all the rest of it."

"*If* there is somebody behind all the rest of it," Magnus pointed out again.

"How can there not be?" she muttered. "It's not as if we've been killing ourselves off."

"No, there haven't been any suicides, as far as we know."

"Including Scott," she muttered.

He nodded. "Believe me. We're not thinking that at all. I think he went out for a smoke, maybe walked a few steps away, and lost his bearings."

"That's not good because that would really suck." While the men were busy eating, she got up and refilled their coffees, then sat down again.

"Will you keep working in the kitchen?" Magnus asked her.

"I don't know," she answered. "I was kind of hoping that somebody wanted to relieve me, but I'm afraid that, having stepped into this position, I might find myself pigeonholed into it."

"You probably will right now at least, while everybody's in shock," Magnus noted. "I'll see what I can do about that, but, if you're okay to help out for a day or two, it would be great."

"How about one day?" she suggested, with an eye roll.

He nodded. "It might be a couple days."

"*Great.*" Yet she smiled brightly. "At least I get coffee this way."

Barret nodded. "And apparently so do we, so thanks."

She laughed. "If I'm staying to help for the rest of the day, I guess I better get back there. It's amazing how much food is required to feed everybody around here." And, with that, she quickly headed back to the kitchen. Chef looked up, and she nodded. "They're chowing down pretty well."

"What about you?" he asked, giving her a long assessing look.

"I ate earlier, and, for the moment, I'm here to help. I don't know how long that'll last, but, as long as I've got some time on my hands, I don't mind pitching in."

"I appreciate it," Chef noted. "I'll throw a bunch of roasts in the oven, and we'll do up some pasta with it for dinner. We also need to get some lunch on, but we have some leftovers for that."

He quickly launched into a discussion that she understood, even if she didn't see how they would get it all done. Shaking her head, she said, "Just tell me what you want me to do. I'll pick it up as I go along."

He did exactly that, and she spent hours peeling potatoes, setting up rice, and making pasta. He tossed her a couple recipe cards which she looked at, nodded, then quickly made four spice cakes.

By the time she had them in the oven, she turned toward him and asked, "What's next?"

He laughed. "Anytime you want to work in my kitchen, you're more than welcome."

"Yeah, well, that would imply it was a choice," she pointed out, with a grin.

But, sure enough, lunch came and went, and she was

still working and had settled into a rhythm. By the time dinner was served, she felt the fatigue hitting her.

Chef looked at her and said, "Go eat, and then you better crash."

"Yeah, but you haven't had a break either."

"No, but I'm used to it," he muttered. "No breaks for me."

"What about dishes?"

"Oh yeah, don't worry. I've got hot water on for those."

She winced. "Of course you do," she muttered. "I'll come back in a bit and get those started."

And she did just that. By the time she had the bulk of those wrapped up, she felt pretty done in. As she turned to look to see if anything else needed to be done, she caught sight of Barret, standing there, studying her.

"You look wasted."

"Not exactly the kind of work I was expecting to do today, and, with just two of us doing it all, it's been pretty intense," she muttered.

He nodded. "Not a bad thing though."

"Meaning that I don't have any spare time or energy to think about other things?"

"Exactly." He smiled. "It is what it is. And we all appreciate that you did step in—especially Chef."

"*Great*," she muttered. "So, what are you up to?"

"I'm about to sit down and have a hot chocolate before I crash," he admitted. "It's been a long day for me too."

"I'll grab one too and some food." She looked around, frowning. "There was some soup left, I think."

"Didn't you eat earlier?"

"I did, but since then it feels as if I've done another full shift." She groaned. "The mountain of dishes after a meal is like … insane."

"Maybe everybody needs to start doing their own."

She looked at him and nodded. "I think I'll check in with Chef and maybe set that up for the morning."

"Good idea," Barret agreed. "No reason people here can't wash their own dishes. Everybody's short-staffed, and, if nothing else, they need to pitch in."

"Oh, I get it," she stated. "I'm just sad that I didn't think of it earlier. I spent hours washing dishes today."

He laughed. "Come on. Let's go sit for a bit and relax. Then you can head to bed early."

"Early to bed," she repeated. "God, I don't know that it's early at all. Feels as if I've done a sixteen-hour day."

"You pretty much have," he noted. "It's well past nine."

She frowned, checked her watch, and whistled. "You're right. How the hell did that happen?"

"It's called being busy."

With him sitting beside her, she asked, "How about an update?" He looked over at her and shook his head. She frowned, and he frowned right back. She groaned and then whispered, "You can't tell me, can you?"

AVALON DOESN'T NEED to know, Barret thought to himself. Maybe not, but, then again, maybe she does. Trying to put his wry thoughts into order, he faced her. "I can't tell you much, that's for sure," he replied. "Our investigation is ongoing."

"Nobody came and talked to me."

He frowned at her, looked around, and asked, "Seriously?"

She nodded. "I mean, I've been in the kitchen all day though, so I gather I've gone invisible," she added in a sarcastic tone. "Nice to know my highly-vaunted naval career put me here in a kitchen."

"Hey, it's honest work."

"It is, indeed, but somehow—when you get ignored while investigating Scott's death, when I was the one who reported him missing—it feels as if you've been slotted into *women's work.*"

"I don't think that's the intention," he stated.

"Probably not, and I'm just tired, so ignore me," she muttered, shaking her head. "Why the hell would I even want to be questioned anyway?"

At that exact moment, Magnus walked over. "There you are."

"Exactly where I have been all day," she snapped, looking at him warily. "In the damn kitchen."

"All day?" he asked, surprised.

She nodded. "Yeah, all day. Chef hasn't had a break, and neither have I."

He frowned at that, then turned and walked out again.

"Now will that make me a troublemaker?" she asked.

"I don't know," Barret admitted, "but, considering we've got a lot of people here, no reason they can't do shifts."

"You say that, but …"

At that, Magnus came back, sat down with them, and said, "The CO will think about it."

She raised an eyebrow. "As long as I'm getting overtime, make that triple overtime," she joked.

"Which, of course, up here on the base, you are not."

"I know. I was kidding." She sighed. "But believe me, this makes me consider wanting to get out right away."

"Even after one day?"

"Yeah. Volunteering seems to have put me into a permanent position, hasn't it?"

"No, it won't be," Magnus corrected. "I hear Egan is good in the kitchen, but, at the moment, we're doing all these interviews, so …"

She shrugged, not sure how that was supposed to make a difference. "I'm okay for a while," she shared, "but Chef will burn out if he doesn't get a break, and I'm not sure he's had one since the beginning of this mess. Plus Scott isn't the first helper Chef's lost. Chef has cooking with little to no help down to quite an art. Yet, at the same time, it still makes for a hard day."

"No, I get it," Magnus agreed, looking back over at the kitchen area. "I think spiritually he's pretty low."

"Well yeah, he's the one who deals with it all. I don't even know how they take breaks here," she shared, looking back at the kitchen, "because there hasn't been one all day. I got a few minutes, but then I tossed a few cakes into the oven and went straight into working on dinner."

They looked at her. "Cakes?"

She nodded. "I made a bunch of spice cakes."

"They didn't come out," Barret noted, nudging her.

She looked at him. "Didn't they?" She frowned and shrugged. "Maybe Chef has plans for them for later."

"There was no dessert."

"I won't go get them," she declared, with a laugh. "That would be overstepping my authority, especially since Chef asked me specifically to make them. So, if suddenly they're not there, that'll just get me in shit."

"Tomorrow?" Barret asked hopefully.

"Maybe," she murmured. "Guess it depends on what

Chef's got planned." At that, she yawned and groaned. "I have to crash."

"And I need a good night's sleep tonight too," Barret chipped in.

"I guess we all do," Magnus stated, looking back and forth between them curiously.

"Yep, you sure do. Come on. Let's get you down to your quarters," Barret suggested, looking over at her.

"I can get there on my own," she replied, as she slowly stood up, but Barret wouldn't take no for an answer.

"Come on. Let's go."

He walked her down to her room and waited until she got inside. At her door, she looked around, then whispered, "Is there a reason you're being so protective?"

"Not any more than usual," he replied, with a gentle smile. "Just get some sleep."

He waited until she went in and locked the door, knowing that the lock was completely useless in this military base. However, it gave some people a sense of security, and, if it helped her sleep tonight, then he was okay with it. In truth, she looked to be absolutely exhausted.

He made his way back to the kitchen and sat down across from Magnus. "Is nobody helping out in the kitchen?"

Magnus smirked, rolled his eyes, and said, "The brass seems to think it's all fine."

"So they're supposed to work all the time without a break, while the rest of us hide in our rooms, is that it?"

"You and I won't be hiding in our rooms," Magnus confirmed, "but apparently some of the international people don't have to do these kinds of jobs, not if they don't want to."

"Do they want to eat?" Barret asked in a conversational

tone.

"That's the way I feel, but the colonel says that we already have enough problems right now and that he's not expecting too much cooperation."

"But he's not putting out a call for volunteers either, is he?" Barret asked in a monotone.

"No, he has, however, requested somebody new to come up and help out in the kitchen."

"And yet, how will that fly with these people, when they aren't allowed to leave, yet we're still bringing in more replacements as the days go by? Doesn't that create more dissent?"

"Yeah, but the reality is, as we lose somebody, we get another to fill the void."

"God, that's awful," Barret muttered.

"Believe me. I know, and it's not how we want to look at it either, but that's how it's working out."

Barret frowned at him. "Do you really think Amelia is involved in all this?"

He nodded. "I do. Not hurting but helping. Mountain has done a deep dive into her background. Dr. Amelia has one hell of a name in her field, and her reputation precedes her. She's hard-headed, yet fair. Everyone we talked to back home is impressed by her. I don't know how she's been able to hide whatever the hell she's doing out here, and still we don't seem to find her. I have to give her credit for that alone. Her team equally has usually been pretty independent and impressive. Anna was one exception obviously, and Myles had some trouble, but everyone else seemed to be on the up-and-up."

"Man, what is it about this session that both facilities were having trouble? Especially when we were working independent of each other—unless someone needed help."

"I don't know, but I sure want to find out. I want to get to the locals' village tomorrow. You want to come?"

"Absolutely. I'm pretty good at reading people. I very much want to see if they have any idea what's going on with this Amelia person."

"I highly suspect that they've seen her several times and that they're covering for her."

"Yet, she's not done anything wrong, has she?"

"Not that we know of, but the locals are all very close-knit, and she's been up here to the Arctic a lot over the years. A lot more than we have been, since we have different people here for each training session. So naturally she's bound to have better personal relationships with the locals than we do."

Barret nodded. "Okay then, what time do you want to leave?"

"Crack of dawn—almost," Magnus replied, with a smile. "We'll wait for the sun to come up and to start warming up the day a bit," he murmured. "Crack of dawn up here is a whole different story."

With that, Barret headed to bed. He passed Avalon's room, and, when he heard movement inside, he called out, "Are you okay?"

A surprised squeak came, and then she poked her head out the door. "What are you doing here?"

"I'm just heading to my room, but I heard you moving around, so I was worried."

"I'm fine," she said, "but you know how it is when you're overtired. Every time I close my eyes, I just keep seeing the kitchen, with pots and pans piling up in front of me again."

"Sorry about that. Apparently a request has been made."

"Good," she replied. "Chances are it'll still be a few days though, won't it?"

"Yeah, it sure will."

"*Great*," she muttered, "so what I really need is to get some sleep so I can get up early."

"If it makes you feel any better, I'll be getting up early too."

She rolled her eyes. "How is the fact that you'll suffer too supposed to make me feel better?"

"I don't know. Isn't there some saying about that?"

"Yeah, how misery loves company." She groaned. "Anyway, good night. I'm going in to bed." And, with that, Avalon smiled up at him and closed the door in his face.

As he headed to his room, he couldn't help but think how adorable she was, even with sleepy eyes and her long johns all rumpled, cold but not cold enough to ask to be warmed up, tired and yet not tired enough that she looked completely stressed. He was also pretty sure cake batter or flour was on her forehead, so she hadn't managed a good wash up either. Too tired.

Morning would bring a complete change of heart for the both of them, at least he hoped so.

DAY 3 EARLY MORNING

AVALON WOKE THE next morning and bailed right into the kitchen to help. When she finally brought out the first coffeepot, Mountain was there. She stared up at the huge man. "Coffee's ready."

He smiled. "Thanks."

"You guys figure anything out?'

"Not yet, sorry."

She nodded. "It would just be nice to have answers."

"And kitchen help people," Chef stated, as he came behind her. "This isn't what Avalon wants to do with her life, much less her military career. She may not say it, but she really doesn't want to do kitchen duty."

"No, but I'm okay to help out for now," she stated, with a roll of her eyes at Mountain, "because I know how stressed you are, Chef, being in here, with all this work."

He waved his hand. "I'm used to it."

"Maybe, but you haven't had a break since all this happened."

"I know, but nobody else can get away from it either," he shared gently.

She frowned but gave him points for that, as she handed Mountain a coffee. She had barely seen this man before. She knew he was around, but he seemed to have a status that nobody really understood. He came and went at odd times, and she had heard rumors about what he was doing, but nobody seemed to really know. She wanted to ask him but, at the same time, didn't want to open a can of worms that wasn't meant to be opened.

But finally she just couldn't resist anymore, and, when he came back for a second cup, she asked, "What do you do here?"

He looked over at her, smiled, and replied, "Put ghosts to rest." And, with that, he poured his coffee and walked out.

Behind her, Chef chuckled and said, "I'm surprised you even asked."

"I've seen him around here off and on, but he just seems to come and go."

"One of the guys who went missing early on was his brother. He's looking for him."

"Oh, shit." Avalon turned toward Chef. "Really?"

He nodded. "And, now that you know, please don't mention it to anyone, especially him."

"Well, hell," she murmured. "I'm sorry I asked him now."

"Don't be. He's kind of hard to miss."

"And yet," she said, cutting him off, "he moves like a ghost."

"I know, and, for his name and his size, the man moves like a panther. I can tell you that, when he wants something, he's a guy who can make it happen."

"How come you haven't asked him to get you some help then?"

"Because Scott and I were doing okay. We could have asked for a third guy, but sometimes, in a small kitchen like this one, you're better off with just two anyway," Chef explained. "It keeps the peace, and, as long as you can get into a rhythm that works, you're fine. Yet now with Scott gone …"

"It's got to be hard."

At that, his face turned sad. "He was a bright kid."

"He was a good kid. I'm not sure how bright he was," she pointed out.

He stared at her and then nodded. "You do like to call a spade a spade, don't you?"

"I'm not trying to insult him or anything. I really liked him, but he wasn't …" And she stopped.

"I know. I know what you mean, but he was brilliant in the kitchen, and that's what I needed."

"Of course," she agreed. "I feel so bad for his family."

"Yeah, me too," Chef replied, "but let's get going. We've got a long day ahead of us."

And a long day it was. She didn't even have a chance to stop until dinnertime, when she collapsed at a table, after everybody else had been served. When two shadows fell on top of her, she looked up to see Magnus and Barret, looking beyond weary, heaping platefuls in hand as they sat down. "Hey," she greeted them. "You look the way I feel."

Barret smiled and nodded. "I hate to say it, but you look the way we feel."

"Ouch," she grumbled. "That bad, *huh*?"

At that, he laughed and added, "Yeah, somewhat."

"Any news?"

"The village has not exactly opened up and welcomed us, but one person from Amelia's apparently two-man team came back not all that long ago, and he has already taken off for civilization."

"Seriously?"

Barret nodded. "Yeah, when one of the supply trucks

made it in, he left with it. It's unclear whether he has been with her all this time or if the two of them had left the scientists' camp separately, going their own way."

"Well, hell," Avalon exclaimed, "then what about Amelia herself?"

"Apparently she headed back out again. She hasn't been talking, but she did get some interesting supplies."

"Such as?'

"She got more medical supplies, dried food that can be easily stored, and some ammunition."

"Bullets?"

He nodded. "She does hunt, if need be."

"Jesus," Avalon said. "And the villagers wouldn't give you any more info than that?"

"No, and of course Dr. Robinson, the other scientist with Amelia, has already left—probably on purpose, so he didn't have to answer questions."

"Jesus, can't somebody get a hold of either of them?"

"We're working on it," Magnus stated. "They were probably afraid they'd be held back."

"So, there's just her out there," Avalon muttered, shaking her head, as she tried to get her befuddled brain to work her way through it all. "What do you think's going on?"

"I don't know," Barret said, looking to Magnus.

Magnus shook his head. "I don't know if she's found somebody and if she's trying to nurse them to health or if there's a bigger problem, like she's the one injured," he offered. "We're still working our way through that."

"It's been weeks," she pointed out. "Do we trust the villagers?"

Again Magnus shook his head. "No. I assume they've kept some information to themselves. We don't necessarily have the best reputation with the villagers, not with all our problems from the beginning of this training session, which makes the locals want to stay away from us. We've got a bad name—and, in their eyes, probably beyond a bad name. It's as if some sort of evil or bad voodoo surrounds us. Even as we approached the village, they came out to talk to us, rather than letting us in. They were friendly enough. They didn't try to stop us, but they're not being completely open either."

"So, they could be helping somebody, and you wouldn't know," Avalon suggested.

"Maybe, but the only way they're doing that is if they have a reason. And it could easily be because they don't trust us."

"Or they are protecting someone. Which is also kind of crazy when you think about it. Nobody else can survive out here."

"Yet the villagers do, and their hunters do," Magnus pointed out calmly.

Avalon didn't say anything because it just seemed to be a far-fetched idea to even hold out hope that anybody else could still be alive out there. "I don't understand why Amelia wouldn't have left with the other scientist."

"There's still plenty of confusion about that too," Barret noted. "That's why we need to talk to the scientist who did leave. There was talk of going back to the scientists' camp and getting other information that was needed."

"That could be what Amelia's doing," Avalon said. "Amelia does a trip there, spends a few days, collects what she needs, shuts down the camp, goes back to the villagers— knowing ahead of time when they're scheduled for supplies coming and going. She times it so she can get out or can order in what she needs. In all fairness, she's not beholden to us, and she doesn't have to check in with us."

"I've thought of that too," Magnus confirmed. "Mountain will go talk to the villagers a few more times. He's making some inroads in terms of getting their trust. However, so far, they aren't very open to discussing what anybody else is doing."

"Which isn't all that far wrong," she admitted. Then she looked them in the face. "Are we sure that Scott's death was an accident?"

"Sydney is," Magnus replied. "Outside of an autopsy, which we can't do here, the body does seem to confirm that he went outside, got lost, and froze to death."

"Right. Unless drugs were involved," Avalon added. When both men remained silent, she continued. "Funny how we have too many drugs in this base, yet we need food supplies here." She shook her head. "That's definitely becoming an issue in the kitchen."

"It is, and hopefully more supplies are coming soon," Barret murmured. "In which case, Scott's body will return to the States."

She nodded. "It seems as if the only way people leave this place is either in handcuffs or a coffin."

At that, Barret leaned over, put a hand on hers, and asked, "Could you keep your voice down when you say that?"

She groaned and nodded. "Sorry. I'm not trying to be negative here, but … it just seems as if that's the truth."

"And we don't want that kind of truth being what everyone thinks. Speaking of which, you're in a unique position here. Are you seeing any strange interactions with people, anybody upset, anybody furtive, anybody hiding anything?"

She frowned at him. "If you guys want me to spy on

everybody," she whispered, leaning in closer, "I'd need to be a whole lot less exhausted and a whole lot less occupied in the back."

They both studied her for a long moment and then nodded. "I guess that makes sense. So, the answer is no?"

She pondered the initial question, as she thought about the day and the people she had encountered. "Most people aren't terribly friendly. They come in, look at the food, grab what they want, and leave," she noted. "I don't hear or see much, even if I'm serving or if I'm refilling containers or putting food out," she explained. "Those are the only times I would really be in a position to see anybody. On the other hand"—she considered it with a growing frown—"they're kind of blind to me being in the back."

"Has anybody teased you about being on KP duty?" Barret asked.

She shook her head at that. "No, but they might be afraid to bring it up, in case they end up being next."

Barret laughed. "Maybe. Sorry to say, sometimes it is a punishment."

"It shouldn't be a punishment to help Chef," she argued.

"Hey, I'm not saying that it is, but, for some people, that's the way they look at it."

"Right," she muttered. "I'll keep my eyes open, but so far the answer is no. I haven't noticed anything."

DAY 4 NEXT MORNING

HOWEVER, SHE HAD a chance to change that impression the next morning, when she was helping serve breakfast. One of the guys that she knew, Ralph, was joking about the fact that she was in the kitchen, right where women belong.

She gave him a bright smile and a retort. "I guess maybe you'll be the first to rotate in and to do your time back here."

"Only if you all want to get poisoned," he grumbled, and, with that, he took his plate and walked away.

But one of the other people turned and looked at him sharply, as if afraid that the guy *was* poisoning people. She reassured him by saying, "Look. He's just kidding."

"But is he?" the guy asked. "Who handles the food here?" he asked suspiciously.

"Chef and I do," she stated. "I've been in here all day."

He nodded but still didn't look very placated.

"I also handled all the food yesterday," she added. "It's just been the two of us, me and Chef, back here. Believe me. We could use some more help, if you're up for it."

He gave her a haunted look, then quickly took his plate and sat down.

She watched him as he played with his food instead of eating, as if the words that Ralph had thrown out in a casual joking manner had taken root, and, just like bad news, those words were settling into his soul in an ugly way.

When she mentioned it to the guys later, they just nodded. Barret said, "That's an unfortunate example of what happens when people are confined to this base when there is trouble. It can create all kinds of issues, including mutiny."

She shook her head. "There sure as hell shouldn't be anybody who's got a problem with the food," she muttered. "We do the best we can."

"No, I know that," Barret acknowledged, "but the minute anybody gets sick, it doesn't matter what it is that they're sick from. They always look to the kitchen."

"Is somebody sick?"

He nodded. "One person went to sickbay last night."

She stared at him. "Really? I didn't hear anything about it."

"No, because we don't think it had anything to do with the kitchen. He's got some stomach bug, but the minute that happens, it can run rampant through a place like this."

"*Great*," she muttered. "That's the last thing we need."

"It is, and we've got to keep that in mind. So if anything else is said about it, just let me know."

IT WAS FRUSTRATING to Barret that the special investigation guys hadn't gotten anywhere, despite all their questions. Scott's death had been ruled an accident, and nothing else had gone wrong since. For Barret, having just come into this scenario, he found himself watching everybody closely, looking at their foibles and personalities, from the jokesters to the depressing ninnies and everyone in between. A certain amount of people would always be out there who had absolutely nothing good to say about anything.

Ralph was one of them, and yet he did it in such a questioningly manner that it was setting off other people.

Barret sat down beside Ralph, faced him, and said, "You want to knock off all the depressing talk about this place, like being poisoned and not leaving except in a coffin?"

"Hey, I didn't say that first," Ralph stated in protest. "Everybody's talking about it."

"And yet you're perpetuating the discord," Barret added.

"What's it to you? You haven't even been here the whole time. You just get to waltz in, when the rest of us have been stuck here with some sort of murderer."

"Really? So that's your answer right there? I'm new, so I don't know what it's like? I did get assigned to come in here, even though none of this has been solved. You know that, right?"

"Maybe you did something to deserve this," Ralph snapped at him. "God, we just want to get out of here. I was supposed to go home weeks ago. And, until they decide something, nobody's going anywhere. And what if nothing happened? What if a couple guys went AWOL and just decided to commit suicide? I mean, nobody ever said that the kid Scott was very stable. In fact, going outside like he did, not fully geared up, yet stepping out for a cigarette, was an idiot move. It's not as if the Arctic is like anywhere else in the world. Maybe he did it on purpose."

"Are you thinking Scott might have just walked off?" Barret asked Ralph.

"Sure, why not? Look at what happened to him. Honestly that makes the most sense. It's sure as hell better than another murder. And we solved all those, so why the hell can't we leave?" Ralph demanded, his voice getting louder and louder.

"I'll take your complaints to the brass," Egan noted, as he walked past.

"What do you care? You're another one who came in late to the party. All you guys just sit around, acting as if you're some special deal, yet nothing's solved. Maybe that's because there isn't anything to solve. Maybe that bloody kid just decided he'd had enough and took a short walk outside, knowing it would be a quick and easy death," Ralph said.

"Why don't you keep that talk to yourself before it gets you sent to the slammer," Barret suggested.

"What's that, the storeroom? Oh, gee, I'll just sit there and eat food all day," he retorted, with a sneer.

Barret studied him. "If you've got a problem with me, feel free to make it clear," he stated in a mild tone. "Other than that, keep your mouth shut."

"You going to make me?" Ralph stood up, his fists clenched.

"I don't think I even need to bother because you're completely out of order."

"I don't give a shit," Ralph bellowed. "I just want to get out of this fucking place. It's ridiculous that we're being kept here as prisoners. You can bet I've got an awful lot to say to my superiors back home about this supposed cooperative venture," he stated, with a sneer. "And I've been sending all kinds of reports, don't you worry."

Barret nodded. "Nice to know exactly where you stand. And nice to know how desperate you are. Maybe you were desperate enough to do something completely off the wall to hurt people here, just so they'd shut down the camp, just so you could finally leave."

At that, Ralph froze. "No, no, no, no, no. You're not

pinning any of that shit on me," he yelled. "I didn't do anything."

"Yet I wonder," Barret murmured.

At that, Ralph stared for a moment, his frustration getting the best of him, then turned and stomped away.

Beside Barret, Egan muttered, "You better watch him. Tempers are very short here."

"I can see that," Barret mused. "I'm just not sure whether it's *just* that or there's something more."

"Not sure there *is* anything more," Egan shared. "And I know that the idea that Scott may have intentionally just walked off to his death is gaining momentum."

"Yeah, but who put that idea in his head in the first place?" he muttered.

"I know in this place, it doesn't take much to set people off, but we want to keep the accidents down as much as we can."

"Yeah, but accidents aren't the problem, are they? Looks to me as if there's more to it." But still, there wasn't anything Barret could do tonight.

DAY 5 WEE HOURS OF THE MORNING

W HEN BARRET WOKE to yells and alarms going off at four in the morning, he bailed out of bed, dressed. and raced out to hear shouts of a fire. And, sure enough, part of the kitchen was on fire, and standing off to the side in shock was Avalon. He noted her singed hair and eyebrows, and light burns on her face and hands. He quickly raced her down to see Sydney in the medical clinic.

"I'm fine," Avalon protested. "I was just lighting the propane, and it just torched off to the side on me." She shook her head. "That stove, I've never had a problem with it before."

"And it could be just a regular maintenance thing," Barret suggested soothingly.

Sydney checked over Avalon, as she tried to explain what had happened. "But I've never had a problem," she argued, looking back at him. "It's almost as if it got stuck open or something. And then, when I lit it, it just shot out flames, and I couldn't stop it."

"They've got it under control now," he told her. "So it's not a problem. It's you we're worried about."

"It's just one more thing to go wrong in this damn place."

"Maybe, but it's not your fault."

"And yet yesterday, when Ralph joked about poisoning

the food, it felt as if a pall hung over the place. With that one guy getting some stomach bug, people don't really think I poisoned anybody, do they?"

"No, they don't," Barret stated. "Don't worry about that. Just try to calm down, so we can get this dealt with right now."

She closed her eyes, as Sydney smoothed a soothing salve over her burns. "I'm not badly hurt," Avalon said. "I need to get back up there and help Chef. He'd just stepped out for a few minutes." Barret frowned at her, and she nodded. "He wanted to check the generator to ensure everything was okay—something he does every morning, I think. Anyway I was trying to light the stove when he came back in, and everything just kind of blew. Jesus, I've never seen that happen before."

"It can happen, even on barbecues," Barret noted. "Don't worry about it. Somebody will figure it out."

"Yeah, and, in the meantime," she noted, "people will want food."

"Doesn't matter. They can live on rations for a while," he snapped.

She nodded and hunkered down.

He took one look at her, turned to Sydney, and said, "I'll be back in a little bit. Keep her here for now." And, with that, he quickly disappeared. Back in the kitchen, the flames were out, and the damage was not that bad at all.

But when he saw Chef and Mountain arguing, Barret stepped forward and interrupted, "Maybe I can help by telling you what Avalon just told me." Then he related that it seemed as if the burner had been stuck on open, and, when the gas shot out, too much came out at one time. So the flames shot up, and she couldn't turn it down, causing some grease to catch fire beside it.

Chef faced him in worry. "That hasn't ever happened before."

"That's what she said. So, normally you were there with her."

"Sure, but she's lit that burner lots of times without any trouble," he replied. "It's off and on many times throughout the day."

Mountain just stared at Chef, then walked over and examined the stove. Fussing with the knobs, he noted, "This one opens a little too wide," he announced, taking a wrench and adjusting it. He quickly lit the fire, shut it down; lit all the different burners, shut them down; then turned to face Chef. "It seems to be fine at the moment."

"What did you just do?" Chef asked, staring at him. "It must have been adjusted because you just had to adjust it back, didn't you?"

He nodded slowly. "Yes." He looked at Barret. "And this doesn't go any further, but my guess is that somebody fiddled with the gas settings before you guys started this morning, so they wanted this to happen."

"They put this kitchen in that kind of danger?" Chef cried out in fury. "And it wasn't me who was targeted, it was her."

"Yet that may not have been the purpose of it," Mountain reminded him. "It could just as easily have been you who turned it on."

"It usually is me," he stated. "I get the fires going and the water on. She's the one who set up the system for the dishes to make it easier on us. So we were putting the hot water on earlier, and then we were just adding extra teakettles to it. But it's always been me who's turned it on."

"And yet this morning, it wasn't you, right?"

"No, it wasn't."

"Would anybody have known that it wouldn't be you today?"

He just stared at him and shrugged. "I don't know how, since I didn't even know myself. It wasn't something that we'd arranged or decided. No telling what people might have thought though."

"And that's where we're at. It didn't matter because it could have been either of you," Mountain stated. He looked over at Barret. "How is she?"

"Shocked, upset, a little scared about the propane, but I think she's fine. She's a little singed and has some minor burns, but she's not seriously hurt. I think it was more the scare of it all."

"Of course," Chef muttered, running a hand through his thin white hair. "Jesus Christ, what next?" He walked over to the stove and deliberately lit the burners himself, then nodded. "It all seems fine now." He sighed, turning back to look at Mountain.

Mountain nodded. "And you and I both know that sometimes they need adjustment."

"Sure," Chef admitted, "but, outside of the adjustments made when the stove arrived after transport, it's never needed anything up until now. It's one of the things I always check out on an assignment like this though, where things aren't used for a time."

"We can't keep a guard here all the time."

"Of course not," Chef stated, as he looked around. "So, I guess I'm sleeping in here from now on. In the back room." He turned, looked at Mountain, and suggested, "You want to find a way to make room for that to happen and do it on the sly? If somebody comes back here to try to kill us, they'll have to shoot me, so there will at least be some evidence of it."

Mountain nodded. "I'll take care of it." He stepped into the back storeroom and then winced. "Except for the fact that you already have a visitor back here." Scott was being kept in the back, until he could be moved, and that was an issue.

"I hate to say it, but that visitor needs to move anyway," Chef replied. "I've got him up against the cold northern exterior wall to keep his body at a temperature so we can move him. We'll just have to put him into the generator shed," he suggested, with a groan. "I don't mind sleeping with a dead body, but I need some heat. Yet I don't want to warm things up to the point that he starts thawing."

"No, we can't have that either," Mountain agreed. "Don't worry. I'll take care of it." And, with that, Mountain motioned at Barret. "Can you give me a hand?"

They headed out to the generator shed, and Mountain checked the temperature here. "We can keep him in here just fine. Though I suppose we should warn anybody who comes to check on the generator. Not everybody handles that sort of thing so well."

"True enough," Barret noted, "but how many people come to the generator shed?"

"There shouldn't be many. We were watching it pretty closely for a while, after we'd had some problems, but we figured that out."

Barret shrugged. "I've checked it a couple times myself," he admitted. "Sometimes I hear an odd sound, and I keep thinking that it's hiccupping. Then I come out to check to ensure that everything's fine."

"You and me both," Mountain shared. "We both know what will happen if this thing goes down."

"Life would get a little more difficult," Barret pointed out cheerfully. "We all have outdoor survival training, but, in these temperatures, with this many people, it would be a tough deal."

"We would have to get emergency supplies dropped," Mountain noted, "but it would happen, and maybe that's why a fire was a better bet."

"You really think it was done on purpose?"

"Oh, I know it was done on purpose," Mountain declared, with a nod. "I mean, I really had to wrench those settings back," he explained. "The question is, was it her or him who was targeted, or, as Chef said, maybe it didn't matter as long as it was somebody."

"Just to create more havoc or trying to shut down the camp?"

At that, Mountain stiffened and nodded. "That's really what people here want, isn't it? They want to go home, and getting this place to shut down is one way to make that happen. So, any kind of chaos will push it in that direction. That makes sense."

"There's also talk …" Barret hesitated, then continued. "And I know it won't be what you want to hear, and it's probably come up because of Scott, but there's also talk that says your brother took that hike and that he did it on purpose anyway."

"I've heard it," Mountain confirmed, staring at Barret steadily. "But I also know my brother, and that wasn't anything he wanted."

"And yet," Barret added hesitantly, knowing that it was a touchy subject, "maybe you didn't know what he was like recently."

"Oh, I did. And drugs? Nope. No way. I won't believe that one, unless the drugs were administered to him, and he didn't know," Mountain declared.

"With the drug problems here already that we know of, it's a possibility," Barret concluded, "and that just takes us back to murder. Because, if Scott did take that walk and if he was under the influence of drugs that he didn't know he had been given, that's still murder."

"It is," Mountain agreed, scrubbing the back of his head. "I wish we could get a hold of Amelia."

At that, Barret looked at Mountain. "Why? Just to see if she is the one who's dropping off the bodies here or at the scientists' camp?"

"I think she is," Mountain declared. "And you're right. It would be nice to find out why she's doing that and not coming in to talk to us, but that's the least of our worries. She's not doing anything but helping, right? She obviously doesn't trust us and probably doesn't want to get in here and get involved in something that takes her out too," he guessed.

"When we were at the village yesterday," Barret murmured, "there was some inkling that she was going back to the scientists' camp to work on some things or whatever and then return. We didn't get proof, but that was intimated by somebody."

"Yeah, they're good at that," Mountain said, with a half laugh. "They don't really come out and say something and have it be wrong, and they don't want to get her in trouble either."

"And the rest of the scientists?"

"I've got a call in to some people about trying to talk to

them, so we're hoping to hook them up for an interview soon."

"That would be good," Barret stated. "It would also put some people's minds at rest, if Amelia came in. There was an awful lot of time and energy put into searching for her and Dr. Robinson in pretty tough conditions."

"That's one of the reasons we need to talk to them. We spent a lot of man-hours trying to get out there to help them, and I understand there may not have been any need. Plus it wasn't wanted in the first place, so they don't feel responsible for us jumping the gun on it."

"I suppose," Barret muttered, shaking his head. "But after Magnus described what happened to the rest of them with the carbon dioxide poisoning from the generator or whatever, I can understand the sense of urgency to find the others. Particularly since there has been so much confusion over how many were unaccounted for. In the end, since it was a great training opportunity anyway, it's not as if anybody should be upset that a search effort was launched. A lot of people were sincerely worried about the scientists, and that's a good thing because you should be worried in this Arctic climate."

"And the bodies?"

"It's the same thing really. If we can talk to the other scientists, maybe we can figure it out. Surely they won't have anything to say against our questions."

"No, and I'm hoping to talk to them soon," Mountain shared. "Meanwhile I think I'll make a trip up to the scientists' camp." He looked at Barret. "You want to stay here and stand guard or you want to come with me?"

Barret was torn because he really wanted to go. "Do you think somebody will make another attack on Avalon?"

"I have no way of knowing," Mountain admitted, his voice low. "Never mind. You stay here. I'll take a snowmobile, so I'll be there and back in no time." And, with that, he quickly disappeared.

Barret looked at his watch and noted it was five o'clock in the morning. It would still be biting cold out there. He headed down to the medical clinic to see how Avalon was doing and found her curled up under a blanket, shivering.

He made a startled exclamation as he walked over. "That again?" He hopped onto the bed beside her and pulled her into his arms, wrapping her body up tight.

"SYDNEY SAYS IT'S shock," Avalon explained, her teeth chattering.

"I know," he murmured, "but that's all right. I got you."

She settled into his arms and just let him hold her. When the shivering finally started to ease, she whispered, "I should go back and help Chef."

"Only if you want to," Barret said. "Obviously schedules are off right now, but people will need something, even if it's rations."

"We should do better, for the sake of morale, you know? We need to get the kitchen back to normal right away and chalk it all up to a freak accident," she murmured.

He smiled at her. "And yet you're injured."

"No, I'm not," she argued, with a weak smile. "Just a little singed. Honestly I'd be better off doing something. I just …"

"I know," he said, when her voice went silent. "You're worried it will happen again. We've turned the burners on several times and adjusted the gas lines to ensure you don't get so much gas coming out again."

"And I'll let Chef light them," she stated defiantly.

He laughed. "Believe me. He already feels bad that he didn't light it for you in the first place."

She groaned. "And yet it's not on him," she whispered. "He does a hell of a job here."

"He absolutely does." Barret shifted back and looked at her. "You're still very cold."

"No, I'm not."

AT THAT, MOMENT Sydney walked in, surprised to see Barret sharing the hospital bed with Avalon.

He smiled. "I came to check up on her, and she was shivering so badly that I decided some extra body heat would help."

Sydney chuckled. "And obviously Avalon didn't decline the offer."

He flushed, then nodded. "Nope."

Avalon groaned. "I'm right here, you know?"

"That's good," Sydney noted. "I couldn't get any hot water yet, but the kitchen is getting set back to rights."

"Good." Avalon sat up. "I might as well go down there myself and give Chef a hand. I'll do better keeping busy, and"—she gave an eye roll—"at least down there, I can get coffee."

"If you think you can get coffee," Barret stated, "I'm coming with you."

She looked at him suspiciously, but he gave her a bland smile. "Why does this sound suspiciously like you are trying to keep an eye on me?"

"I am," he admitted. "You've been injured and had a shock, and I want to confirm there are no lasting effects." He turned and looked at Sydney. "You wouldn't argue with that, would you?"

"No, absolutely not," the doc agreed calmly. "And the way things are going around here these days, I would very much appreciate it if you would keep an eye on her."

He turned and gave Avalon a sunny smile. "See? That was easy."

She glared at him. "That sounds very much as if you two are conniving together."

"Nope, not at all." Barret chuckled. "Come on. Let's go see if we can put on some coffee."

"Oh, now I get it," Avalon said, adding to the teasing atmosphere. "You just want coffee."

"If coffee's coming," Sydney noted, "I could use some too."

"I know you could," Avalon murmured. "Give me a few minutes to get down there and to get some started."

WITH BARRET AT her side, she headed back to the kitchen. The minute Chef saw her, he raced over and gave her a hug.

When he finally stepped back enough to look at her, she smiled up at him. "See? I'm just fine. Honest."

"Are you sure?" he asked, studying her face intently.

"I'm fine. I lost part of an eyebrow and a little hair is all." Wrinkling her nose, she winced. "I think I'll have to trim some of that because that smell is just driving me nuts." She walked over to where he kept the utility scissors, then quickly cut off the small amount of singed hair, and then she declared, "We need coffee, and I understand the burners are working okay now."

"Yes." Chef pointed. "I have coffee on, thinking we could use a shot ourselves. It's not done yet, but it won't be long. I was hoping to tank up before I get going on breakfast."

He looked at her hesitantly, and she repeated, "I'm fine. I'll be here for breakfast at least. You know, back in the saddle and all. I don't know if we'll get a change in staff anytime soon, but I'm not quitting on you." She saw the relief on his face and smiled. "Listen. I don't know whether we were targeted or if this was an accident, but I'm not a quitter."

"You might not be a quitter," Chef noted gently, "but nobody'll knock you for wanting to change jobs."

"It's fine." She gave a wave of her hand. "I'm quite comfortable in a kitchen, and, besides, this way I get coffee and food too."

He laughed and turned to Barret. "So, are you here to help too?"

Barret smiled at Chef. "That's a damn good idea. What I'm here for is to ensure she's okay, but—"

"That's what I figured," Chef interrupted, "but, if you'll be underfoot, I'm putting you to work."

"Done." Barret smirked. "We'll make sure that nothing else happens," he stated, with a look back at Avalon.

"Good. I can't say I want to deal with any more of that BS."

"Nope, none of us do," Barret confirmed. "So, how long before that coffee's done?"

And, with that, the day began.

DAY 5 LUNCH

A VALON DOVE INTO the day, working in the kitchen again. Later she looked up to see Mountain standing there, frowning at her. She frowned back.

He motioned at her, and she stepped away and asked, "What's up?"

"You doing okay?" he asked, his voice low.

She nodded. "I am. Barret's been keeping a close eye on us." Avalon rolled her eyes. "Matter of fact, Chef put him to work in the kitchen."

Mountain's eyebrows shot up at that, and he looked behind her to see Barret flipping pork chops on one of the big grills. "Now that is a sight to see." He chuckled.

"I know, right? He seems to think that I'm still in danger." She searched Mountain's expression for any kind of hint.

"We hope not," he replied, "but better to be safe than sorry."

"Any chance of getting out of here anytime soon? Or at least a shift change and more staff coming in?"

He shook his head at that. "No, probably not for a few more days anyway."

Just then Barret joined them. "Did you go to the scientists' camp?" he asked in an equally low tone.

Mountain nodded. "Amelia's been there. The camp's

been shut down for a while, yet some more of the stuff inside has been put away. Closets are closed. Things are locked up that weren't before, and it's just looking more secured for winter than it was before. Also I found fresh tracks in and out."

"That's good news," Barret replied. "Did she leave a note?"

"She did, plus she may have taken some books with her. Our notes we left are gone, where we shared that the scientists had been poisoned by carbon monoxide and were removed to our base, so obviously Amelia knows what happened and is choosing not to come in to deal with us in any way," Mountain explained. "I still can't talk to her, which would be nice, but she did leave a note saying she was clearing out in the next few days, but I don't know if I believe her."

"Are you thinking it was just to send us off on a wild goose chase again?"

"Or to give everybody the idea that she's long gone but isn't."

"Why would she do that?"

"I don't know," Mountain admitted. "I have my suspicions, but, until I talk to her, which is something she seems to be going to great lengths to avoid, I'm not getting very far. Short of my making an all-out campaign to track her down, I left her another note, and we'll go from there. I've also gone to the locals' village and told them, just in private, that I was looking to talk to her, that she wasn't in trouble, and that it was important because we did have other people missing. So we were looking for any kind of hints or clues she might have to help us out, including talking to the scientists who had been here."

"Did anybody connect with them?"

He nodded. "The brass did. Apparently all they got was how they were very sorry to hear about what happened to their teammates and how they have tried to reach out and connect with Anna, but we all know that's not happening. Some of them also tried to contact Amelia, but that is a long shot too. We'll follow up with some more questions with them because again I wasn't involved in the original questioning."

"Of course not, but it's good news to have Amelia and Dr. Robinson somewhat accounted for—if we can believe what Amelia has said—so we're not out there looking for them."

He nodded. "And we think Amelia found the body of Yegorahn and brought him to the scientists' camp but wanted to avoid explanations because such a mess was going on here at the training base. We can only surmise on her reasoning."

"Right. So, a comedy of errors, miscommunications, or just bad timing."

"Exactly, but the others are all in the clear."

"Except for Amelia."

"Yes, except for Amelia, who was back out again at the time."

"All alone?"

He nodded. "It seems so."

"And yet she took a lot of supplies."

Mountain's expression changed, and he nodded. "Exactly. And she's female."

At that, Avalon looked at him. "What does that mean? She might be helping with something?"

"With *somebody*," he clarified, his voice thick. "That

doesn't mean that she's helping anybody in a bad way," Mountain added. "A lot of people are up here, and almost all of them don't want anything to do with anybody from our base."

"Right," Avalon agreed. "It takes an independent and self-reliant loner to live up here, doesn't it?"

"And yet how old is Amelia?" Barret asked.

"Mid-thirties," Mountain stated. "She's done a lot of time up here, and she's beloved by the villagers, so I don't think anything in particular is going on with her—outside of the fact that, for whatever reason, she's decided to avoid us entirely."

Though it was more than they'd had, it was still too little information and too much confusion surrounding Amelia, and they all scattered to their duties, yet again with more questions.

DAY 5 DINNER

AVALON GRABBED A quick nap but woke sore and stiff, feeling as if she had run a marathon, but she still raced to the kitchen. Chef looked up as she walked in, with a note of relief on his face.

She smiled. "I told you. I'm not a quitter."

"And yet a lot of people would," he noted.

She shrugged. "Just not built that way, I guess."

"That's to my benefit," Chef stated, "and is much appreciated."

As they quickly got down to the final prep for a belated dinner, she asked, "Has anybody mentioned anything to you about this? The fire, I mean."

He shook his head. "No, I think most of them are talking among themselves, and the ones who aren't are just trying to ignore it."

She laughed. "I can see the ignoring part."

"Sure, if you're the kind to stick your head in the sand," Chef quipped, with a fat grin. "It could have just been an unfortunate accident."

He didn't say anything else, and neither did she, but they were both fully aware that it was no accident at all, and they had yet to deal with the fallout. "Are you still sleeping here?" she asked, pointing to the back room.

He nodded. "Yeah. I have to admit I'll sleep better when

poor Scott's picked up."

She winced. "God, you're sleeping there with him, aren't you?"

"No. Not in the same room but I didn't want anything else to go on. So he's in the generator shed."

She smiled at that and nodded. It certainly wasn't an attitude that most people would have, but, in a way, she understood it. "He was a nice kid, wasn't he?"

"He was," Chef confirmed. "And he sure as hell didn't deserve whatever happened to him."

She looked at him carefully. "Do you expect them to find that something untoward happened?"

He shook his head. "I don't know, … maybe not," he muttered, with a shrug. "I just … it's such a senseless death, put it that way."

"That I can agree with," she murmured. "It was maybe an easy death though."

"I don't think there is such a thing," Chef noted. "Sure, you freeze up, and you go to sleep, and I know he was tired already, so maybe he just got caught up in the cold and didn't realize how dangerous it would be."

She pondered that, and, when dinner was finally done, she grabbed a plate of her own. "I'll go sit in the dining room and eat."

"You do that," Chef agreed, with a warm smile. "And setting up everybody to do their own dishes has really helped."

"It really has," she said. "I can't say they do a great job of it, at least not all of them, but it gives us a break."

"It does."

With that, she grabbed her food and headed out to sit in the common area. As she approached, Barret looked up, smiled, and waved at her. She walked over toward him and his team. "May I sit here, or am I interrupting?"

"Sure, join us," Barret replied. "We were just talking."

"Yeah, everybody's just talking," she quipped, with an eye roll.

"Anybody talking about anything in particular?" Egan asked.

She shook her head. "Not so you'd notice. At least not to me."

"Do you think there's a reason they won't talk to you?"

"*Yeah.*" She sent a wry look in his direction. "Look where I'm sitting. Your team's here, except Rogan."

Barret glanced around and nodded. "Rogan's scouting the area. So, you're seen as part of the enemy band, is that it?"

"I'd hate to think so, but I wouldn't be surprised if I was cast that way."

Egan shook his head. "It's a sad day when attitudes get to that point."

"I'm guessing at least some people wonder if I did cause that accident all on my own," she shared, as she looked down at her meal. "I haven't heard anybody say as much, but it wouldn't surprise me."

"Of course anybody who's not had anything to do with you probably doesn't understand either."

"Even if they do, I don't think they give a crap," she stated cheerfully. "Right now, everybody is just in maintenance mode, until they can get out."

"I'm not sure when that'll happen though," Barret stated, looking at Mountain and Magnus, the two long-timers here at their table. "There's still enough going on in this area that we're pretty well on our own. Besides, as I understood from the brass, it may be a case of, can we or can we not survive this?"

"Meaning, it's a test of the human spirit and all that garbage?" Avalon asked.

"Meaning, it's a test of our survival skills," Mountain corrected her. "Because survival—and this is really an important point—survival isn't just about enduring or overcoming Mother Nature. It's also about surviving each other."

Silence fell around the table at his words.

She had to admit that he had a point. "And I guess there's no point in surviving this Arctic weather if we kill each other off because we can't handle the isolation and the stress."

"I would think that could be a large part of what's going on here," Barret murmured. "Of course I don't know for sure, and who knows just what is really happening, but I do know that an awful lot of data is being collected, including medical data."

"That's true. We do constantly get tested," she noted. "I can't imagine Sydney's appreciating that."

"It's part of her job," Magnus noted, with a shrug. "She sometimes rolls her eyes at the instructions she gets, but orders are orders. Plus, in this situation—where it's too easy to see people going a little stir-crazy—maybe it's for the best."

"Maybe," Avalon muttered, "but it does give you an odd feeling to think that the brass is measuring how this is affecting us."

"Of course they are," Mountain declared, studying her. "Why wouldn't they? They do studies like this all the time, and not just studies for the sake of studies. The military really needs to understand what isolation does. Can we cooperate and work together to get through it, or is somebody here to sabotage that, so we all go home again? It's necessary data to accumulate and to study and to plan for."

"And yet the brass probably doesn't want to let us go home, not if they are that far into the research," Avalon pointed out.

Magnus nodded. "I don't think they want to let us go home until the outstanding mysteries are solved. Even the other countries have stopped requesting the release of their people at this point, although they are doing their own investigations."

Surprised, she looked at him with her eyebrows raised.

Magnus shared a knowing look with Mountain, who shared with Avalon, "You are new here, so you weren't part of the trainee program from the beginning of this session. However, we had two suspicious deaths early on—one a Russian and the other a German."

"Oh my God," she muttered.

He nodded.

"And here I am in the kitchen."

"And," Barret added, looking at her directly, "that's a very valuable place to find yourself."

She swallowed hard, as she stared at him. "And there's clearly something behind that comment."

"Of course." Barret smiled. "Isn't there always?"

"Sure," she replied hesitantly, "but, if you need me to do something, then I might need it to be official."

"It is official," Barret declared, "but all we need you to do is keep watch."

"I can keep watch as much as I can, but, as I told you before, I'm in the kitchen, doing food prep, exactly the same thing pretty much every day. I don't see anybody during the day between meals, outside of those who come for coffee. I don't hear anything, and I'm not sure, but, maybe because of the fire, I haven't quite faded into the background yet."

He looked at her, as she shrugged.

She continued. "You know how staff people—such as housekeepers, maids, and waiters—all just tend to blend into the background? So you don't ever really think about what you're saying around them? But, in this case, that may not have happened yet, though it probably won't take all that long," she shared, with a half smile.

Barret nodded. "Interesting take on it."

"No, not so much," Avalon disagreed. "I used to work as a waitress, so I know what people are like, and they tend to ignore you, as if you're a second-class citizen or not even that, maybe just wallpaper," she noted cheerfully. "But if I hear or see anything, I'll help out, not so much because it's official but because something is rotten here, and Chef and I want to make sure that nobody else dies."

At that, she winced and added, "Especially me." Concerned, the men frowned at her. She shrugged. "I'm fine, really. That was just one of those off-the-cuff comments that slipped out."

"Was it though?" Mountain asked, eyeing her intently. "Are you sleeping well?'

"Sure, I'm sleeping," she stated, "the whole four to six hours that I get."

He nodded. "Nobody is getting a whole lot up here anyway, I know."

"Did you hear the winds last night?" she murmured. "I mean, I know they get ugly weather up here, but wow. That was something else."

"We've had an unusually long spate of it," Magnus murmured, "but it's been interspersed with really nice weather."

"Oh, I missed the interspersed part," she teased on a laugh. "And that has made it a little more difficult to get up and smile every day. It was fine until … what? I don't know."

Magnus nodded. "Almost about when I arrived, some three weeks into the original twelve-week session." He looked at her and shrugged. "The attitude changed somewhere around then. And I'm not saying my arrival changed the general attitude here at the base. I'm just saying that it happened in that time frame. That worries me too," he added, his voice low. "The question is whether it was the arrival of somebody new and knowing these trainees weren't allowed to leave, the impact of one more suspicious death, or was it the whole scientists' camp thing?"

"Maybe it was all of it," Avalon suggested, looking at him. "I mean, when you think about it, an awful lot is going on here that didn't make anybody happy, and then finding out that the scientists' camp wouldn't be any better than what was going on here was just another strain that made everybody hit rock bottom."

"That's an interesting thought too," Magnus said, pondering it.

She shrugged. "I don't know. I just … It was just an observation. Don't take it the wrong way."

He laughed. "I won't, but you're right. The timeline fits with Anna's sabotage of the scientists' camp. If you're right, then that timing is also interesting."

Avalon replied, "Only in the sense that I think people finally realized that they were stuck here and that they weren't getting away anytime soon."

"This is military training, part of their job. This isn't some vacation they can cut short. They were under orders and were stuck here regardless of whether we had all this shit happening or not. However, once we do settle up who and what has gone on here, that should change."

"I still think everybody here will want to leave," she stated, shaking her head. "And would be grateful for an opportunity to do so."

"That bad?"

"Yeah, that bad," she declared, with a clipped nod. "Me too, honestly. I mean, I hate to say it, but this isn't where I want to be long-term. It's already dragging on longer than expected, and, once things get problematic in terms of people and supplies getting in and getting out, the desire to do so is magnified. I just want to know that I'll get out."

"You will," Barret stated.

She looked over at him and smiled. "You see? That's the good old cheerleader part of you, but you haven't been here long enough to see how down and depressed everybody else is."

"No, I haven't," he acknowledged. "Good point. And I'm not trying to be so much of a cheerleader that it pisses everybody off."

"On the other hand"—she chuckled—"maybe we all need a cheerleader, at least somebody who's bright and cheerful. It helps counteract all the gloom-and-doom thinking going on here."

"Well," Magnus said, "if you hear anything specific that's nasty, negative, or in any way *not* what we want happening around here, let me know." With that, Magnus and Egan got up and left.

She looked over at Barret. "I don't even understand what role those guys play here."

"Investigatory. Yet the roles are changing," Barret noted. "Mostly due to the added problems."

"If you say so. It seems as if Magnus and Mountain have been in the forefront of it all anyway. At least, you guys are trying to handle it."

"Yep, that sounds about right. We are all the good guys, so don't worry about us."

"No, I'm not worried about your team," she admitted. "It's just that I worry I'll end up getting in trouble myself because I'm seen with you guys all the time."

"Has anybody said anything?" he asked.

She shook her head. "No, but I don't think they would either. I think it'll just be the typical behind-my-back kind of talk." He frowned at that, and she shrugged. "You have to expect a certain amount of it here right about now, and I do notice an awful lot of conversations going on that stop when I get near," she murmured. "I don't know that they're all bad. I think people are just upset and worried and want to go home. And then are wondering what it'll take to no longer be a prisoner here," she shared, with an eye roll.

"Do you think they are thinking that? The last thing we really want is a revolt of some kind."

"I think it's quite possible that some of them are think-ing that," she stated, staring at him. "The minute you stop people from leaving, you know they will resort to all kinds of things."

"Sure," Barret noted, "but it's a different story if people believe the rumors and innuendoes."

She shrugged. "I don't know whether they believe it or not. It's not been anything that I've come across at that level, but I wouldn't really want to either."

"No, of course not. Anyway, if you hear anything that sounds wrong, let us know." And, with that, he got up, then asked, "Are you staying here?"

"No, I need to go crash," she murmured. "If I don't get to sleep early in the night, I don't get to sleep at all because it's already well past time for any quantity of sleep. When I get overtired, I just can't … can't do any more," she shared. "And then I'm up so early now that, well, you know." She shrugged. "No point in bitching about it. It's just the way it is for the moment. I'm adjusting to kitchen duty and all that it entails."

"You're being a good sport about it."

She laughed. "I don't think anybody particularly cares whether I'm a good sport or not," she noted, "as long as somebody is there to help out in the kitchen. I'm happy to help. I like Chef a lot, and I don't appreciate whatever is going on in this place, so it keeps me busy and stops me from fretting, especially when the weather keeps everybody inside." She gave a wave of her hands. "When you go to bed exhausted every night, there's really no energy left for worrying."

He gave her a gentle smile. "Then come on. Time for bed for you. I'll walk you back down to your room."

"Do I need an escort now?" she asked, with surprise, but she was happy to visit with him along the way. When they got closer to her room, she stopped and stared.

"What's the matter?" he asked, as he went to walk past her.

She pointed out, "My door's open."

He frowned, stepped in front of her, and muttered, "Just a minute." Then he pushed the door open cautiously.

She gasped as she appeared behind him. "My God, they destroyed my room." He glared at the room and turned toward her. She shook her head. "No, obviously that is not how I left it this morning. No, I don't know what happened, and, no, I don't know who would do this," she snapped, glaring at him.

His eyebrows shot up, and then he grinned. "At least that saves me from having to ask all those boring questions myself."

She groaned, as she stepped inside, wondering who would have done this. She looked around, shaking her head.

He asked, "The biggest thing right now is, do you see anything missing?"

"I didn't even really have anything here to speak of. My phone is with me, and I had a laptop here." She searched for it and found it with her pillows. "So, if they were in here searching for something to steal, they didn't do a good job because my laptop wasn't exactly hidden."

"And yet you put it inside the pillowcase, inside with the pillow?"

"Sure," she murmured. "It's just an old trick."

"And apparently a good one," he noted.

She shrugged. "I don't even know that it's necessary. It's something I've always done as a habit."

"It's a good habit, and, if they were looking for the laptop, they didn't find it."

"No need to steal it," she stated. "Everybody has access to laptops here." Then she stopped and asked him, "Don't they?"

"I would imagine so," he agreed. "I don't know of anybody who hasn't been allowed access to any electronics or communication devices." He frowned. "So that's another question to ask Magnus or Mountain. The real question is, why toss your room, and why now?"

"I don't know," she stated, as she stared around the room, hating that sense of invasion. "God, and to know that I am one of what? Maybe thirty people here on base?" she noted. "That to me is the most depressing part. I mean, everybody knows where I am during the day. It's not as if I've had a chance to go anywhere and to do anything. So, my room is completely open for anybody to search, should they want to."

"Did you lock it?"

She frowned and shook her head. "I can't say for sure. These past few days I stumble out of here exhausted in the morning. I'm not exactly sure whether I locked it or not. I usually do, and it's kind of a matter of habit, but did I this time? I don't know. I would guess yes, but I can't swear to it," she confessed.

When another man spoke, the room spun as she turned, surprised to see Magnus studying the space.

"What happened here?" he asked.

She sighed. "Seems my room was searched, while I wasn't here."

"Searched?" he asked, an eyebrow shooting up. "More like destroyed."

"I don't know what else you want to call it," she said. "Let's just say that I didn't ask anybody to come in here and destroy it."

"Of course not," he murmured, as he looked around. "Okay." He nodded. "Barret, look for anything with prints. I do have a way to track fingerprints, if any are here. I'll see if anybody's been around her room."

"I doubt you'll find any witnesses." She glared at her

room. "Even if nothing is missing, it's just that sense of violation."

"Anything missing?"

She shrugged. "I have my laptop, and I have my phone. … Other than that, my clothes. I don't really have much else. We all came up here with minimum baggage."

"I know, so what is it that they could be looking for?"

She snorted at that. "I don't know. After that whole drug scene on base had been exposed, maybe they're after drugs."

"I hate to ask," Barret said, with a small smile, and left it at that.

She rolled her eyes. "No, … I don't do drugs. No, I don't have drugs. No, I wouldn't have any in here. So, if they're in here, somebody planted them," she snapped.

At that, Magnus stiffened. "That's a really good point. Why don't you step out in the hallway and let me take a look."

She glared at him and then shrugged. "Fine." She stepped out, arms crossed, leaned against the nearby wall, and waited.

Inside, she was fuming. Who would have done this, and why? It's not as if she had anything of importance, nothing of value, and nothing that was even sellable really, especially in this Arctic locale, at least nothing that anybody else would want. She never spent very much money on anything except for, she would admit, she had a good phone and she had a good laptop. But both of those items were here with her, so that didn't make any sense either.

The men stepped back out again, and her gaze went from one to the other. "Anything?" They both shook their heads, and she sagged in relief. "I hate to admit it, but that is a huge relief," she muttered. "I scared myself a little bit with that idea."

"Still, to know that somebody rifled through your room is not the status quo on how we want this camp to run," Magnus muttered. "And now I have to take that to the boss."

She gave a laugh. "Better you than me."

"And yet"—he gave her a hard look—"you can't expect to walk away from that."

"What do you mean?" she asked, glaring at him.

"He'll want to talk to you."

She swallowed and nodded. "Not to mention the investigators. What happened to the MPs?" she asked. "Isn't that something fairly normal for a situation like this?"

Magnus nodded. "It would be, except that they were the first two who died—suspiciously. One Russian and one from the German team."

At that, Barret stared at him. "What?'

"Yeah, didn't you know that?"

"No, I didn't know that. So why weren't more sent up?"

"Yeah, that's one of the questions I want to get answered myself," Magnus stated. "I'm heading off now to have a little talk with Ted and maybe the colonel."

"Yeah, let me know how that goes," Barret said heatedly.

"I will, but I'm not holding my breath." With that, Magnus quickly disappeared.

She looked up at Barret. "So, can I go back in my room?"

"I would think so. I didn't see anything to try and pull prints from. Let's go get your bed made up." He gave her a hand, and, when it was done, he asked, "Are you sure you're okay to sleep in here?"

She nodded. "Honestly I'm so tired that it wouldn't make any difference." He didn't like that answer; she could tell from his immediate frown and the uneasy glance around. "What are you expecting?"

"I'm not expecting anything, but whoever searched your room now knows that you're here alone," he pointed out, "and that makes me nervous."

"And yet it shouldn't."

"Do you remember what drug was found here on the compound?"

She nodded. "Yeah, a date rape drug, and I get that but—"

"No but, no but at all," he murmured. "It just makes me uneasy."

"So, what do you want me to do?" she asked in exasperation. "I can't exactly change my sleeping arrangements on the fly. I'm way too tired tonight to even go apply, or worse, to make a big fuss over it, and honestly I really prefer my own personal space. They'll just put me in with somebody else, and I don't want that."

He nodded. "I hear you, and I get it. So I'll just include you in my rounds now."

She stared at him. "What do you mean, in your rounds?"

"I'm one of several of us who do rounds all night long," he replied, "trying to keep the place safe."

"I didn't know that," she murmured.

He gave her a ghost of a smile. "It's not something we advertise. We don't want any more trouble, so we've upped our presence, just to try and keep some of the shenanigans down."

"And yet during the day …"

"Exactly. During the day we don't have the same presence. We don't have the same manpower because most of us are out doing other things," he explained, with a casual shrug. "This will be part of the unfortunate discussion that Magnus has to have with the boss."

She winced. "Better him than me."

He laughed. "I'm not even sure it's him directly, as much as it may be Mountain."

"Yeah, well, I think Mountain can handle anything that comes his way," she said. "Now that is somebody who intimidates me."

"Mountain?" he asked.

She nodded. "Maybe it's just his sheer size alone. I mean, he's huge."

"He is. He's a big man, but he's also a really good man and fair."

"If you say so. I honestly don't have much experience with him, so I don't know what to say about that."

"I don't think anything needs to be said either," Barret noted. "Just know that he's on the side of right—always."

She smiled. "That is a very interesting statement."

"Why?" he asked.

"Because I don't think most people would agree with that. The size that he is, he could be doing any damn thing he wants, and nobody would say no."

"All the better that he's on the right side of the equation," he murmured.

"And you're sure about that?" she verified. He nodded, and she felt relief wash through her. "In that case, okay, but I'll head to bed because morning comes damn early." She stopped at the doorway, looked back at him, and smiled. "Thanks for the help tonight."

He nodded and smiled at her. "You have a good night."

And he quickly walked away.

BARRET FOUND IT hard to leave Avalon. He wanted to sit down and guard her all day and all night, an impulse that was both foreign and felt right at the same time. He didn't know how he'd become so attached to her, yet the circumstances were definitely part of the drive behind it. She was somebody he wanted to know a whole lot better, but, at the moment, things were just a complete and utter mess.

He quickly found Magnus, who told him, "I've already talked to Mountain."

"I'll add her quarters to my list of places to keep an eye on overnight," Barret noted. "We shouldn't have anybody bunking alone."

"But several people are choosing to," Magnus pointed out.

"Of course. In her case, the fact that her room was already searched is another dubious point."

"Why didn't you just suggest sharing her room?"

He laughed. "If I didn't think it was way too early for that and that she would freak out, I might have, but I don't think she's in any way ready for that suggestion."

"That's too bad," Magnus replied, "because I know those of us who have bunked in with our women are infinitely safer."

"Or at least delusional," he murmured.

"That too," he teased, with a half smile. "It does give us a sense, maybe a false sense, of security though."

The men discussed the issue for a little bit longer. Barret muttered, "Hopefully we won't have more issues."

"I still don't understand why they would go after her room though."

"Unless they thought that she had access to something from the kitchen, but what would anybody want from there? That is the question." It made no sense to Barret, and he pondered it throughout the night. When he got up to do his shift, he passed Magnus, who was headed to bed.

"All is quiet."

Nodding, Barret headed to Avalon's first. He would end his shift doing the same thing again. Once he took his first sweep by her room, stopping to hear nothing behind her door, Barret headed to check the generator shed. Before coming back inside, he made a trip to see Joe, and the dogs gave a warning. He called out to them to find Joe opening the door.

"Problems?" Joe snapped.

"No, just checking to make sure there aren't any." Barret walked toward the dogs and was engulfed with slobbery kisses and tails whacking his legs. He laughed and tried to cuddle as many as he could. One called Ratchet, due to the big black ring around one eye, was persistent. He'd met this one several times. If Joe ever wanted to sell these dogs, many of the men here on base would be interested. Barret knew he would be.

Joe nodded. "It's a sad day."

"It is, indeed, but we won't worry about that. We'll just keep going forward, as if there's no problem, but we won't take any chances in the meantime." Barret bent down to greet Chaos, one of the younger huskies that was one of the favorites. He was always friendly, a hard worker, and absolutely loved being outdoors all the time. He was also one of the first ones to greet anybody who came to visit.

He scratched Chaos on the back. "Sorry, I didn't mean to wake you." He looked at Joe and then went back to pat the dog lightly.

"No, it's better you do wake me," he grumbled. "I want to make sure that nothing else goes wrong."

"You and me both," he muttered.

And, with that, and one last round of cuddles, Barret left Joe, so the animal keeper could go back to sleep in peace. Then Barret headed to the kitchen, checking on everyone's room as he went. It appeared that all the room doors were closed, and everybody was out like a light. He headed into the storeroom, checked on Chef, who grumbled but didn't argue. Barret didn't turn on the light, just heard the older man snuffling in disgust.

He smiled and kept on going. Chef might snuffle in disgust at the need for nighttime sentries, but, at the same time, there was also a certain sense of relief that Barret and his team were out there, diligently keeping the peace. And, with that, Barret headed to make his second pass at Avalon's door, then back toward his room, bypassing Mountain at five in the morning, as he stepped up to take a shift now. "All is well," Barret softly called out to him.

And, with that, Barret quickly passed off the shift and went to grab a few more hours of sleep himself.

WHEN HE HEADED for the kitchen the next morning, everything appeared normal and fine. He found Avalon working away in the kitchen.

She looked up, cast him a bright smile. "See? I had a good night."

"Glad to hear it," he replied calmly. "You probably got more sleep than I did."

She cast a glance at him and nodded. "Anybody who's up doing those kinds of checks isn't getting much sleep."

"I'm also quite used to it," he noted.

"Maybe, but it still wears you down."

"Perhaps, yet, at this point in time, I don't want to say we're at war but—"

"We're at war. I get it. Great way to think about it."

He winced. "Sorry, that wasn't quite the way I wanted to present it."

"No, but it's a good way," she agreed. "It keeps the motivation quite clear." She handed him a big heavy mug and said, "Here. Take this coffee, go sit down, and wake up." He looked down at the mug, and she shrugged. "It's one of our kitchen mugs."

"Hey, it makes sense to me. And it looks as if it keeps the drinks a little warmer."

"It does. Not that you guys have any problem with getting it down beforehand," she added, with a laugh.

He smiled and headed out to the dining area to see several other people gathering around, looking for food. A few came up and talked to him, and he was friendly with everybody, just keeping his eyes open and watchful.

One of the guys approached and said, "Hey, I just … I don't want to trespass, but you know Avalon there? She's quite something."

"So, you don't want to trespass in what way?" Barret asked, his voice hard.

At that, the other guy winced. "Hey, not saying anything. I already got the message from your tone of voice. Glad I asked." And, with that, he quickly disappeared.

He remembered his name was Ralph, one of the regulars. Behind him, Magnus chuckled. "You sure you don't want to move into her room?"

"I'd love to, but I won't bring that up right now," he shared, with a smile, as he turned. "But you can damn-well bet I'm not letting any other punk in there."

"No, I get it." Magnus smirked. "Interesting that he asked."

"I'm not exactly sure why he asked though," Barret admitted, looking over at Magnus. "That was completely unnecessary."

"And the fact that he felt it was necessary is a very interesting state of affairs."

"I don't think she would agree with that," Barret noted. "In fact, I'm pretty sure it would just piss her off."

He had a chance to ask her, just before he headed out for an afternoon training shift on skis. They were doing long-distance rifle training and dealing with avalanche training on another team. As he packed up some water and jerky, he looked up to see her standing there, watching the trainees all disappear, a wistful look on her face. He realized just what she'd given up by agreeing to help Chef in the kitchen. "I'm sorry."

She turned to him and shrugged. "We can all be sorry, but it doesn't change anything."

"No, but this isn't quite what you came for, is it?"

"No, it sure isn't," she admitted, with a laugh. "However, at this point, I would count just getting home in one piece as an equally positive thing."

"As far as I know, more staff is coming. I just don't know when."

"I'll believe that when I see it." She snorted. "I think once they get somebody in their clutches, they're pretty happy to just stick with the status quo."

Barret asked, "Do you know Ralph very well?"

"Ralph, Ralph, Ralph?" She looked a little confused for a moment, then realization dawned. "Which one is he?"

"The guy talking about the kitchen help poisoning the food."

"Sure. I remember him now. I know him at little but not well."

Barret nodded. "I may have put the kibosh on him trying to get to know you better," he shared apologetically. "He asked me, in a roundabout way, if he'd be stepping on toes if he got to know you better."

Her eyebrows shot up. "Did you say he asked you?" her tone dropping, as her gaze narrowed.

"Not so much that," he replied hurriedly. "He just … I think he was asking whether he would be stepping on anybody's toes if he headed in that direction."

"I see." She studied Barret for a long moment. "So, what

did you say to him?"

"I guess I didn't need to say a whole lot," Barret replied. "I didn't appreciate him asking, and he got his answer from my tone of voice."

She snorted. "So, the real question is, did you not appreciate him asking because you're interested yourself, or you didn't appreciate him asking because I'm perfectly capable of dealing with my own problems?"

He looked at her, knowing a minefield had just opened up in front of him. "A whole lot of everything."

She glared at him. "And that sounds like a cop-out."

"Okay, straight-up then. I'm definitely interested. I definitely don't want anybody else to step in the way, and, given the circumstances, I was also not impressed with the idea of anybody else getting between us," he admitted, firing off the answers just as if she had asked him to. "And, of course, you're perfectly capable. That goes without saying," he added, hoping he had made a quick recovery.

She looked at him and then a slow smile broke out. "Good to hear on all counts," she said. "Now, get lost and go do your afternoon games. I'll be in here baking cookies." He froze, then turned and looked at her hopefully. "Yes, cookies. Apparently we have enough supplies," she stated, with an eye roll.

"There's always enough supplies to bake cookies," he declared, with a smile.

"I wouldn't have said that myself, but cookies it is for me today."

He grinned. "Good, just make sure you save me one or two."

"We'll see," she hedged. "Depends on how late you are."

And, with that, he headed out, a big smile on his face.

DAY 6 DINNERTIME PREP

AVALON THOUGHT ABOUT Barret's words throughout the rest of the day to the point that Chef even called her on it a couple times. "Who are you mooning over?"

She winced. "I hope I'm not mooning over anybody," she muttered. "I don't understand how you can moon over somebody and then have that also be the phrase where you drop your drawers and shoot them a good look at your tushy."

"That one escalated too quickly," Chef teased, with a snicker.

"How does that equate to love?" she asked him. He just gave her a lopsided grin. She rolled her eyes. "Better yet, don't answer that question," she corrected, with a smirk in his direction.

She got busy with the dinner prep. When she heard a sound in the kitchen later, she noted the colonel coming in, looking for something. She walked over and asked, "May I get you something, sir?" He stared at her, then frowned. "I know. I wasn't originally assigned to be in the kitchen," she explained. "I'm just helping out."

He didn't say anything, just eyed her suspiciously.

She regretted approaching him now, but she added, "If you need anything from the kitchen, just let me know."

And, with that, she made a very awkward exit. As soon

as she got to the back, she motioned out to the front and told Chef, "The colonel's out there."

Chef just nodded and didn't say anything.

"Does he not get any special treatment?"

Chef shook his head at that. "Nope, not unless he asks for it," he replied in a comfortable tone that really surprised her.

She shrugged. "Okay then. He seemed kind of suspicious when he saw me."

"That's because you're not a part of this training group, as the others would be," he replied, with a smile.

"I guess," she noted. "It just seems kind of weird. Yet, hey, happy to stay out of it."

With that, he nodded, but Chef ended up heading out to the front anyway.

She kept an eye out and listened, and, when she heard low voices, she wondered what was going on. She looked out to see the two of them sitting down and talking, as if old friends. She studied their body language for a moment, but it seemed as if everything was fine, and that surprised her.

She headed back to the kitchen to do her work, but when Chef didn't come back after another half hour, she had a few questions she needed answered in order to keep her work on schedule. She hesitated, then popped her head around and asked, "May I interrupt for a moment, please?"

The colonel frowned at her, but Chef nodded and hopped up. "What do you need?"

When she explained, he gave her the answers she needed, and then he rejoined the colonel, while she returned to work, pondering the mysteries of life and likely relationships.

She quickly buckled down and worked her way through the tasks before her, keeping her mind occupied with other things. When Chef did come back, she looked at him sideways. "Didn't realize you and the colonel were such good buds."

He laughed. "In a way, yes, we are. We go way back."

"Oh, good for you, although it blew me away."

"Not really," he said, with a smile as he faced her. "We've done a lot of missions together. Worked on a lot of bases together and in particular circumstances. I came here because of him," Chef shared comfortably. She stopped and turned, frowning at him. He laughed. "That surprises you, doesn't it?"

"It does kinda, yeah," she admitted. "Guess I didn't realize that was a thing."

"Sure, it is, but it's not as if I get special treatment for it."

"No, not that I've seen anyway." She chuckled. "Yet maybe you get special consideration at the back end that I don't know about."

"Nope," he denied, giving her a flat smile. "That's not the way I operate."

Maybe she shouldn't have said that out loud, but, in the back of her mind, she wondered.

She kept working to get dinner underway, but eventually she told Chef, "I need to go sit down and get off my feet for a bit."

"Absolutely. You didn't even take lunch, did you?"

"No, I was too busy getting everything prepped for dinner."

"Well, go on then, go." Chef shooed her away. "I'll need you back again, so you grab your breaks when you can."

She nodded and headed out. At the same time though it kind of felt weird to leave, while Chef would obviously still be working. She hesitated and then asked, "Are you sure? I mean, I could keep working, if you need me."

"Nope, you go. Everything's fine."

Not sure, but now that she'd asked for the time, she felt bad at even trying to take it. Still he shooed her away again. She headed back to her room, sat on her bed, and completely collapsed. These early mornings and the persistent cold, and the steady kitchen work on her feet just seemed to take the energy right out of her. She took several slow deep breaths and tried to just unwind and to enjoy being where she was.

When she heard an odd sound in the room beside her, she wasn't at all sure what she heard, but it stopped her from crashing properly and definitely from going under. She listened again. A woman crying. She thought about the women on the base and couldn't even begin to picture who resided in that room, not with all the room reassignments going on and her stint in the kitchen. Yet the cries sounded female. Avalon hesitated and then got up and walked out of her room and knocked on the other door. All sounds stopped.

She winced and then in a soft voice said, "Hey, look. I'm not trying to intrude, but, if there's anything I can do to help, just let me know."

"I'm fine," said the woman, in a muffled tone.

Avalon winced because it was so obvious that *fine* wasn't a word that went along with this. "Okay. I mean, I get that, and I'm sorry. I'm not trying to get in your face about anything, I just … If you need something, you can always knock on my door and say that you need help. I'm right beside you."

No answer came, but she'd already declined her help, so what was Avalon supposed to say now? Frowning, she went back to her room. At least the sobbing had stopped. Yet maybe that wasn't a good thing. Maybe the poor woman needed some sort of a release from all the heavy emotions she was feeling, and now Avalon felt bad about ruining that for her.

She lay in bed, tense, wondering if she could have done something else for her, when, out of the blue, came this horrific set of screams. She got out of her bed and stepped into the hallway to find a woman collapsed on the floor, holding her throat tight.

Avalon raced over to her, screaming at the others, "Get Sydney. Hurry up. Get the doctor!"

When she tried to lift the other woman, one of the men brushed her aside, picked up the woman in distress, and raced her to the medical center. Avalon followed along right behind him, not at all sure what was going on. The woman appeared to be choking, and yet nobody was offering first aid.

As soon as they got to the center, Sydney jumped into action. It seemed that the woman's throat was seizing up, so she needed oxygen and apparently adrenaline to reduce the swelling. With Sydney having the matter firmly in control, Avalon hesitated at the doorway.

Sydney looked at her and asked, "Did you see her?"

Avalon hesitated and then shook her head. "I didn't see what happened. I was lying in my room, trying to catch five from work, when I heard the screams. First, someone was crying, I think, and then …"

Magnus was almost behind her, when he asked, "Who was screaming?"

"I thought it was the crying woman," Avalon replied in confusion. "I'm not sure who else it would have been. I don't know how many women there are on base."

"We have seven right now," Magnus noted, "and three of you are right here."

"And the others?" she asked him, looking around.

"Berry's one. Cherry, her twin sister, is gone, and two more newbies are now on base."

"Here's the problem," Sydney noted, as she checked the distressed woman's vitals. "This one is incapable of screaming, so it wasn't her."

Magnus looked at Sydney sharply and quickly disappeared.

"So obviously we have another person out there in trouble," Avalon muttered.

Sydney eyed Avalon. "Did you see her?"

"No. I just talked to the crying woman through the door to her room." Avalon frowned. "People were milling around." Then she shook her head. "Honest to God, I don't really know who I saw. I don't know whether I saw just men or women. One of the guys brushed me aside, picked up this woman, and raced her here to you."

"Which is a good thing," Sydney stated cheerfully. "She's had an allergic reaction to something."

Avalon stared at the doc. "Please tell me it's not food-related." When Sydney studied Avalon curiously, she shrugged. "I'm in the kitchen all the time, and I would hate for anybody to think I was poisoning people, like Ralph said one day," she noted bitterly.

"Right," Sydney murmured. "I don't think that's exactly what we're looking at here, but I won't know until I get a better handle on it. She is breathing comfortably now, so we'll hang on to that."

"I'm grateful for that," Avalon muttered, "but it's pretty

damn scary to think it could be something I did."

"If it was," Sydney replied, "I presume it wasn't something you did deliberately."

Avalon stared at her in horror and quickly shook her head. "No, no, of course not," she declared, "but I'm in the kitchen all the time now—it's just Chef and me. As long as it's not food poisoning," she muttered. At that, Sydney looked at her sharply, and she shrugged. "I just don't want it to have anything to do with me."

"Interesting you would jump to that," the doc acknowledged. "What's going on here? A guilty conscience?"

"I am new to the kitchen. And so much goes on back there. And I've been thrown into that job to fill a void. Human errors happen. And I would be the likely suspect. However, everything we put out is safely labeled as such," Avalon noted. At Sydney's frown, Avalon added, "The labels on certain dishes. We have to note which items have peanuts or soy or dairy or whatever that someone on base has noted as an allergic item in their file. … But that doesn't mean there isn't something else going on here."

"No, and, until I get a chance to talk to her," Sydney stated, "I won't know. So go back to work. You do whatever you need to do. I'll follow up with you in a bit."

And, with that, dismissed, Avalon headed back to the kitchen.

As she got in, Chef took one look at her and said, "You don't look as if you rested much."

She shook her head. "No, not at all." Then she quickly explained, first about the woman crying and then about the screams and finding a woman in the hallway, choking. He looked at her in astonishment. "Sydney said it was an allergic reaction?"

Avalon nodded. "That's what she thought, at least for the moment."

"Then we'll do the same," Chef acknowledged. "Let's not borrow trouble."

He walked out, checked the foods that they had out and the respective labels, and he nodded. "Everything out here is properly labeled," he murmured. "Still that doesn't mean that somebody who's trying to cause trouble couldn't have done it another way."

She studied the labels. "You mean, by just switching the labels?"

He nodded. "We do have some people with bad allergies, and Sydney's patient is one of them."

"Well, Jesus, then surely she wouldn't take something off a tray clearly marked as something she can't have."

"Unless she thought for sure it was safe," he pointed out.

Avalon winced and nodded. "Unless she thought it was safe. God, I hope it had nothing to do with us."

"Even if it did," Chef replied, "it wasn't deliberate on our part."

"No, but there's already been a couple comments about poisoning the food to poison the personnel," she shared, looking over at him.

He snapped, "I hadn't heard anything about that. Who's saying that?"

She winced. "First it was Ralph. Then just a couple guys joking about it. … I told them how that kind of talk wasn't welcome, and one of them got kind of stuffy about it."

"He can get stuffy all he wants," Chef snapped again. "We don't tolerate that kind of talk. Looking after as many people as we do, with as many special diets as we have, we put up all food with proper warnings," he declared. "So anybody saying otherwise is just trying to cause trouble."

"Which is exactly what a lot people here are trying to do," she agreed.

"Right now, yes," he confirmed, "I've never seen this many troublemakers in one group in my life." He glared, looking around.

"I'm sorry. I didn't mean to upset you."

He frowned at her. "Why the hell wouldn't you tell me?"

"Because I figured he was just being an asshole, and we didn't need to pay him any attention."

"Yet it's been bothering you."

She shrugged. "Maybe not bothering me as much as being very aware that we potentially have some ugly talk going around."

"Potential ugly talk is more ugly talk than I'm interested in having," Chef stated, "so we'll deal with that one too."

"Especially if this turns out to be food poisoning," she muttered.

He nodded. "Honestly, in this case, it wouldn't be anything to blame us about. She has quite the list of allergies. She warned me at the time and told me that she carried an emergency kit for it."

"Which is also something Sydney would have known."

"Exactly, so why didn't the woman use her EpiPen or whatever? Regardless it's not your fault. It's not my fault, no matter what triggered it. And you tell me immediately the next time some asshole makes jokes about the food."

Avalon nodded. And, with that, she headed back to the kitchen, where they continued to work on food prep.

When Magnus stepped into the kitchen a little later, he announced, "It was food poisoning, ... of a sort anyway. She had a cookie labeled as nut free."

At that, Chef looked at him and shook his head. "For one, we don't ever label anything that way. For two, she should have known better, and, for three, … I'm already very aware about her food allergies and sensitivities. She gets a special diet all the time, so what the hell is she doing eating a cookie off a tray like that?"

"She told me that it had been given to her with a special note, saying that it was made just for her."

Chef sucked in his breath, shook his head, and asked, "And she believed it?"

At that, Magnus nodded slowly. "So, the question is, why would she, and why would somebody do that in the first place?"

"To cause trouble," Avalon stated. "As we well know, an awful lot of troublemakers are at work around here."

"Oh, I get it," Magnus noted, "but was this some sick joke? Was it somebody who didn't really understand just how sick she could become? Or was it something more sinister? Any ideas?"

"No, no ideas," Avalon said. "Believe me. It makes me sick to my stomach to think that somebody might have done that to deliberately hurt her."

"They did it deliberately all right," Magnus confirmed. "No doubt about that. The question is whether she'll be okay enough to stay here."

"Can she really get out that way? If she can, then that's another reason for her to have eaten that cookie."

"Are you saying she would have eaten it just so she could leave?" Magnus asked in astonishment.

"I don't know her personally, but you have no idea what the mood is around this place," she explained. "I'm just saying it's another possibility, and, yes, it's an ugly one. I know that."

He nodded. "It absolutely is an ugly one, but I hear you, and it's something I'll keep in mind."

She nodded, then turned but stopped. She faced Magnus and added, "Unless it was directed at the two of us here in the kitchen."

Magnus quickly nodded. "That's another possibility we're keeping on our radar too. Just stay safe, both of you, will you?"

"They'll just try using us as scapegoats, you know, for reasons or methods to get them out of this training session and off this base or to expel me and Chef," she snapped.

"Still won't work," Magnus replied cheerfully. "Chef's here for the long term, and you might be too."

"Not if anybody else gets sick while I'm still doing kitchen duty," she pointed out. And, with that, she turned and walked away.

BARRET, WHO HAD been standing behind Magnus the whole time, studied Avalon carefully. She was worried, nervous, angry, and yet at the bottom of it all was fear.

As soon as Magnus stepped back, Barret asked him, "Did you see that?"

"Sure, she's afraid, but I don't know why."

"Could be a lot of reasons at this point, and one of the biggest is the fact that she feels targeted—that somebody will blame her," he pointed out. "Not so much that she's targeted, just that whatever this is, it's directed at them."

"I don't even know that it's directed at them," Magnus

corrected, "or if it's directed at anybody. You know that it could be just causing trouble for the sake of causing trouble."

"With very serious consequences. Not sure anybody would have known how serious though, especially someone without such life-threatening responses," Barret added. "Plus, just because she's got food allergies doesn't mean that it's the life-threatening kind. And most people who have life-threatening food allergies don't work in a place like this."

"I'll check in with Sydney, as I need to talk to her patient as soon as I can," Magnus noted, "to find out who gave her the cookie and why she would believe it was okay to eat it."

"The part that surprises me is, if she has that many severe allergies, why would she trust somebody outside of close friends and family?"

"That would suggest that it was somebody she trusted, and, if so, who was that person?"

And, with that, they both headed to the medical clinic, where a weary Sydney smiled at them. "She'll be fine, but her throat's pretty raw. I did end up making her vomit to clear it out of her system quickly, and her body's still in reactive mode at the moment, but she'll be okay."

"Good," Magnus replied. "We need to talk to her."

At that, Sydney cast a glance back at her patient. Barret stepped closer and smiled at the young woman and asked, "Hey, how're you feeling?"

"Pretty crappy at the moment," she said, talking slowly and wincing with pain, "but better than I was before. At least I know I'll survive." She shook her head. "I haven't had a reaction like that in a very long time."

"Which brings us around to why you had this one."

She shrugged. "A cookie was sent my way, and I absolutely adore cookies. I was told that it was fine for me, by somebody I trusted."

"And that is who we need to talk to."

She shook her head. "They wouldn't have known the difference," she stated too quickly for Barret's liking. "They went to the kitchen and brought it back, saying they had spoken to somebody who told them that special cookies were being made and that I would be allowed to have some. Obviously some ingredients were in there that either they didn't know about or …"

"Or they assumed that you were okay to have, which is also a little bit dubious or downright …"

The patient shook her head. "I don't care to hear about how many others were affected or could possibly be this time. I've never had a problem here before."

"I know," Barret confirmed, "and that's the good news because we don't want you to have any problems like this ever again."

"No, God no," she whispered.

"But I do need to know who gave you the cookie."

"I thought it was from Chester." She pulled a note from her pocket. "This was under the cookie." She looked at the note, shook her head, and added, "I don't know for sure that Chester wrote it."

"We'll go talk to him."

"No need. I'm right here," stated the burly young staff sergeant at the doorway. He smiled at her. "Hey, Helen. How you doing?"

"I would have been a whole lot better if I hadn't eaten that cookie."

He frowned. "I can't imagine that you ate a cookie up here, when you're on such a restricted diet."

"I wasn't even going to come here because of all my allergies," she explained, "but I really wanted the experience."

"Like a lot of people." Chester nodded. "And the base kitchen accommodated your special diet, so you're all good."

She smiled. "I mean, I just stick to basic food. I don't get any special diet, but I do get my own meals prepared just for me," she shared. "In this case the cookie was with a note from you, by the way, saying that it was perfectly safe."

Chester stared at her in shock. "From me? What?" She held out the note, so that he saw it. He turned and looked back at Magnus, shaking his head. "I didn't write this. Oh, no, no, no, I did not write this."

He was too loud, too vehement, in Barret's opinion.

"I know that she's deathly allergic to so many foods, so I would never have done this," he cried out. "Who would write this?" he asked, his shock quickly turning to fury. "This was deliberate, wasn't it?" He spun around, looking at the two men, now glaring when they didn't respond fast enough. "Wasn't it?" he cried out.

Helen tried to calm him down. "Chester, look it's okay. I'll be fine."

He stared at her, shaking his head. "Yeah, but you almost weren't. Do you have any idea what it did to me to see you in the hallway like that?"

When she gave him a wan smile, he walked over and gave her a hug, leaving no doubt about the relationship between the two of them. "My God," he whispered.

"I know. I'm sorry," Helen murmured.

"What are you sorry for?" he cried out, his temper once again flaring.

She groaned. "Easy, just take it easy."

He took a deep breath, then turned and faced the two

men. "You'll find out who did this, right? Because if you don't, I will."

"Best that you not do anything," Magnus suggested, but with absolute authority in his tone that Barret wholeheartedly approved of.

Barret stepped forward and added, "We will find out who did this."

The young man looked at him and slowly nodded. "And fast, right?"

"As fast as we can," Barret stated cheerfully. "Which is why we were just here talking to her, and she mentioned that you wrote the note and left the cookie for her."

"Which I didn't do and would never have done, as somebody who knows perfectly well what she goes through when she eats the wrong food. No way I would ever put her through that."

Barret turned to Helen. "It has been brought up that you've made several requests to leave."

She nodded. "Yeah, just like almost everybody else here."

Chester nodded. "Hell, I did too," he agreed. "None of us want to be here right now. And I get it. All kinds of reasons hold us all here, but it seems as if they should be moving a little bit faster."

Barret wouldn't argue with him; no point in arguing with somebody who was already irate. Then he turned to Helen. "Look. This is a question that is bound to make you angry, but I do need to ask it. Can you verify that you didn't intentionally do this in an attempt to get yourself out of here?"

She stared at him in shock. "I don't think you understand how bad my allergies are. One slight miscalculation or even being a little bit farther away from Sydney here, and I wouldn't have made it," she murmured. "So, the answer to your question is absolutely not. I did not and would never take something deliberately to cause a medical crisis in an effort to get myself released from this hellhole. Although, if I didn't get anywhere near as sick as I do, it would be a hell of a good idea, and I do understand the question." Then she looked at him and smiled sadly. "But, no, I did not do this intentionally."

Chester brimmed with fury, as he stared at Barret. "You really had to ask her that?"

"Of course he did," Helen stated calmly. "Come on. You know he had to, and, if you weren't so irate over the whole thing, you would be calmer and would understand it from their point of view."

"It's pretty hard to understand how anybody could suggest that you would do this on purpose," he snapped, now glaring at her.

And she just smiled, reached out a hand, and said, "That's because, right now, you're just afraid and in shock because you thought you might have lost me."

He bent over and gave her another hug and then whispered something in her ear.

She blushed and smiled. "As you can tell, gentlemen," she shared, "the two of us have a relationship, and we care very deeply about each other. As much as I want to leave, I was hoping that both of us could leave together," she added. "So making myself sick and pointing the finger at him would only make that impossible."

Barret nodded at that. "You know I had to ask."

"I do know you had to ask," she said, with half a smile. "I understand, and I won't hold it against you."

"I might though," Chester declared, glaring at Barret.

"You can if you want. Absolutely you can. It won't impact me either way," Barret said, eyeing him. "Just don't get in my way while I'm out there talking to other people." And, with that, Barret gave Magnus another look, then turned and left. At the doorway he stopped, turned back, and asked, "Where was the note exactly? And the cookie?"

"They were on my bed," she stated right away.

"Do you lock your door?"

She winced and shook her head. "No, I don't generally lock my door." Chester rounded on her, and she held up a hand. "I know. I told you that I would, and I haven't bothered. I mean, we live in close-enough confines as it is," she muttered. "I can't say it was anything I thought I needed to do."

Barret nodded at that reasoning. "Maybe from now on you should."

"Yeah, okay, fine." She winced. "I don't have a room to myself though," she noted, "so I can't guarantee that the door will always end up locked, since it is not just me using the door."

"Right." Barret looked over at Chester, half smiled, and suggested, "Maybe you should change your sleeping arrangements." And, with that, he was gone.

BACK IN THE kitchen, Barret walked over to Chef and asked, "May I have a word?"

He looked up, nodded, and stepped a bit away from where Avalon was working. She glared at Barret but didn't say anything, and he knew how she felt, but he needed to talk to Chef. He quickly explained about the cookie.

Chef just stared at him. "Jesus, anybody could have done that."

"Exactly the problem," Barret confirmed. "And, if you didn't see anybody around here in any way, talking to people or doing anything like this, then we don't have any way to know who might have set it up."

"And somebody could have grabbed the cookie for themselves," Chef protested, "and then dropped it off for her."

"Which is another consideration."

"Can you get the handwriting analyzed?" Chef asked.

"Not likely," Barret noted, "and I hope to get it solved much sooner than the time that would take. Of course I had to ask Helen if she might have done it on her own just to get removed from this place."

At that, Chef chuckled and nodded. "No, she's severely allergic. One wrong move on her part, and it could easily be fatal. It's made me kind of nervous even having her here. But I think she must have some pull with someone and wanted to come up for a few weeks, but that few weeks has ended up being a whole lot longer," Chef explained.

"Understood, and that pretty well confirms everything she has told me so far. Anyway, I just wanted to let you know that's where it came from."

"Great. I mean …" He stopped, shook his head. "I still can't believe that she would even eat anything offered in here. Her food is kept completely separate, … as in I cook it especially for her. She gets a stir-fry pretty well every night, or, if I'm doing ribs or something, I don't put anything in it that I know can upset her system. Usually I just cook hers separately." Chef shook his head. "I even use a special pan for her meals, so what you're saying doesn't make any sense to me."

"It may not make sense now, but it will when we get down to it," Barret declared. "That much I can promise." And, with that, he turned and left, smiling at Avalon as he went, hoping that the smile would at least let her know that everything was okay.

WHEN AVALON RACED down the hall and caught up with him, she asked in an urgent voice, "Did I have anything to do with it?" She knew her expression must clearly reveal her woebegone feelings.

He looked at her and shook his head, pulling her in for a quick hug, smiling when she sagged into his embrace.

She whispered, "I've been so worried." He told her what happened, and she just stared. "That means it was deliberate," she said in a hoarse voice.

He nodded. "Absolutely it was deliberate, but it wasn't you, and it wasn't Chef, and Helen's on guard now to ensure that she doesn't eat anything that she's not supposed to."

"She shouldn't have anyway," Avalon stated, staring at him.

"I suppose maybe the note and the thought that Chester had done something special for her got her guard down. Of course now she feels like a fool for buying into it. Trust me."

"God." Avalon stared at him. "I would feel so awful if anything happened to her while I was in the kitchen. Now I just want to get out of there, so, if somebody does something else like that, … it can't be put on me."

"Hopefully it won't be put on anybody," he said pointedly, "because hopefully it won't happen again." And, with, that he leaned over and gave her a light kiss. "Now I have to head out. Take care of yourself, I have to keep asking questions."

And, with that, he was gone.

DAY 6 DINNERTIME

T HAT NIGHT, AS Avalon was serving dinner, one of the guys came up to her, leaning in over the counter, almost towering over her. "Is it safe to eat?" he demanded.

She looked up and flatly stated, "Yes, but, if you don't want to eat, that's fine. I don't care either way."

He glared at her. "We never had a problem in the kitchen until you started working in there."

"Anytime you want to take over, feel free," she said, her voice equally flat as she glared at him. She knew the names of most the guys around but couldn't remember this one and didn't really care to remember at this point. He was just being an asshole, and plenty of those were around when everybody was stuck here and fed up. Already there was no shortage of people letting others know their opinions on life.

As she continued to serve people as they came by, the asshole watched every move she made, as if she were doing something completely wrong. Finally, when she'd had enough, she walked back to Chef. "You need to go serve."

He looked at her and didn't say a word, then walked to the main dining area, where everyone was sitting. "Apparently some of you guys are having trouble with my assistant," he began, his voice booming. "The next person who says one word will be off the list of people being served here. I don't care. You can go to rations or prepare your own damn food.

It's my kitchen, so you know what? … Eat it as is or get out." Then he stood there, a fuming volcano, and waited to see if anybody wanted to say anything.

Then the one punk turned and glared at him and asked, "How do we know she didn't poison us?"

"You don't," he quipped. "It's kind of like Russian roulette, isn't it?" he said, his voice soft, but his gaze was hard as he looked at him. "If you've got a problem with her, you come to me, young man. And, if you want to see tomorrow, you make sure that when you do come to me, … you come to me with respect in your voice because I don't talk to shitheads, and no one will disrespect her again." And, with that, Chef turned and walked back into the kitchen.

She stayed in the back, waiting until the crowd died down. She looked over at him. "Do you think I should go out there and serve?"

"They're not babies. They can serve themselves," he replied, with a careless shrug. "We don't have time or energy to deal with that kind of crap," he muttered.

She nodded. "I was kind of hoping to get some food myself."

"If you want to, sure. We need to check and see how much is left out there in terms of quantity anyway. We can fill up some of these containers for them—but, if you don't want to go out there, I don't blame you."

She looked at him and smiled. "The trouble is, if I don't go out there, they'll just think that I can't handle it."

He nodded. "That's exactly what they'll think. So, if you can stomach being out there and serving them food, go for it. Otherwise let the shitheads go without."

She laughed as she stepped out, still grinning, and there was Magnus and Sydney. "Hey, Sydney. How's the patient doing?"

"Helen's doing pretty well. I wanted to see if Chef could make something up for her."

"We were wondering about getting her some food but weren't sure if she had the stomach for it yet," Avalon admitted. "I can only imagine what all you had to do to get her stomach empty and to reverse the effects. So I can't imagine anything will go down too well so soon."

"I suggest a little bit of soup or broth, if you have something easy on her throat."

"Yeah, I'm sure Chef's got something set aside for her that will work." Avalon turned to find that Chef had come out at the sound of this conversation.

He nodded. "I'll get her something. I've been cooking for her since she arrived, so I sure won't stop now."

"Appreciate it," Sydney replied cheerfully. "She's feeling much better."

At that, it seemed as if everybody in the dining area had stopped talking, while this particular discussion was going on. As soon as Sydney reported how well Helen was doing, several people went back to eating, as if they'd been thinking that maybe Helen wouldn't survive.

As Avalon served up everybody in front of her, Barret asked her if she could sit down and join them for a bit.

She winced. "Not sure I want to."

He nodded. "I heard Chef's voice booming down the hall. I presume somebody mouthed off at you?"

She nodded. "Some guy was an asshole," she murmured. "Don't worry about it." Yet it was obvious that Barret wouldn't let the subject drop. She sighed. "Okay, look. I'll come out and sit down, but no badgering anybody." He gave her an innocent look, and she rolled her eyes at that.

"Really, … no badgering."

"Wasn't planning on it," he replied cheerfully.

"*Great*, that just means you'll get worse, doesn't it?"

At her side, Magnus laughed. "He might. We don't particularly take too well to bullying."

"And yet it happens so much that you can't really get that upset about it," Avalon noted.

"I can," Barret declared. "I can absolutely get upset about it. You didn't do anything wrong, so don't you let that hinder you one bit."

"Maybe not, but, when everybody else is judging you and looking at you sideways, it makes you feel pretty rough."

"Only if their opinion of you matters more than your own opinion of you. Regardless, you didn't do anything wrong." Barret gave her a look. "Grab some food and come join us, if you can."

And, with that show of support, she looked back to see Chef nodding at her.

"Go," Chef said. "We won't have a ton of time tonight, so go eat while you can."

And, with that, she served herself a plate and walked over and sat down beside the guys, feeling some of the stress and the tension ease, as she avoided looking around. She was pretty sure everyone was looking at her, but she ignored it and tried to just let it go.

AS AVALON SAT down, Barret asked, "Is the asshole here?"

She shook her head. "Looks as if he cleared out."

"Good thing," Barret said, with a cheerful smile. "He'll sleep better tonight for it."

She snorted. "Yeah, well, he knows you'll probably track him down anyway."

"Absolutely I'll track him down. That's hardly acceptable behavior in a military base. We do not allow that kind of abuse." When she looked at him, he shrugged. "I don't know how many specialized training centers like this one you've been to, but that'll never be an acceptable way to behave."

"I have to admit that it was a little unnerving."

"Don't worry about it. We'll talk to him."

"That'll just make me feel even worse," she muttered, "and Chef already ripped him pretty hard, right in front of everyone." Barret stared at her, shaking his head. She shrugged. "It's not as if I'm trying to get him into trouble."

"Maybe you should be because that kind of attitude will get him in trouble all on his own."

"Then he gets in trouble on his own," she stated, "but I don't want to be the reason behind it."

He smiled. "Are you always this nice?"

She rolled her eyes at that. "No, I'm kind of a bitch all the time."

He burst out laughing, and she grinned. "See? You're already feeling better," he noted, returning her smile.

"And that's why you said that?" she asked, with a head-shake. "You have to be nuts."

"No, not nuts," he corrected, "but I do understand when things get to be too much. I've done a lot of military base time, and you see a lot of people out there. Some of them handle base life very well, and some of them don't handle it at all. You just came up against one who's struggling."

"Yeah, you could say that," she replied, with an eye roll. "And it's kind of sad that he is struggling quite so much, and obviously he was supposed to be gone already."

"Yeah, the asshole probably was, but nobody's going anywhere. Everybody's stay was extended by another three weeks. Therefore, if they were scheduled for three weeks, they're here for six," Barret explained. "I'm not even sure that everybody will be allowed to go home at the end of their extended stay, but they've all been given notice as of today that they're here for an additional three weeks. That alone could account for some of the crankiness."

"*Great*," she murmured. "I'm sure nobody wants to hear that."

"Nope, they sure don't, but it doesn't matter. Orders are orders," he noted cheerfully. "And it doesn't matter whether you're here or somewhere else. Particularly in this case."

"What matters is that they would be a hell of a long way away from whatever is going on here, and that is what matters to them."

"They'll get out of here in a few weeks," Barret noted. "That much has been determined. We have until then to sort it out. After that? I'm not sure what the brass will do, but I don't imagine any of us will like it."

DAY 6 AFTER DINNER

IT GAVE AVALON an odd feeling, knowing she was being watched constantly, knowing that such a level of distrust of her was a part of her life. She didn't like it. When she talked to Chef about it, he shrugged.

"Things happen." He half smiled at her. "Let it go. It'll die down. We just have to keep our nose clean and make sure that none of this has anything to do with us, and we'll deal with it another time."

"We can't deal with it another time," she said in exasperation.

"Hey, this is all we've got. We're here for a few more weeks."

She rolled her eyes at him. "You mean, you're *hoping* we're here for a few more weeks, and then it's off to whatever." At that, she asked him, "What will you do next?"

He smiled. "I'm heading to Coronado. I've always liked the idea of staying near open beaches, views, and people to see."

She nodded. "Good for you."

"You?"

She shrugged. "I'm not sure. I had applied for a transfer. I've got a couple more years, and then I was thinking of leaving."

"I'm a lifer," Chef stated, with a proud smile. "This is

where I belong."

"Good for you," she murmured.

But she didn't feel the same way, and she knew it. She just didn't know where she wanted to go after her military commitment was complete. Life was many things, but an ugly surprise—like the one she had found here—wasn't what she expected. She wanted to come for the experience because, in the back of her mind, she had often wondered about ending up in Banff, doing avalanche control or as a tour guide or something. She wanted to do something with people, not war, not weapons. Maybe something along the survival line.

She didn't have a problem at all with the weather. She didn't have a problem with the cold. Yet she did have a problem with being locked up like this. That was the issue.

DAY 7 BREAKFAST

NOTHING HAPPENED AT breakfast the next day, and she started to relax a little bit. By midday she was too bored and needed something to do, other than cooking and prepping food. "I don't want to bake any more cookies," she announced.

Chef laughed. "The spice cakes went over pretty well. How about something else?"

She shrugged. "How about bar cookies?" she asked. "I could do up a bunch, like sheet cakes."

He nodded. "Sounds good. Go check what we have for ingredients."

She went into the storeroom and hauled out raisins and walnuts, thinking she could make a butter tart.

As she came back out, he looked at the ingredients, nodded, and said, "Good choices. We have lots of those."

"Just as long as we put up allergy notices," she muttered.

He laughed. "Yep, that and a few others."

It didn't take long to mix up the batter and to get it into sheet pans and in the oven. With that done, she smiled and realized he was cutting up ribs. She groaned. "Ribs again?'

"Ribs again." He nodded. "We have lots."

"Good enough, I guess."

And these were beef ribs, so, between the two of them, they soon had them in pans, ready to go into the oven.

"Should we just bake potatoes to go with it?"

Chef shrugged. "That would be an easy answer."

She laughed. "I was just trying to think of something different." With that she scrubbed up and filled several racks full of potatoes. By the time she was done, he was making a pot of tea. She smiled at him. "Now that sounds like a good idea."

As she sat here with a cup of tea, she shared, "I have this sense of waiting, a sense of, I don't know. ... Maybe like something's about to happen."

He stared at her, shook his head. "Or is it just that you're expecting something bad to happen?"

"Maybe," she muttered.

An odd feeling of waiting, a stillness inside her, all told her that whatever the shit was about to go down, it wasn't done. Still something weird was happening here. She looked around the kitchen. "Every time I see all the burn marks in here ..."

Chef nodded. "I know, but we're not going there. I check the burners every night, and I check them every morning before I turn them on." She raised her eyebrows. He nodded. "Hey, somebody intentionally tampered with it before," he noted, with a casualness that amazed her. "Don't think for a moment that I've forgotten."

She swallowed hard and nodded. "Agreed. I hear you, and I appreciate the extra caution. My burns are healing," she noted, "but I can't say that I'm sleeping all that well."

"How could you?" he said. "I mean, knowing that somebody out there was trying to kill us is a whole different story."

"Do you really think that's what it was?"

"I don't know," he admitted, "but, if the kitchen doesn't

work, at what point in time do they send people home?"

She nodded. "I do think that's what this was all about, as in they're just trying to get the place not so uncomfortable for themselves, not intent on burning down the entire thing, but stalled enough so that we're stuck out here and have to go invade the poor village of locals or something," she suggested, with a shiver. "Somehow make it bad enough here that maybe some people can get shipped out."

"In which case, they should just be talking to their superiors."

"I think they all are." Avalon stared at Chef. "As far as I know, every single person here has asked to leave."

"I haven't," he declared, with half a smile. "I don't mind this at all. I like the cold."

"What about the dogs?" she asked. "I miss them. Can't get over there as much as I want. Patches is a sweetheart, but a young one over there called Ratchet is a hoot. I'd love to take him home with me."

"Not really much of a canine person myself, although a couple come to the back door, and I give them scraps."

She raised her eyebrows at that. "Does Joe know?"

He shook his head. "Joe would never let his dogs get that far away from him like that. Not in these conditions. Of course some of them are determined."

At that, she froze and then slowly turned and looked at him, as a possibility dawned on her. "What then? Who? … Oh my God, are you helping Amelia?" He just gave her a flat stare, as she swallowed and sank back against the chair. "I presume you won't answer any questions."

"You got that right."

"Okay, fine," she replied. "Just be warned that I might get you in trouble."

A ghost of a smile drifted across his face. "Kid, I've been on the edge of getting in trouble for a very long time, and I really don't give a shit at this point. I do what I know I have to do, and I do it for all the right reasons, and I accept the consequences and don't worry about it."

To her amazement, he was still smiling at her.

"Other than that, life is just … the rules. You have to know and to understand the rules," Chef explained. "That way you know which ones you can bend, and bending them means not breaking them. When you got that, … you've got life in the service all figured out."

She laughed. "I can tell you right now that I don't have it figured out."

"Nope, I get that too," he acknowledged, "but you haven't been in the military as long as I have. Now don't you go telling anybody." And he pointed a finger at her. "Do you hear me?"

She winced. "You know that some people need to know."

He shook his head. "What I can tell you is that all the people who need to know already do."

"Oh." She frowned, as she pondered that.

He nodded. "I'm not keeping this from those who need to know," he stated. "I'm just keeping it from all the assholes who don't need to know."

BARRET SAT IN the small room, looking over at Mountain. "We're not getting anywhere on your brother."

Mountain just glared at him.

"I know. I know, but I'm thinking that we need to go

back to the beginning and sort this out."

"You think I haven't tried?" Mountain bit off. "There isn't anything to go on. He was collecting some sort of information on something wrong up here, but he didn't tell me what. So, by the time I understood what he was trying to say, and I was warning him off, he'd already gone missing."

"So we want to backtrack that."

"Good luck with that. He left no notes, not even a clue left behind. There was nothing."

"I know I'm not privy to all that's been going on here," Barret began, "but the two original deaths of the MPs look more suspicious now, plus every other one ensuing—Helsky, Ron, Yegorahn, Scott, even Joy and her boyfriend and Dr. Myles, those that we know of so far—would be …"

Mountain groaned. "Too many deaths, along with too many missing."

Barret studied Mountain and nodded. "It's no wonder such a pall is over this place."

"We're not bringing in more men to replace them," Mountain stated. "Outside of the few people who have been coming in one at a time," he added, with a glimmer of a smirk.

"Meaning, people like me." Barret gave him a quick nod. "Understood. At the same time, I do think we'd be better off if we had a little more intel."

"But you have a limited pool of suspects," Mountain pointed out. "And, with the original deaths, they happened on training missions."

"Okay, so war training, ice training, what?"

"A little bit of everything."

"So, who had access to both those first deaths, those MPs?"

"That's what we don't know. We have thirty-plus people here, and I don't want too much more suspicion thrown on anybody, so we'll have to find answers ourselves."

"Yet, so far, there just haven't been any answers popping up."

"No, and that's why you guys are here," Mountain said, with a smile.

"And you?"

"I'm looking for my brother," he replied, with a clipped nod. "And trying to figure out if the village has anything to do with this."

Barret stared at him. "Why would the locals be involved?"

"I don't know. Potentially there's money, potentially there's revenge, plus always the possibility that they want the military out of here. I don't know," Mountain admitted. "As far as keeping an eye on everybody in here, you're in touch here, and I'm the outward liaison," he noted, with a mocking smile.

"What about Avalon and Amelia?"

"You keep an eye on Avalon because I don't believe for a second that the deal with the burner was an accident."

Barret shook his head. "No, obviously it wasn't an accident."

"I don't understand how that and the other kitchen fires fit into any of this—unless purely a distraction, maybe even thinking the brass would shut down this place without a kitchen. I got news for them. We'd be eating rations and drinking cold coffee made with a snowdrift. This is an Arctic survival training camp, after all," Mountain said, with a shake of his head. "So keep an eye on Avalon. However, at the same time, if you want to go back to the beginning and try to sort out something with Teegan, go ahead. Pick one of our guys to help you, and we'll figure it out."

"Sure. Do you care who I pick?"

Mountain hesitated, then said, "You may want to try Whalen. … I've known him in the past. He's a good man."

"And you're sure he's not involved?"

At that, Mountain nodded. "Yes. He's not involved."

"Good enough," Barret replied. "I'll contact him then."

And, with that, Mountain strode off.

Barret then found Whalen in the kitchen, lingering near the coffeepot. He asked for a few minutes to speak with him, and then explained how he was looking for a clear head to analyze some of the information that had gone on and to help Barret possibly sort out some of the issues.

Whalen stared at him. "Why me?" he asked.

"Mountain suggested it."

At that, Whalen relaxed. "Then I suggest you bring in Jerry and Ted, the two investigators."

"I'm not sure I want to," Barret hedged. "We'll have to on a certain level because they'll feel as if they're getting their toes stomped on if we don't," Barret noted, "but I don't know that I want to let them in on too much."

"Yet they've already done a lot of the work," Whalen pointed out.

Barret nodded. "Yes, but they've also been here, so technically that would add them to the suspect list. You're new."

Whalen's gaze widened as he studied Barret, then slowly nodded. "I see," he replied, settling down. "So, we can't get their help, and yet, if we start asking questions from the beginning, we'll be going over the same material and making everybody suspicious."

"I do have a copy of the investigation files up until a

couple days ago. So, I suggest you curtail your personal life," Barret stated, with a motion at one of the women behind Whalen.

"What personal life?" he asked a bit sheepishly. "I can't say I'm getting anywhere anyway." And he laughed. "Not that I'm trying."

"Of course you're trying," Barret declared. "It's second nature."

"Not really trying because she's a nice girl, and it's obvious she's pretty nervous about having anything to do with anybody."

"That just means she's got brains too," Barret replied, with a sudden smile. "Anyway, considering where we're at, it would be appreciated if you could clear some of your schedule to give me a hand."

"Sure, I don't have a problem with that part," Whalen clarified. "Still, hanging with you guys will ostracize me though."

"Maybe, but there are a few benefits."

"Like what?" Whalen asked, with a smile.

"Coffee and cookies, if that interests you."

His gaze widened. "So, are they in on it too?" He motioned his head discreetly toward the kitchen.

"It's not so much that they're in on it, but, due to circumstances, they're in the know a little more than most other people."

"Right." Whalen nodded, as he turned and looked around the area. "Coffee and cookies aren't a bad bribe, considering where we're at and all."

"Yeah, not bad at all. Of course there's always the official line that your services would be appreciated."

He snorted at that. "I just want to get out of here with

my life."

"And yet you haven't been here from the beginning, have you?"

"No, I came in with Mountain, three weeks into this session," he replied. "And you're right. The two of us have known each other for a very long time. If he wants me on this, I'm definitely there."

"Good," Barret agreed. "Let's get started then." And, with that, he and Whalen walked to Barret's quarters. He pulled out his laptop and asked, "Have you got one?"

"I do."

"Good. This data must be encrypted at all times, and nobody has to know anything about this," he stated, as he inserted the USB key into his laptop. "This is the investigation so far."

Together the two of them went over it page by page.

"Jesus, we don't have much," Whalen noted in concern.

"No, we don't, but what we do have is a lot of suspects. A lot of people have been through this place," Barret pointed out, "and we can't be sure that people weren't lying in those interviews."

"It's not even the lying that concerns me," Whalen pointed out, "and I know it probably should. However, when you have this many people around, you would think that someone may have seen something, may remember something. We should keep track."

"And they were, in the beginning," Barret said. "However, as the weather brought everybody back inside and kept us all locked up, then we ended up with more incidents happening. We did have some people more than willing to tattle on each other. However, they were not necessarily worrying about it being the truth."

"So, they're lying," Whalen snapped, his voice sharp as he eyed Barret.

"I won't even say that they're lying as much as … I think they're seeing what is suspicious to them, or, given the circumstances, things that feel suspicious, and they can't let it go."

Whalen thought about that and asked, "Is that what all these statements are?"

"It is. I want to do a timeline of who was where when, then see if we can come up with any kind of overlap."

"They've already done that though."

"I know," Barret agreed, with a groan. "But, outside of starting back at the beginning and taking a look with fresh eyes, we don't really have a whole lot of choice for ideas."

"*Great,* so not only are we looking for a needle in a haystack, we have a limited number of suspects in place here in one area."

"And friends potentially backing up each other, even if things don't add up, because *He wouldn't have done anything wrong of course,*" Barret repeated in a mocking tone. "That's part of it, for sure, and we're more than a little concerned that we could be dealing with more than one person."

At that, Whalen sat back, looked at him. "That makes more sense, doesn't it? To have all these events happen, you would think that somebody had access, and I mean a lot of access, and a lot of freedom here. … That first one was a shooting accident, right?"

"Yes, and we put it down as an accident, friendly fire, and, because of where we are, all the forensic material was shipped out. Thus, to date, we haven't had any confirmation that the killing shot came from any of the weapons here."

"So why wouldn't they have gotten back to us?" Whalen

asked.

"Yeah, well, that's another problem," Barret shared. "I don't know whether it's just a communication problem or if Ted and/or Jerry are keeping that information close at hand. However, I presume that, if they had actual proof that somebody here had done something wrong, then something would have been done about it."

"Sure, that makes sense. But, if they don't have any proof that it came from friendly fire, then it came from unfriendly fire, and that's a whole different story that needs to be addressed."

Barret nodded slowly. "It was also fairly close to camp, as in anybody could have come out and joined up in the training. An awful lot of friendly rivalry, a lot of team spirit, a lot of competition is here on any military base," he shared, with a miserable expression.

"That was the first death, so that makes sense. Then, after that, things went downhill, correct?" Whalen asked, looking over at Barret.

Barret nodded. "That's my understanding, but again I wasn't here."

"Maybe we should be talking to the locals about that."

"On the sly absolutely," Barret agreed, "but without any kind of probing. We can't antagonize the Inuit settlement or any locals in any way, shape, or form."

"Right, because nobody'll be allowed to know, and, as soon as anybody does know, the relationship here will change."

"Exactly, and, as somebody who's been around a bit, you'll probably have more luck asking questions than I will," Barret noted.

"You kind of come across as a strong-arm protector in

the midst of everything," Whalen shared, with a chuckle. "So, I'm not sure anybody'll give you very much in the way of information regardless."

"Exactly, yet I didn't have a whole lot of choice when I came in. It was trial by fire. We arrived, and a new man went missing."

"So, are we counting Helen's allergic reaction accident into this?"

"I would consider that a bit different, like the kitchen fires. By the way, Chester's been cleared on Helen's allergic reaction. It's definitely an incident we'll keep track of, but I don't think we'll put it on the same level as these missing persons and the dead," Barret specified. "I don't think the first death was criminal, but let's not make the mistake of knocking it off too early and not knowing or not having any way to bring that information back into the case. Let's just keep our eyes open. I want you to go through each of these case files, the same as I will, and make a list of who you think are possible suspects. I've done it once, and I have fourteen names."

"Fourteen names? That's a lot."

"It is, and unfortunately it's not the same fourteen names that Ted listed."

"At some point in time will we communicate with Ted?"

"I will, and we'll keep your name out of it."

Whalen nodded. "That would be great," he said, clearly looking relieved to stay out of the mess that was in front of them. "For the moment, I'm getting along with everybody. The minute you alert them to the fact that I could be part of the investigation, that will go right out the window."

"That's why we'll do our best to keep you under wraps, at least for the moment."

"Great," Whalen agreed, with a smile.

When they were finally done, Barret added, "Remember. Don't let anybody know."

"Including the women, I presume." Whalen grinned.

"Especially the women."

At that, he stopped, looked at Barret, and frowned. "You can't be serious. You're not thinking they're involved?"

"Absolutely serious. Think of the women we've had issues with already. It's not that I'm thinking they're necessarily the prime target, but we can't overlook the fact that they could be part of a team or have some key information."

Whalen's face shut down, as he contemplated that for a long moment. "That would really suck. Only a few aren't spoken for by now."

"But even the ones spoken for need to be investigated, just to make sure that they're in the clear."

"I presume that includes the one you're hooking up with."

"As much as I want to 'hook up' with Avalon, at this point I'm just trying to ensure that she's safe."

"Yeah," Whalen agreed. "I was thinking the same thing with Katya."

"She's Russian, isn't she?"

"Yes," he said almost defensively, and then he groaned. "As you can tell, I'm a little bit hooked."

"I get it, just don't let it cloud your judgment," Barret murmured. "Do not take it lightly because it's happened before."

"I understand, but, if you're talking about me, she may be Russian, but she's on the German team."

Barret stared at him and shrugged. "Born to a Russian

family, then emigrated to Germany? She'd make a great double agent."

"I don't think she would agree with that," Whalen said. "She's taken quite a bit of flak over her nationality as it is."

"Of course, and I'm not saying that she's guilty in any way. I'm just saying we can't afford to make a mistake."

With that, Whalen, turned and walked out, leaving Barret staring behind him.

DAY 7 DINNER

NOT AT ALL happy that she was still assigned full-time to the kitchen, though prepared to keep working her way through it, Avalon asked Chef, "Any chance I'll ever get out of here?"

He laughed. "Next supply run, we're supposed to have a couple guys coming in to help me."

"Oh, good," she said, with a beaming smile. "It's just not what I came for, you know?"

"Oh, I get it." Chef gave her a cheeky grin. "As much as I appreciate the help, I understand you not wanting to stay in the kitchen."

She shrugged. "It seems, once you're in a kitchen, it's hard to get out."

He shook his head. "That's not true," he murmured. "It's got nothing to do with it."

"Maybe not, but it sure feels that way."

He just dismissed it, but she didn't feel as if he was dismissing her, and there was a big difference. By the time she had everything prepped and was putting dinner out, she looked around to see a steady stream of people coming in. By now she knew everybody by name, and, as long as nobody made any crass remarks about poisoning or raised any dissent, she got along with almost everyone. She had served up the first half and was waiting for the second half to show up. When nobody did, she looked back at Chef. "Do we have a group still out?"

He frowned, as he looked around. "Maybe." He stepped into the back and picked up his phone. When he came back out a few minutes later, he nodded. "One group was due back twenty minutes ago, and they're late."

"But not problematically late, right?" she asked hesitantly.

He looked at her a bit too pointedly. "Not that I know of."

She had to be satisfied with that, though she wasn't. When Barret came in a little bit later, she looked up and asked, "Any word on the other group?"

He frowned. "I didn't realize we were missing a group."

"Where have you been?" she asked lightly. "We're waiting for them to serve dinner."

"No, as far as I know, everybody due back was in already."

"The other team is just on the late side."

"A little late is to be expected out here."

"Fine." Avalon stared at the food, frowning.

"If you have to put it away, you have to put it away," Barret stated.

"Yeah, and, in this place, we know only so many people are here. Plus we don't want any of them going without food, so I'd just as soon give them a few more minutes to get in."

Only a few moments later, caterwauling could be heard outside, and she smiled. "Seems they're back."

"Good," Barret replied, as he turned and looked around. "I would hate to think we had any more bad news waiting for us."

"You and me both," she agreed. He glanced at her sharply, and she shrugged. "Everything's fine, as far as I know."

"I'm glad to hear it," he replied. "And how about you? Nobody else getting ugly?"

"No. It seems maybe the word got out that you'll be there as my backup—in case anybody decides to get shitty."

"I'm glad to hear that." Barret smiled. "I always wanted to be a hero."

She rolled her eyes at that, but it brought a grin to her face. "Hey, I just appreciate it, though I hate to think it was even necessary in the first place."

"Don't blame everybody here for the actions of some, and remember, everybody reacts differently to stressful situations like these. Things have calmed down a little bit now, and maybe it'll continue to stay that way."

"But have they calmed down?" she asked, frowning at him. "I sense ... people waiting, a doomsday attitude that people are anticipating."

"Do you think so?" he asked. "I thought people were starting to handle this better."

She shook her head. "Maybe in your world," she said, with a mock smile, "But I don't agree. ... I wouldn't agree with that at all."

"Okay then," he noted.

She studied his face, wondering at the shift. He looked around a little more uneasily, then back at her almost too quickly. She frowned at him. "What are you trying to hide?"

He looked at her steadily. "If I were trying to hide something, I sure as hell wouldn't hide it from you, would I?"

She shook her head. "No, you wouldn't, and I would hope you wouldn't even try." He winced at that and nodded. "I gather something's going on," she stated.

"Something is, but it's part of the investigation," Barret shared. "So, if people come and talk to you in any way, shape, or form, … just don't take it the wrong way."

She groaned. "More investigative work? We're all tired of it."

"Sure, I know, but we're not all tired of living, are we?"

Taking his meaning, she nodded. "Oh, fine. I can't imagine it'll make anybody happy though."

"I don't think this shit makes anyone happy," he added, as he turned and looked around. "On the other hand, if we can get all get this to stop, it shouldn't piss people off."

"Maybe not," she agreed, yet with a quick headshake. "On the other hand, I'd just as soon call it a day, even if we don't catch somebody." He eyed her, and she shrugged. "I think a lot of us probably feel that way. … I mean, what if they were just accidents? What if it really was just …" At the look on his face, she sighed. "Fine, so clearly, as far as you're concerned, none were just an accident."

"Nope, sure weren't," he declared, "but I can understand why a lot of people would need to normalize the situation and to do that by thinking it was multiple accidents."

"That doesn't say much for the safety of the base and the teams," she noted. "And I agree with that, but I'd still rather it was ugly accidents than anything else."

"Maybe after this investigation is done, we'll come to the same conclusion."

"And, if you do, will that be the end of it?" she asked hopefully.

"Yeah, I would think so," he said, "but we still need to talk to Amelia."

"I don't think she wants to talk to anybody," Avalon suggested, with a smile.

"And you don't know who she is?"

"No, not at all. I've never met her." Avalon asked Barret, "Have you?"

He shook his head. "No, I haven't."

"Okay, good. Sometimes I wonder how much people here know and how much they don't. And some people are definitely in the know." She gave Barret an eye roll. "Lots of other people aren't, and those who aren't tend to feel a little bit left out, I think. So, I don't want to say it in the wrong way, but it's as if they're not being trusted."

"Considering what's going on, would you want everybody to know?"

"No, of course not," she replied. "You're right. It's an investigation that needs to be kept confidential in order to sort all this out, but whoever would have thought any of this would be happening?"

"Right?" he said, with a gentle smile. "Let's hope that we come to the end of it pretty fast." As he grabbed some food, he turned and looked back at her. "Will you be eating?"

"I will be. I'm just not sure it'll be right now. I'm waiting for this other team to come in."

"Okay, whenever you can, grab some food. Then come join me."

And with that invitation still fresh in her mind, she smiled. "Give me a few minutes."

But it ended up being another twenty minutes before everybody came in and grabbed some food, and then she was busy cleaning up and putting food away. By the time she had a plate of her own, she sat down in the dining room, where everybody else was, automatically just grabbing a chair at a table, where other people were around, asking them how the day had gone.

Everybody was laughing and joking, and it was good-hearted banter which made her feel much better. It certainly made her consider her stovetop mishap really could have potentially been an accident. It hurt to think that anybody here could be the kind of person who would deliberately hurt the rest of the team. She was enjoying the conversation with everyone, but, when it stopped suddenly, she knew without looking that either Magnus or Barret, possibly Egan or maybe even Mountain, had showed up.

She looked up and smiled to see Barret, standing there looking at her. She picked up her empty plate and walked over to him. "Hey, are you looking for me?"

He nodded and smiled. "You did manage to eat, *huh*?"

"Yeah, but it was a lot later than expected, so I missed you."

He nodded. "Sorry, I had to go out and check with Joe." She frowned, but he shook his head, as he glanced around and murmured, "Not here."

Hating to even contemplate something happening to the dogs, she quickly cleaned up her dishes and walked out with him, heading toward her room. When they got to her door, he motioned her inside. "What's going on?" she asked.

"One of the dogs came back, carrying a note."

"A note?" she repeated in astonishment. "That's about the last thing I expected. A dead body, some weapons, covered in blood, injured, or hurt maybe, but a note?" He nodded, his face grim. "What did the note say?" she asked, studying his face. "Whatever it was, it's obviously upsetting you."

"It was a simple note, but more or less a call for help."

She sat back and stared. "What?"

He nodded. "That's exactly what I was thinking."

"Is it a joke?"

"No idea yet. Is anyone missing? Did anybody not show up for a meal today?"

She looked at him blankly, as she mentally ran through whoever hadn't been in. "I wasn't keeping track or anything, but I knew a whole team was out. When they all came in, I waited until they were done before I put away the food, but I certainly wasn't looking to see if anybody else didn't show up," she stated. "God." She rubbed her temples. "Will I need to record when people eat meals, so I can check everybody off?" she cried out.

"No, I just … I guess I'm asking, do you know of anybody who didn't show up?"

"Let's walk back and ask Chef."

"Would he know?" Barret asked. "I mean, he's not out in front all the time, is he?"

"No, but not a whole lot passes through this place that he doesn't know about," she replied calmly, as the two of them walked back to the kitchen.

Chef, as was his routine, had already retired to his makeshift bedroom in the storeroom. He looked up when they appeared. Barret crouched down because Chef was sitting on the floor, atop his pallet. "Hey, do you know if anybody didn't show up for food tonight?"

Chef's gaze turned to hers, and she shrugged.

"I was keeping track of eaters," she replied apologetically. "I mean, not for real, but I was trying to keep track, just so we knew when the team had been through. Since I knew the whole team was late, I wasn't keeping track any closer, and then, when they came in, there was a big hullabaloo. Afterward everybody grabbed food, so I just assumed at that point that everybody had come through."

Chef nodded, then turned toward Barret. "What she said. Yet you're expecting a different answer than that from me?"

"No, not necessarily," Barret admitted, "but one of the dogs came back with an odd note hidden in his collar from someone asking for help."

Chef's gaze sharpened, and he quickly climbed to his feet. "But everybody returned to base tonight, right?" he repeated, frowning. "What else was in the note?"

"There was a little bit more to the note, but nothing that made any sense, and nothing that I can tell you about."

"Of course." Chef rolled his eyes. "All this cloak-and-dagger bullshit. If we were in any other circumstance, I'd be happy enough to just beat that right out of you."

"In any other circumstances, I'd be happy to share. Can't say I fancy getting the crap beaten out of me for something like this."

"No, of course not," Chef murmured, as he shook his head. "Any chance it was from Amelia?"

"That is under consideration," Barret shared, "and it would be great if we had any idea of anyone else out there."

"The other thing is," Avalon added, suddenly looking at Barret, "what if the note's old?" He frowned at her, and she shrugged. "What if … I hate to say it, but what if Joe missed it? And what if it was just dislodged from somewhere?"

Barret pondered that for a moment. "It is a theory, and God knows we could use a few of those right now because we don't have much to go on."

"It could also be a practical joke," Chef suggested in an odd tone.

"I know, and that is a problem because, in our current situation, practical jokes are not well received."

"And again we don't know for sure that it's recent," Avalon repeated.

"I think they'll call for a headcount, just to make sure everybody is here. So be prepared. Don't be shocked when it comes through."

Just as Barret stood there, the alerts went out, and everybody was ordered to head toward the small common room off the kitchen. By the time everybody had piled in, grumbling but curious, they did a call-out headcount, and, when they got down to Xavier, one of the Swiss team, there was no answer. The name was called two more times, as everybody looked around at each other, searching for him.

Magnus, who had been running the call, asked, "Has anybody seen him today?"

One person spoke up. "I saw him at breakfast," he stated loudly. "He wasn't feeling great, and he wanted to skip today. I assumed he wanted to at least check in."

At that, Magnus nodded. "I'll go check for him myself." He quickly ran through the rest of the names, and, when everybody else appeared to be present, he nodded. "Okay, everybody is dismissed. That was just a check to make sure everybody had returned from today's missions."

As they all disappeared, Magnus looked over at Barret, who squeezed Avalon's hand. "I'll be back in a few minutes."

She watched nervously as the crowd disappeared, but her gaze was on Barret and Magnus. The last thing she wanted was to have somebody else hurt or injured or even feeling sick. Not when they had just finally gotten the rumors to die down.

She walked back over to where Chef stood and looked at him intently. "I hope Xavier's okay."

"I haven't seen him all day," Chef admitted. "Normally

we do kind of keep an eye on everyone. I'm not sure why we didn't notice."

"I think it was just the fact that everybody came through in big groups tonight. I assumed he was on that team running late tonight."

"His name's on that team, and, as far I know, that's where he was at. Nobody told us that he was staying in either, and that's another thing they need to fix," Chef declared. "Particularly under the circumstances."

"It wouldn't normally happen though, would it?" she asked curiously.

"No, it sure wouldn't. Normally everybody would be checking in and out, and we would all know exactly where people were and what was going on."

"So, the fact that he was here for breakfast and then wasn't here later would suggest he's in his room."

"Let's hope he is." Chef glanced around the almost empty room. A few people were still mingling, picking up drinks and visiting, but nobody appeared to be terribly concerned.

When her phone buzzed a few minutes later, she saw a message from Barret, then looked over at Chef and whispered, "Aw, shit. Xavier's been found, and he's fine, but, according to him, nobody's seen Jerry, the second investigator. Ted's now raising the alarm for him."

"Why wasn't he called out then?" Chef asked.

"He's probably not on any of the lists because he's here as part of the base's investigation team," she murmured.

"That's just BS." Chef pondered that. "I don't think I've seen him all day either."

She looked at him and then slowly nodded. "I guess I have to agree because I don't recall seeing him either."

"So, when did you see him last?" asked a man, his hard

voice, coming from behind her.

She spun to see Magnus, his hands on his hips, glaring at her. She glared back. "I don't know." She raised both hands in frustration. Then she stopped and frowned. "He was here at breakfast yesterday."

"And then?" Magnus turned to Chef.

He shrugged. "Yesterday for sure. I don't know about this morning though," he replied apologetically. He looked back at Magnus. "Things get a little hot and heavy when it's just the two of us in the back, and we have to really move it."

Magnus nodded slowly as he stared around the room. "So, now we have to go door to door and find out when anybody saw Jerry last."

"But wouldn't Ted have been the one to see him last?"

"He said he last saw him yesterday, after breakfast but before dinner."

"But Ted didn't show up for dinner himself," Chef pointed out.

Magnus stared, then nodded. "I asked Ted about Jerry myself, and Ted told me that Jerry just hadn't been feeling great and wanted to give his stomach a day off. It wasn't a day off really. It was just a meal off."

"That happens sometimes with the guys, when they feel a little bit tired," Chef noted.

"Yeah, especially if they're coming down with something," Avalon added.

Magnus nodded. "I'll go door to door, mark down who was there to speak to, and see if anybody has seen Jerry and when and where that was," he stated. "I've got both Egan and Barret helping me, so that'll be fun."

"Yeah, I'll bet," she murmured. "If there's anything we can do, speak up."

"There is something. Rack your brain for the last time you saw Jerry, and let's hope it was more recent than yesterday," he noted, with a grim tone. "If he's been missing that long, not only do we have a problem in this camp but we've got a bigger problem with people not noticing who's around them. We'll have to set up a much more stringent tracking system."

And, with that, he was gone.

BARRET LOOKED DOWN at the list in his hand and headed to the next room. Two men were assigned to this room. When he knocked, the door opened quickly, as if they were expecting somebody else. He was greeted by double frowns. Barret nodded. "Just checking to see if either of you have seen Jerry at all today."

"Jerry?" they asked in a reaction that Barret was becoming accustomed to.

Jerry apparently had the ability to be here, yet not be noticed. It was a good trait when it came to being an investigator. However, since the investigation hadn't really gone anywhere, maybe not the best for his own health. When Barret explained a little more, their faces cleared.

"Right. He's that older guy, bald head, looks completely out of place here."

Barret nodded. "He's an investigator, with many years of experience, and well accustomed to being in the shadows."

"The shadows are kinda creepy," the other guy noted sharply. "Particularly right now. We don't like people who stay in the shadows."

"And that's not the question I have for you right now."

Barret kept his tone calm. "We're missing a man and want to know when that happened."

"I thought you were missing Xavier," the first guy said in confusion.

"Xavier's fine. He's in his room, just not feeling great."

"What? More food poisoning?" he asked, with an eye roll.

At that, a third man started to laugh, deeper inside the room.

Barret took note of who else was here. *Ralph.* "Yeah, I'm glad you guys are having fun with this, but I'd appreciate it if you could just answer the question."

At that, the first man snapped back to the subject. "I don't remember when I last saw Jerry," he stated, "and honestly, since he wasn't part of our teams, I just blocked him out."

"Maybe so," Barret acknowledged, "but it would sure be nice if we had somebody who had seen him more recently, so we would have some idea of where and when he may have disappeared."

"The fact that he's gone is a good thing. It's not as if they were getting anywhere anyway," the first guy said in disgust. "And now ..." Then he stopped and frowned. "Unless he *was* getting somewhere?"

"That's the question, isn't it?" Barret noted, with a hard smile at these men who thought a missing man was more of a joke than a concern. "Let's hope if you ever go missing, we treat your disappearance with a little less levity than you're treating Jerry's."

"Hey, hey, hey," Ralph replied, jumping off the bed. "I mean, if he's really missing, that's a whole different story."

"That's why we're here, trying to figure out where and

when he was last seen."

They were no help because the three of them couldn't remember anything. The smell of alcohol hung in the room. Alcohol was not allowed, and several of the rooms had been searched already, so Barret didn't want to bring up the issue right now. He did put a question mark beside their names, however, and he carried on to the next room. There he found two women, and Katya was one of them. He looked at her and nodded. "Hi, we're checking to see when everyone last saw Jerry."

"Jerry?" she repeated, frowning. "God, I don't know. It's been, ... well, I don't think I saw him today. I was in the group coming back late tonight, so the dining room was already pretty clear. I don't know that he even leaves the place, does he?"

"No, I don't think so," Barret replied. "Still doesn't change the fact that I need to know when you may have last seen him."

"If I saw him, it probably would have been at dinnertime yesterday," she said. "Otherwise I honestly can't remember." She winced. "How horrible is that? I'm sorry," she added in a thick accent, unhappy at her inability to pull out an answer for him. "I really don't know, but it wouldn't have been today and quite possibly might have been dinner last night, but I can't even say that for sure."

Barret nodded and moved on. Eventually he met up with Magnus, who was standing in the hallway, staring at his list, his expression one of worry.

"Any luck?" Magnus asked him.

"No, no luck. Nobody knows where he is. Nobody knows when they even saw him last."

"How the hell does that happen?" Magnus asked in frustration. "I got pretty well the same response."

"Jerry was very good at fading into the background," Ted interjected, as he walked toward them from the end of the corridor. "It's what made him such a good investigator. He could just slide into places, and people would talk freely, without really noticing he was even there."

"Jesus, but that just brings up another whole list." Barret hesitated, then leaned forward and, in low voice, asked, "Is there any chance that he may have been making progress on the investigation and was taken out because of it?"

Ted stared at him, then slowly nodded. "We were coming up with some potential conclusions, but we hadn't come up with the final answer. As you know, we had narrowed down the suspect list," he replied, turning to Magnus.

"Sure, but that list didn't get narrowed down very much," Magnus replied. "Fourteen names were still on it."

"No, … unfortunately it didn't, not nearly as much as we needed it to," Ted agreed, frowning. "So, in answer to the question, it's possible somebody thought he might have found some answers. Maybe he did talk to the wrong person, but, even if he did, where is he? He never left the compound because he wasn't into the cold at all. He didn't grouse about being here, which was helpful, but he didn't want to be here. He wanted to head home as soon as this job was done, so he was applying himself as diligently as he could. Yet he was also really frustrated that we were getting nowhere."

"And when you say, *getting nowhere*, that completely belies what you just said."

"No, not at all," Ted argued, raising his hands, palms up. "It's just that we couldn't come up with anything concrete enough to give to our bosses. I mean, you have your brass, but we have ours. And believe me. They're all over us on this because we've been here as long as we have and because we're not finding anything, at least nothing concrete."

"And yet we've found all kinds of things," Barret pointed out.

"Sure, but nothing that applies to these original cases. I know that some of the brass is looking to just call everything accidents and leave it at that," Ted admitted, with a frustrated tone. "I'm not convinced of that myself."

"What about Jerry? What was his take on it?"

"He wasn't convinced either," Ted shared. "And, to be honest, it really bothered him to think that somebody could be getting away with murder. Obviously we've solved some of the cases but were the rest accidents, suicides, or something else?"

"I think that would bother anybody," Barret stated, "particularly anybody related to these cases. So, ... now what?"

"When you say that this other guy Xavier wasn't feeling well, do we have any confirmation that he stayed in his room?" Magnus asked Ted.

"No, we don't," Ted murmured. "He says he did, but, unless somebody saw him, we'll have no way to prove differently. That's a question we'll need to ask the kitchen staff."

"Avalon already told us that she couldn't remember seeing him at all herself after breakfast. Same for Chef," Magnus replied.

"People come and go all day long though," Barret pointed out, "and it's not necessarily something that the kitchen staff have time or even the awareness to clock who's in and who's out. To have somebody keep track of that, we'll need more manpower."

"Hell," Ted grumbled. "I'll have to make a phone call or two." And, with that, looking fairly unimpressed, he took off at a fast clip.

Disturbed, Barret headed toward his room, only his feet had taken him directly to Avalon's quarters. He stood outside her door and waited. When it opened suddenly, and she stepped out wearing a suspicious expression, he winced. "Hey, it is just me. I was … I was thinking I was heading back to my place," he confessed, "but instead I found myself standing outside your door, wondering whether I should even be contacting you or not."

"Come in," she murmured. "I heard the footsteps stop, and, with so much trouble going on, I didn't want to take a chance. So I opened up the door, so I would know who it was at least. However, I find you standing here, looking completely lost."

"Yeah, and that's a good word for it," he muttered, as he stepped inside. "No sign of Jerry."

She stared at him in horror. "Oh God no," she whispered, "please not again."

He nodded. "Yeah, that appears to be a refrain we're dealing with on a regular basis." He ran his fingers through his hair. "The trouble is, if somebody did something to Jerry, this time they did it right under our noses."

"So, you want to compare all the accidents, the outright deaths, the missing people, from the beginning of this training session?" At his nod, she continued. "I wasn't here until recently. However, from what I've heard, those first two looked to be accidents, yet outside of the complex."

"Sure, but still fairly close to base, right?"

"Yes. So, it could have been anybody who was part of

the training mission or the exercise they were on, or it could have been anybody still here on base just because it was close enough for them to travel back and forth. And lots of people did travel back and forth, depending on what was going on some days. They were working in relays originally, I heard."

He nodded slowly. "Which meant that the two original accidents could have really been accidents. Then we have the subsequent deaths. They could have been planned and executed … and again by almost anybody up here," he suggested, with a huge sigh, dropping his head into his hands. "Jeez, I need a whiteboard to keep all this straight. There's got to be a way to narrow this down. Everyone missing or dead could be explained away. Yet we can't just leave the whiteboard standing somewhere for all to see."

She hesitated and then pointed to the plywood floor. "How about the floor? We could always throw a carpet down."

"You have a carpet?" he asked.

"No, but a couple mats are in the kitchen," she offered.

"I like it. One way or another, we should find something to cover it up. You're alone in your room most of the time anyway, aren't you?"

"Yeah, I am," she said, "but the wrong people seeing this is not a good idea. And I've already had the earlier break-in here."

He apologetically replied, "You're right. Jesus, I can't believe I didn't think of that. I need to do this back in my room, just in case anybody potentially sees it, especially if it's the wrong person."

"In that case, let's go do it now," she stated. When he hesitated, she shrugged. "Hey, if I'm in on it, … then I'm fully in on it, right?"

He smiled. "As long as you're okay. I don't want you being uncomfortable with this because it'll be people you've been working with."

"It's people I've been *training* with," she corrected. "We already know that Chef's clear. We already know you're clear, and I guess I'm clear," she added, looking at him a bit nervously. When he nodded, relief washed over her face, and she kept going. "Magnus, Sydney, Berry, Mountain, the rest of your team. I mean, we've got quite a few who we know are clear, so where are the other twenty-odd people in this?"

Barret frowned at that question and nodded slowly. "That's the point," he declared in a flat tone.

"Let's go get something down and start eliminating some of these people. However, if they were anywhere around these training missions in question," she noted, "we have to look a whole lot closer."

He nodded. "I know you don't like the idea of spying on everybody or looking into their activities."

She laughed. "I would say we're well past that now. Definitely more spying is going on among everybody else than ever before. However, if somebody has been causing these accidents, we need to figure it out. Not to mention that we're still missing Teegan Rode, Mountain's brother."

"I know," Barret muttered, his tone grim. "And that's a whole different issue."

As they walked to his room, he checked to make sure that nobody noticed what they were doing. They passed a couple people, who seemed to be in deep discussions of their own. When Avalon and Barret got to his room, he stepped inside and motioned for her to follow.

Once in his room, she looked around and noted, "this is a little bigger than mine. What did you get? Some secret upgrade?"

He laughed. "Not really. The complete fluke of it is that everything I do here is more or less supposed to be under the guise of being here for training."

"But that's not why you came here, is it? You were sent here to work on this investigation, right?" she asked, eyeing him shrewdly.

He nodded. "Yep, and I feel like crap that we haven't really gotten anywhere."

"And yet you and I both know that is not your fault. Besides, with everything else going on—"

"Everything else going on is beginning to make me wonder if some of it hasn't been intended to distract people and to throw us off the trail."

"Let's go through the list of people," she said, "and figure out who is still around. Then maybe we can see if we can find any links between each of these people and the individual victims." He raised his eyebrows at her. She shrugged. "Hey, just because I'm not officially part of your secret group doesn't mean I can't do some sleuthing on my own," she stated, with a half smile.

"No, you absolutely can. I just want you to be careful about it," he murmured. "I don't want anybody to know what you're doing or that you're even looking at this." When she frowned at him, he shrugged. "I really wouldn't want anything to happen to you."

She beamed a smile at him. "Oh, well, *that* I'll accept. Now let's get going."

They quickly mapped out a timeline of the list of people missing or dead on a notepad, tweaking it to get it right on the one page before they transferred it to multiple pages on the floor, with room for notes. Then they quickly marked off everybody's whereabouts regarding each instance. Finally they sat back to look at their work.

They had been at it for hours. When Barret looked up, Avalon was rubbing her eyes. "It's bedtime for you," he murmured.

She blinked several times and then nodded. "I hadn't expected to be at it this long."

"No, but it's never a quick job, as it shouldn't be, I guess. I mean, we've got people's lives and careers at stake here."

"No, you're right," she whispered. "I wasn't thinking it would be so complicated. I thought once you got a lead on it, we'd be all set."

He laughed. "Wouldn't that be nice? It would be great to think this investigative work was that simple."

"Naïve of me, wasn't it?" she noted, with a headshake.

"No, not naïve," he argued. "It's just that, when you've got something that's complex, with so many moving elements, plus potentially criminal or accidental, potentially one crime versus five or six or seven crimes," he explained, "we have to get to conclusions carefully."

"I get it." She stood and stretched. "I'll see you in the morning. I've got to go crash, so I can get up and start all over again. The good news is apparently that I'm to be replaced by new kitchen staff on the next load of incoming supplies."

"Good," Barret said. "I'm sure you'll enjoy getting back outside again."

"That depends. Is the weather taking another ugly spin? If that's the case, maybe not."

He shook his head. "Up here you never can tell, so don't count on it. You could be better off in the kitchen."

She laughed at that, then gave him a quick hug. "Thanks for an entertaining evening."

He winced. "Hardly date material."

"Are we looking to have a date?" she asked in amusement.

His grin flashed. "I wouldn't mind."

"Yeah, well, I'd just as soon not, … especially here," she added. "There's already enough talk, and that makes me uncomfortable."

"Does it bother you?" he asked.

"Not that it's just talk," she explained, "but, with the lack of trust so bad that the base thinks I'm poisoning them, next they'll be saying that I'm hooking up with you in order to get the benefit of the doubt."

He shook his head. "I might as well tell you, if that's what you were doing, it wouldn't work anyway."

She nodded, with a smile. "I know, and that's another reason why I wouldn't even bother trying." And, with that, she laughed. "I'll see you in the morning." Then she headed to bed.

He was left sitting on his bed, wondering if she'd really been joking about what everybody was saying, if people really were looking at what was going on here at that level. It didn't say a whole lot for people if they were. But then people were just that, … people. Some would go one way, and some would go another. Only when the tide started to turn did it become an issue, and that's when gang mentalities could kick in, and he didn't want any of that happening here.

DAY 8 EARLY MORNING

AVALON WOKE EARLY the next morning and dragged her sorry butt out of bed and headed to the kitchen. First thing she did was pour herself a cup of coffee, knowing that Chef had no doubt done exactly the same thing.

When she checked the storeroom for him, she slumped onto the floor beside him, sipping her coffee.

Chef looked over at her, still tucked into his makeshift bed. "Aren't we a sorry pair?" Chef asked.

She nodded. "That we are," she declared. "On the other hand, we're both still alive, so …"

He laughed. "You know what? I'll take it. There are worse things to be grateful for."

"I know, and, while we're here, we'll get it sorted out," she stated. "At least I hope we can get to the bottom of all this."

"But it sure would be nice if we did it in some sort of decent time frame." Chef glanced over at her. "For now, they seem to be moving in a circle."

She winced. "It's not as if we have a whole lot else to do around this place."

"No, and another ugly storm is coming our way."

"And today is all about searching for Jerry," she noted.

"It pretty well has to be. Nobody has any idea when he went missing, and that's one of the biggest concerns."

"It is for me," she murmured. "How can anybody not know?"

"But you don't know," he pointed out.

"Yeah, great, thanks." She sighed, giving him a raw smile. "I was trying to figure out how that could even be, but you know? Everybody's busy. Everybody's off doing their own thing. Plus the weather's crappy, and everybody's buckled in against it. Even when they're outside or busy, they're not looking around at everybody. I wonder if Jerry didn't have a friend or any group that he could relate to—I guess it's probably pretty normal for an investigator. Or normal*ish* anyway."

"His natural friend group would have been Ted," Chef pointed out, "and Ted hasn't seen him either."

"Last I heard," she added, "nobody can pinpoint when they last saw Jerry—other than the day before yesterday. And that means, if he's not somewhere inside the base, then he's likely …" She didn't finish the sentence.

Chef stared morosely at his coffee cup. "And that would really suck," he whispered.

"I know. But guess what? We'll still have a bunch of hungry people in here after a bit. And, unless we get orders to the contrary, I'm still here with you. So we might as well get busy and do what we do."

He gave her a bright smile. "It's been really nice having you in the kitchen, you know? If you want to stay, I'd be more than happy to keep you."

She laughed. "Don't take this the wrong way, but I very much want to get back out and do some training."

"How about a combination?" he suggested.

"Can we do that?" she asked, frowning at him. "Because at least I'm warm in here, and I get food and coffee," she said, with a smile.

"We can make all kinds of things happen," Chef replied cheerfully. "You just tell me what you want, and I'll see to it."

"Just like that?" she murmured. "Abracadabra?"

"I don't know about *just like that*,"—Chef laughed—"but most people are reasonable when it comes to this type of thing."

"I don't know about that," she hedged. "Right about now I don't think there is such a thing as people being reasonable. I think everybody is panicked and the opposite of reasonable."

"Jerry was known for going for walks though, wasn't he?" Chef asked, looking at her.

"I don't know." She winced. "I hate to say it, but I always avoided him, and we'll find out that's what most people did. He was part of an investigation, and, short of answering his questions, most people probably responded the same way."

"And, yeah, now that he's gone missing, none of us know anything about it, which is another part of the problem," Chef added, with a nod.

By the time they had breakfast served, she realized that some hadn't shown up for breakfast. "Did a team go out early?" she asked, looking around. "Did I miss them?"

"Several went out at the crack of dawn," Chef pointed out, "looking for tracks."

"Just going out in this ugly weather is putting the team at risk."

"And that's the next problem," Chef noted. "If Jerry went out on his own, even just to grab a few minutes to himself, he did it with the knowledge that it's dangerous as hell out there. And now we're putting more people at risk looking for him."

"What about Joe? Did anybody check in with him?"

"I saw him at breakfast, but when you mean *checking in?* … Did you mean. asking him? If so, I'm sure somebody has, since they would have wanted to know if Jerry had taken off with a dog team."

"But Jerry wouldn't have," Avalon stated. "I thought I heard somebody say he was terrified of the dogs." At that, Chef stopped and frowned. She shrugged. "No, I don't know who mentioned that or if it's even true," she added, with a half smile. "It seems as if everything's just this big blur now."

"Maybe, but it's a blur that we need to come to terms with. So let's get some work done because, either way, short of what seems to be a miracle at this point, there'll be some very upset people today."

With that in mind, they quickly tweaked the menu and got at the preparation work. When she turned around much later, Barret stood there, his hands on his hips, watching her.

Surprised, she stopped and asked him intently, "Problems?" She kept her voice low.

"No, I'm just really happy to see you."

She walked over, gave him a quick hug, and said, "Thank you. That's nice to know." However, when she realized that his hug was a little more intense than expected, her shoulders sagged. "You found him?"

"We found him," Barret replied. "And, yes, he's dead."

"Do we know what, why, how?"

"Sleeping in the snow, wrapped up in his jacket, potentially the same as Scott."

"No, no, no. Everybody knows better than that, and they've all been talking about it constantly since Scott was found.”

“I know,” he replied. “Sydney is examining him right now.” He looked over at Chef, who was sitting there, suddenly looking very gray in the face as he stared at him. “You okay?”

“Sure, I’m okay,” he said. “We were joking earlier about being grateful to be alive. While, of course, it was something to be grateful for”—he shook his head too vehemently—“I wasn’t thinking of it in the sense that, … that it was reality. Jesus, I just don’t understand,” he muttered.

She walked over and sat down beside him and patted his hand. “I don’t either.” She looked back at Barret. “How close to the center was he?’

“He was just outside the generator room. He had a pack of cigarettes with him,” Barret described, “and one was still in his mouth.”

She blinked several times. “He just went outside for a smoke?” she wailed.

He nodded. “He had a pen in his hand but no notebook.”

At that, she stiffened and looked at him worriedly. “Are you thinking that somebody might have been there and removed it?”

“It’s hard to say.” Barret looked around. “He was kind of half hidden, and quite a few tracks were around, as everybody went looking for him. Both old tracks and new tracks. Unfortunately no way to find what were the original tracks. Nothing remains of the original scene.”

“Jesus,” she said, with a shake of her head.

“Not to mention the fact that anybody checking the generators would have utilized the same pathway.”

“He was out there?” Chef asked, looking at Barret in

horror. "I go out there all the time."

He nodded. "And not very far out either. It's just, I guess, maybe he needed some space or needed something. I don't know, but he wasn't very far from safety. Yet that cold got him."

"And that's where the problem comes in," she stated, staring up at him. "That cold out there …"

He nodded. "Yeah, it's brutal. Jerry wasn't part of the training missions, and, like Scott, it's quite possible it was just a stupid mistake."

She swallowed. "And yet don't we think this is way too many stupid mistakes? Particularly if he had a notebook, and it's missing? Especially as he had just investigated Scott's death and his own mistake?"

"But we don't know that he had a notebook. He just had a pen in his hand."

"No way that you could write notes out there," Chef declared, looking up at him. "No way."

"I think you're right," Barret agreed. "I think, in this case, taking notes out there would be foolish, but he may have …" Then he stopped.

"He always had a pen in his hand," Avalon pointed out, suddenly frowning at Barret. "Every time I've seen him, he's had a pen in his hand."

He looked at her and then turned toward Chef. "Is that your take on it too?"

"I'm not sure," he admitted. "I can't say I'm that observant. Or that my eyesight is that great for that matter," he added, frowning. "Yet I'm sure the other guys could say something about that."

"I'm sure they could but …" She took in the Chef's small quarters. "I hate to ask, but where will you store him?"

"In the generator room," he replied, "or at least out in the back with Scott."

"*Great.*" She muttered under her breath, hating the idea of a makeshift morgue.

"He's already frozen," Barret explained. "Almost nothing that *Sydney* can even say about him, short of thawing him out and doing some sort of autopsy. However, she's not equipped for that here, and, because his body's frozen, any actual timelines, et cetera, will be distorted anyway. She will take some of his blood and send it in for analysis, but it may have degraded with the freezing. Then, by the time she gets the results back, well, … we have no way of knowing anything for sure right now."

"She can check for some things here, can't she?" Avalon asked.

"Sure, she can and she is. However, for the moment, … we're considering it an accidental death." Avalon shook her head at that. "No?" he asked curiously.

"No way," she declared. "I don't know how. I don't know why. All I can tell you is *that* answer, that whole premise, just feels terribly wrong."

"Wrong or not," Barret replied gently, "it is an answer." And, with that, he rubbed his eyes hard. "I'll talk to you in a little bit." And he quickly left.

BARRET HAPPENED TO agree with Avalon. As far as he was concerned, an accident was way too easy of an answer. Yet it was something that would make everybody else feel a little better. Not that giving an answer to make others feel better was the thing to do, but they had enough suspicion and outrage already. As he quickly tracked down Mountain, Barret found him talking to Magnus over a cup of coffee.

He sat down beside the two men. "I gather that we're calling it an accident, but are we really thinking that?"

"What do you think?"

"I think it's bullshit," he snapped. At a glare from Mountain, Barret lowered his voice and looked around. "The first thing Avalon said to me is that there is absolutely no way this was accidental."

"Sure, but we won't just accept her instincts without any kind of proof," Magnus pointed out.

Mountain nodded. "I've checked with Salmo, who works in the gear room. He didn't see either Scott or Jerry in there, which is a death knell here in the Arctic."

Magnus sighed, shaking his head. "I'm waiting for Sydney to get any information she can off the remains, but, at first glance at finding Jerry's body, sitting there, leaning against the back wall, all tucked up, supposedly out of the wind, yet in the cold? It wouldn't have taken very long at all."

"I know, and that's ... just terrible," Barret said. "The sad part is, why did he stay there? Why didn't he just come back in again? Why was he out there in the first place?"

"I don't know, and that will be one of the ever-expanding questions that we have to deal with here," Magnus replied. "So, let's just keep all the supposition and guessing to a minimum and wait until Sydney has gotten whatever answers are to be had."

"Sadly *Sydney* doesn't have any answers," the doc said, as she stepped forward, looking tired and shaken. "I've taken some blood, but everything's frozen. I don't want to cut him apart too much, but I should test for some drugs at least," she noted. "He was apparently smoking that cigarette. It looks as if it had been lit and had burned down to the nub in his fingers. It could have just burned all the way down. We did get that sudden chill out there, and twenty minutes without the proper clothing and protective gear? I mean, it's quite possible this was another accident."

"Yet another accident," Mountain bit off.

She nodded. "And, yes, that's way too many accidents for it to be accidental," she murmured. "So, we'll have to find some answers fast, before there are any more accidental deaths. After renewed safety training being held at this *survival training* base, if it really was an accident, it was a seriously stupid and senseless one. I don't imagine anybody will believe that this is an accident, unless we can come up with some plausible reason as to why it happened at all."

"In Scott's case he had a tiff with somebody and stepped out, but why would Jerry go outside?"

"He did have a phone on him," Sydney noted. "Maybe he couldn't get reception." At that, the other men looked at her. "I've seen other guys do it."

"Do what?"

"Step outside to get better reception," she replied. "Surely you've seen them. I had a talk with one of them when he came back in. I told him it was straight-up foolishness. What I can tell you is that there doesn't appear to be any blood where the body was found. However, in the cold out there, if somebody knocked Jerry over the head, it wouldn't have bled very much or very fast. It also could have been a slow internal brain bleed," she whispered, as she sat down. She looked over at Magnus and reached out a hand, which he gently picked up. "I can't say I had any idea that *this* was what I was signing up for when I joined in."

"No, I'm sure you didn't," Magnus agreed in a soft tone, "but we appreciate having you."

She shook her head. "We need new people in, and we need to move these two out. I want a full investigation and an autopsy done on each, but I highly suspect that, short of what we can see right now, we won't find anything else."

"Unless Jerry was knocked out just enough to keep him outside long enough to freeze to death," Magnus suggested.

"That would be my guess," she agreed, "but again I can't really tell, not without a visible head wound. Not in his current state."

"There are lots of ways to inflict a blow that wouldn't cause any bleeding," Magnus murmured.

"I know," she replied, "and it doesn't help that everybody here knows exactly how to do it."

"The only reason to do something like that," Barret stated, "is if there was a reason to take him out, and the only reason I can think of is if they thought that he was on to them."

"Once again, we're back in that chaos of not knowing what people were thinking about trying to shut down this place. Maybe they thought they could just knock him out, and it wouldn't kill him."

"If they had dragged him back inside again, it wouldn't have," Sydney stated tartly. "But by leaving him out there ..."

"We have to get ourselves on the same page. So is there any way that this could have been an accidental attack?" Magnus asked, looking over at Mountain.

Mountain's eyebrows shot up. "Seriously?"

"Hey, I'm just asking because I want to make sure, before we go off half-cocked with this and report to the lovely and very necessary authorities that we have a good idea of exactly what we're looking at. What do we tell people?"

Mountain nodded. "Yeah, I'm the one who'll be in there talking to the colonel. Believe me. I'm not looking forward to that one bit."

"Of course not. At the same time, we must consider all aspects. So, how could somebody accidentally hit him?" Magnus turned and looked at Sydney. "How long do you think it would have taken him to die out there?"

"In that cold? I mean, really, twenty minutes is more than enough, maybe even less. With a head injury, where he would have just slumped down unconscious, it would have been an easy death, and he would have been gone probably in half the time, and there wouldn't have been any body heat to worry about."

"Interesting," Barret murmured. "So, it could have been done very quickly and without too much effort."

"Sure," Sydney agreed. "In and out. He could have just had an argument with somebody out there, and honestly it could have been as simple as a cigarette he didn't want to share." The guys winced, and she nodded. "Tempers are running hot, and people who may not otherwise be violent aren't holding back anymore," she shared. "I don't know how long it'll be before a real blowup happens."

"You think it's that bad?" Barret asked.

"Oh, no doubt," she stated crossly. "I was just hoping we would have some answers before it got any worse."

"You and me both," Barret added. Then he looked over at Magnus. "I think we need to have a talk about making some things public and letting people know where we're at."

"I don't think that'll help at all," Mountain argued, his voice deep, angry even. "But I can understand the need for being open, considering the amount of lies and innuendoes that appear to be catching up to everybody. Still, as Sydney said, I just wasn't thinking that would be necessary."

"And it shouldn't be. You know the brass won't want to tell anybody anything."

"No, but at this point in time we're well past that point. Even if we just make a ..." Sydney hesitated and then added, "Maybe over the next few days, if you could just, instead of doing regular training, or while this bloody cold is going on, just do training for safety. I mean, I know that it's supposed to be something that's done regularly, but what if you just focused on safety training for exactly these things, taking into consideration that Scott died this way and potentially so did Jerry," she noted. "Just maybe make that a focus, so everybody can see that's how you believe it went down."

"Even if we don't believe it?" Magnus asked.

"Even if you don't believe it," she murmured.

"It's got to help some people stay calmer," Barret suggested, "even if it is a lie."

Mountain looked thoughtful and nodded. "It could certainly go a long way toward everybody accepting that this was an accident," he shared, deep in thought.

"We have to remember that, if it wasn't an accident," Barret added, looking at the others, "at least this will make them believe that we fell for the ruse. And that alone might give us a little more time to sort out what the hell's going on." He was oozing frustration at this point. "We also need to have a full investigation again as to where everybody was."

"If you're thinking that'll catch anybody, I think you're wrong," Mountain stated, the fatigue evident in his tone, as he stared off into the distance. "There's already been more-than-enough opportunity to sort out who's been here and who hasn't."

"Maybe. Or maybe we're just slow at it," Barret suggested, "and I think we still need to keep track. I've been trying to run a timeline at my place to figure out who's involved, but it's just not that easy because everybody's got a reason for being where they are."

"The trouble is, everybody having a reason and nobody keeping watch just really means that anybody could have done any of this," Mountain declared, looking wearier by the minute.

"And that's the point that we've come to, I think," Barret said. "The fact is, this appears to be something that anybody could have done on their own. Not that it's what we want to look at, but we have twenty-odd suspects who I think I've narrowed down to ten, and we're working on those. I want some outside assistance to start separating out those ten to see if there are any connections with anybody else in this place."

Mountain looked at him intently. "You're thinking there's history here?"

Barret nodded. "I'm thinking that so many damn people are dying that there has to be something big, something major behind it all."

"Or," Sydney offered, "it's got nothing to do with that and has everything to do with somebody who doesn't think they'll get out of here alive, maybe because of the weather, maybe because of something else, but they're determined to take as many people with them as they can."

"I don't like that idea at all," Barret muttered, staring at her. "And neither do I want to contemplate that we have a serial killer up here. I get it that a lot of people don't have the same conscience and the same level of care or empathy for other people." He looked around to see the effect of his words on the others here but saw nothing askew. "However, I want to think that isn't the case here. Yet it's all too methodical."

"And yet it isn't," Sydney spoke up. "There are a couple cases with the same circumstances—like Scott and now Jerry—where there doesn't appear to be any thought process involved. It's almost as if someone saw an opportunity to commit murder just because. Only, in each case, they could be passed off as accidental. Except it's too many accidents."

"What does that opportunity do for somebody?" Barret asked her intently.

Sydney looked at him, surprised, and then nodded. "It throws everybody off the scent and causes more chaos, more disruption."

"And," Barret added, "it hides the trail. So I wouldn't be at all surprised to find out that some of these so-called accidents may have had a nudge in that direction. People do stupid things, no doubt," he confirmed, "but there appears to be just a little bit too much of this kind of chaos going on. As far as I'm concerned, a very methodical mind is in the background, arranging these diversions, maybe even while we have a serial killer on base. Now we must catch both of them. Or is just one person doing both?"

DAY 8 MORNING

AFTER THE EARLY morning bad news, Avalon had stepped outside to say hi to Ratchet, who'd escaped Joe's barn. She stood right at the door, so she could get in and out without threat of getting lost in the whiteout conditions. The cold-loving, tail-wagging, friendly sled dog had been the perfect answer to clearing her head of all the ugliness here. After a minute she sent him home—particularly when she heard Joe whistling for him.

She remained outside, despite the cold morning. She took several gasping breaths of fresh air, as she tried to get her mind back on track. She couldn't stop thinking about what had happened to Jerry. Shivering slightly, she turned to head back in.

And yet, as she pulled the door to her to get back inside, it was locked. She stared at it in shock and then, in a panic, started banging on the door. It opened a few minutes later, even if it felt like ages.

Chef stood there, frowning. He dragged her inside and cried out, "What the hell are you doing?"

She wrapped herself up against the warm oven and stove, turning the burner on to try and heat up, while he grabbed blankets and threw them around her. She shivered, and her teeth chattered. "I'll say that this is how stupidity happens."

He glared at her in shock and asked, "Seriously? You

went out there, wearing only that, even after what just happened? *Twice* happened?"

"I just … I was so tired all of a sudden, and it was so stuffy that it seemed to be a good idea," she explained. "I didn't get any sleep last night. I was feeling all maudlin and upset and depressed," she muttered. "God, and then the door wouldn't open."

"What do you mean, it wouldn't open?" He walked to the door, opened it, pulled it back, and opened it several times.

She shook her head, not being able to control that movement. "I couldn't get it open from the other side, and then? Well then, I panicked."

He looked at her and pulled out his phone. Within minutes she was staring at Barret, who studied her in shocked horror. He wrapped her up in his arms and asked Chef, "Seriously?"

"Yeah, seriously." Scrubbing at his face, Chef announced, "I'm putting on more damn coffee." Then he grumped his way past them and set about doing just that.

She curled into Barret's arms, until her shivering and teeth chattering somewhat died down. "I was just going to stand out there for a minute. I needed fresh air. The air in here was really, really ugly," she muttered, as she took a deep breath. "I was so upset through the night. I had a bad night. I was just …" And then she stopped. "I guess none of that really matters because you guys will still be pissed at me."

"Pissed? No," Barret disagreed. "Shocked, upset, terrified, sure, and we really do need to give more classes on safety."

"But," she added, looking up at him, "I couldn't open the door. It wouldn't budge."

Frowning, he stepped off to one side, headed outside, closed the door, opened it, closed it several times, letting in a blast of cold air that made her shiver all over again, and he shook his head. "The only thing I can think of is that it might have gotten sticky," he suggested, "if it stood closed for a while."

"Maybe," she muttered, and she started to shiver yet again. "God." She dropped her head into her hands. "I forgot how cold it is out there."

"Yeah, not only that, you must consider your lungs too," he snapped. He took a deep breath, then groaned. "Sorry, I'm not trying to get even more irate than I am."

"But it's a reminder that even I—who I think you would say knows better, or should anyway—even I stepped out just to get some fresh air, … and this is what happened."

"And this time you were lucky. What if you couldn't get the door open, and you banged and banged, and no one opened the door for you? Then you were so cold that you just curled up in a ball and sat down?" Barret noted.

She blinked. "And that might be exactly what happened to Scott and Jerry, isn't it? Oh my God." Now she shivered from the shock of what she'd just experienced, plus what could have happened too. "It didn't even seem to be a stupid idea at the time. I was just trying to clear my head," she murmured. "I just couldn't clear my head in here. All these accidents …"

"And then you decided to go prove that it was possible, *huh?*" he asked, as if trying to get his voice back in control, yet, at the same time, also wanting to give her a hell of a talking to.

She blinked at him. "I know. I didn't realize just how stupid it was," she murmured, as she looked down. "I'm not … I'm not even dressed in outdoor gear. I was grabbing a couple breaths of fresh air," she murmured.

"Right," he confirmed. "And you've got it now, but the question is, are you okay? Can you work, or do I need to rope somebody else in to help Chef? And, yes, I will be contacting everybody up the line."

She wilted and nodded slowly. "*Great*," she murmured. "That's what everybody needs."

"On the other hand," Chef interjected, "in a way it is info they need because they'll see that it's possible for it to happen this way too. Particularly those higher above." Chef looked over at Barret. "So, while I'm certainly not applauding or in any way endorsing what she did, it does give me a very clear idea of what happened to Scott, … and that makes my heart feel better. It was an accident because he was upset and went outside for a few minutes. I can see it happening just like that. Maybe that's what happened to Scott, possibly even Jerry …"

"Has the door ever gotten sticky before?" Barret asked Chef.

"No. … Not to my knowledge, but, in this ice, I mean, it's just like any other moving part. When you get a lot of frost build-up, it's quite possible that's what happened."

Barret frowned at that, then looked at the door and nodded. "I suppose you were the first one to open it this morning, weren't you?" She nodded. "How was it to open?" he asked, as she got lost in thoughts.

"It was fine, but, of course, I had to use force," she shared. "Look. Let me just get back to some work, so I can keep busy. It'll help me to stay a little more focused, instead of thinking about what might have happened."

"Yeah, but what about me?" Barret asked, glaring at her.

"What'll keep me focused throughout the day on something besides finding you frozen outside—the same way we found the other two?"

She winced. "I'm so sorry."

"Yeah, I know." He shook off her apology with a wave of his hand. "Just please, for the love of God, don't do anything like that ever again." She could see he was too emotionally charged at the moment. "You may have confused the issue, or hell, maybe you've clarified it. I don't know," he declared, "but I never want to find your frozen body outside. Please, don't do that again." And then, as if overcome by emotions, he quickly turned and walked away.

She stared at Barret's back, then turned toward Chef. "I guess that was really stupid, wasn't it?"

"Ya think?" he quipped. "Even saying that concerns me."

She winced. "Fine, it was very stupid. I just couldn't get myself awake. I was tired. I was cranky. I was miserable. I had a lot of work to do, and I was just looking for some fresh air."

"And you got it, at great risk to yourself," Chef added. "Now I suggest you grab some more hot coffee, then let's get some work done." Muttering something unintelligible, she was too lost to even ask for clarification again.

They got to work, and, throughout the morning, Chef kept looking at her, as if checking to ensure she was okay. She smiled at him several times. Finally she'd had enough and snapped, "Honestly I'm fine. Really I am."

He didn't say anything, just kept working. When she saw him talking to Barret later, she realized that Barret had probably been checking up on her all morning too. She walked over to them and stated, "I'm fine, really."

"I'm glad to hear that," Barret said, glaring at her.

She glared right back. "Look. I know it was stupid, and obviously I won't do it again," she stated, "but I really don't want to be treated like a child for the rest of the day, so thank you."

"How about for the rest of the week?" he bit off. "Or how about the rest of the year?"

She fisted her hands on her hips, stuck her nose up pugnaciously at him, and said, "How about not?"

He groaned. "If you only had any idea how much people care about you and how doing something that stupid could cause massive pain," he whispered, shaking his head.

"I don't know any of that, and up here I wouldn't have said I had anybody who cared," she muttered, frowning at him.

He stared at her, then snatched her up into his arms, ignoring the fact that she was covered in flour. "Maybe it's time you found out." He then lowered his head, and he kissed her hard.

She welcomed the massive explosion of power and the simultaneous release of tension. It was as if everything had been coiled up inside her, and this was unleashed, only she hadn't expected it. This happened so damn fast, and she immediately flung her arms around his neck and hugged him back.

When he finally lifted his head, she was prepared to address this kiss.

"I don't know exactly what lesson that was supposed to be," she teased, "but I'll tell you right now that I didn't quite get it, so you'll need to repeat it."

With a muffled groan that was half-laugh and half-desire, he whispered, "Good. Christ. Surely you must have seen that coming."

"I've been trying to block out damn-near everything that's been building up," she noted, "so no."

He stepped back and shook his head. "I can't believe you haven't been aware this whole time. Wake up and smell the roses," he whispered, "because, damn, a hell of a lot is going on around you, girl." And, with that, he quickly made his escape.

She turned back to see Chef grinning like a fool. Glaring at him, she barked out, "Oh no, don't you dare start."

"Me? I'm not. I'm not starting anything," he said, as he looked at the kitchen around him. "And I've got way too much work to be playing those kinds of games, *girl.*" He emphasized the last word a bit too much. "But he's right. If you didn't see that one coming, you weren't looking very closely."

"I wasn't looking at all," she cried out. "I've just been thinking about trying to stay alive."

"Really?" he asked. "That's what you were thinking when you walked out that door this morning?"

When she glared at him, he shook his head. "Fine, I won't bring it up again, but I also won't be letting you go out on your own either."

With that, he went back to work, leaving her questioning just how in the hell her world had suddenly flipped upside down.

BARRET ACKNOWLEDGED THAT maybe Avalon hadn't seen the energy between them building, but he was still furious over her actions earlier this morning. Mountain and Magnus had both been stunned at her narrow escape. And, when

Barret explained how and what had happened, they both nodded.

"That could have been exactly what happened to Scott."

"And quite possibly Jerry," Barret added. "That begs the question again though. Are we looking for boogeymen where there aren't any?"

At that, neither man had an answer for him.

"Jesus Christ," Mountain moaned, as he pinched the bridge of his nose. "I don't know what the hell to make of all this, but I hope she's had a good-enough scare to not pull that stunt again."

"I want to think so, but I'm not sure I believe it yet," Barret muttered, shaking his head.

Mountain nodded. "Of course not, yet it's got to be one of those top issues."

"We did do some safety training today," Magnus stated, "particularly after that happened, but we'll be doing a lot more over the next few days, teaching some survival skills as much as safety skills." He was frustrated to say the least. "They should go hand in hand, but some people just don't seem to get it."

Barret tossed a glance back toward the kitchen. "I still can't believe she did that."

"You can't? I can't either. Believe me." Magnus shook his head. "I'm sure that, at this point in time, she thinks none of us will trust her again."

"I can see that you won't," Mountain said to Barret, with a smile.

"No, I won't," Barret confirmed, "and I know she was just out for fresh air, but the fact of the matter is that door jammed, and she couldn't open it again."

"Do we know anything about that?"

"I tested it at the time, and it seemed to open, but she doesn't have my strength. Plus, when you're cold, and the metal is freezing, very quickly it may not open."

"So, she did what?"

"She banged on the door, and Chef heard the pounding and opened it. Correct?" Barret turned to Chef, now joining the group.

"Yes." Chef nodded. "Nobody else was around, so nobody would have heard her."

"So, pretty much exactly like Scott."

"Yeah." With that, Chef stalked off again.

"*Great*," Barret said, with a headshake. "On the other hand, as Chef told us, it clarified for him just what happened to Scott, his helper. It makes Chef angry because it's such a senseless, stupid death, but it does make it something that he can set aside now and learn to live with."

"I'm not sure that *living with it* is the goal," Mountain clarified, "but I understand what Chef's saying. It's frustrating as all hell, but it does give us some sort of an answer." He looked back over at Magnus. "Are you comfortable with the knowledge that nothing else is involved in this?"

He nodded. "She was aware, and she didn't lose consciousness at any time," he explained. "So, in this case, I think it really was an accident."

"An accident but a warning for us all," Mountain muttered. "I'll brief the colonel, and we'll set up more safety training."

"Safety training that we never would have thought would be necessary," Magnus muttered. "Yet obviously people are still not getting it through their heads that just one unexpected glitch can lead to an almost instantaneous death out there."

"I don't think Avalon even thought about it before just doing it," Barret shared. "It happened, and she didn't even … she just reacted. When the door didn't open is when the problem began."

"And no locks are on those exterior doors, correct?"

"Correct. And that exterior kitchen door has been damaged over time. It's from the storehouses, and it's the other door in that area, so anyone could have had access to it, but she didn't see or talk to anybody."

"She just went out and grabbed some fresh air, but she almost didn't come back," Mountain reminded him.

"I know." Barret groaned, and he didn't want to think about that. It would haunt his nightmares for the rest of his life. He looked back at the other two. "However, it does satisfy me that, in at least some of these cases, we could be dealing with accidents."

"But are they all?" Mountain asked. "That's the next question we have to sort out. Were some of these accidents? And, if some of these aren't accidents, which are which?" he asked. "Because, dammit, they could all pass for both."

"Maybe not in Scott's case though," Barret suggested. "I mean, apparently he was overtired and angry at the time. So what if he just closed his eyes for a bit and drifted off?"

"Sure. Doesn't that make it an accident then?"

"And yet what would stop it from being an accident?" Barret asked.

"What would stop it is easy," Magnus stated. "Drugs. A hit on the head or a knock-out punch, where the bruising wasn't evident yet. Maybe somebody had closed the door and refused to open it. Then, when Scott realized he was too far gone, he curled up in a ball, and that was it."

"Jesus, that doesn't bear thinking about," Barret noted.

"The same for Jerry. He went out to the generator area, something he was known to do all the time. Especially after all the generator trouble at the scientists' camp. Therefore, if somebody had wanted to do something to him, that would have given them the opportunity. So, he would potentially try to get into the generator room for safety, but this time couldn't get in. And it was too far to get back to the main compound."

"I don't know about that," Magnus argued.

"Sure, but what if it wasn't even an option?" Barret added. "What if, like you said, somebody hit him over the head or drugged him, then locked him out and left him there?"

"You might see a blow on the autopsy," Magnus offered, "but that'll still be days away. Just like any blood test results for poisons or whatever. And nobody'll prove that the blow wasn't caused by him falling."

"That's quite true too," Barret muttered. "So, in other words, we really don't have anything again."

"Except for the fact that we still have a few missing people," Mountain replied.

"Missing, and yet," Magnus clarified, "during some of the legitimate exercises and training missions, there was talk and quite a few jokes and war games and side bets made about who could stay out the longest. Would your brother have participated in unauthorized challenges and those things?"

Mountain shook his head. "No, not only that, he told me that he was actively collecting evidence that some people weren't part of these games. He had a series of names written down that needed further checks, according to him. However, in each case, he could see how the accidents could have happened and yet not been accidents at all. But he didn't pinpoint anybody in particular, and that's where the problem lies. So, if he was taken out by somebody on this compound," Mountain added, "that person is still here."

"Or else he's already dead," Magnus reminded them. "Don't forget the fact that we also have several dead men on our hands."

"Yet somebody knows something," Mountain replied in frustration.

"Sure, somebody knows something, but that doesn't mean somebody will give it up."

"Also, as unlikely it might seem, Scott really could be another option. Maybe it wasn't an accidental death as much as intentional."

At that, Mountain shot him a look of surprise and slowly nodded. "We really need to know if these people have any connections in their history."

"Did you send that information to Mason?" Magnus asked in a low tone.

"I did. I just haven't heard back."

DAY 8 MIDMORNING

AVALON RECEIVED THE news that she was to be replaced in the kitchen with mixed results. She'd really been enjoying her time here with Chef. Yet it was also good to get back to her regular training. When she got the news, Chef laughed at her.

"Hey, if you want to stay, believe me. I'll keep you around."

"*Oh, thanks,*" she quipped, rolling her eyes at him. "A chance to go back to a regular shift and get some real sleep, and find out what sleeping in is all about?" She chuckled. "I mean, it's pretty hard to turn that down."

"Fresh coffee, coffee that you get when everybody else never quite knows," he pointed out. "Food, even though there might be a shortage elsewhere. Not to mention first crack at the treats, and, whenever you're hungry, you can get a snack."

She stopped and looked at him. "You're really working it, aren't you?"

"Is it working?" he asked, with a cheeky grin.

"Maybe," she admitted, as she looked around. "I think you're forgetting the biggest thing when working in the kitchen."

"What's that?" he asked, frowning at her.

She smiled. "It's called being warm."

At that, he burst out laughing. "Absolutely you're very warm here. So, if there was ever a good reason for you to stay, there you go."

"But you've already applied for somebody."

"Yes, but I need more than one somebody," Chef noted, with a sigh. "As you know, with just two of us, we're completely overwhelmed and never get a break."

"Oh, that's true," she agreed. "Let me give it some thought."

Satisfied with that, Chef made her a fancy cup of coffee with whipped cream on top. "There. That's just, you know, a cherry on top."

She burst out laughing at the obvious bribery attempt, and that set the tone for the work so far. It was a consideration, and it's not as if she wanted to be here in the crazy north for very long. She had a few weeks left, even though the camp had been originally set to go for six months straight—hosting two twelve-week survival courses.

With this first course extended from twelve to fifteen weeks, that may apply to the second course, turning the six-month projection into more like eight months. She shook her head. She sure didn't sign up for that and didn't want to be staying that long for sure. It was a unique experience, and she was learning a lot that she would take with her down the road. It was practical life experience.

However, she came here for a reason, and it was to experience these cold conditions. Frowning, she realized she already gotten plenty of that, and maybe she really didn't need to have more. When the crew came in with the supplies, she was surprised to see four more people arrive. She voiced her opinion to Chef.

"We were short anyway," Chef pointed out. "Nobody

replaced Scott, and, as you know, we could use a third body in the kitchen. Plus I have Jerry's body here with Scott's."

She nodded slowly. "Still, it feels wrong in a way."

"Of course it does," Chef agreed, "but that's the cycle of life and death." He gave her a gentle smile. "So, you need to make a decision whether two of these guys are coming to me or just the one."

At that, two men turned up at the kitchen, presenting themselves to Chef.

He looked at them and smiled. "One of you I know." He reached out a hand. "Hey, Steven. How're you doing?"

Steven gaped at him. "Chef Williamson? I didn't know you were here." His tone was friendly, amiable, but not exactly respectful, so it was somebody that Chef knew well enough.

"Yep, been here the whole time," Chef stated, with a smile, now facing the others. "Steven and I go way back."

"Yep, sure do." And then Steven turned toward Avalon. "I hear you're being relieved."

She nodded slowly. "Unless I choose to stay."

At that, the second man stepped forward and stated, "Your choice, ma'am."

She looked at him. "Do you have any experience up here?"

He gave her a boyish grin. "I'm really hoping to get out there and get some survival experience. Not sure how likely that'll be."

And, with that, she made a sudden decision. "You can head off and take my place on the training teams, and I'll stay here in the kitchen with Chef." He looked at her, hopeful, and she nodded strongly now. "This wasn't to be your regular job here, was it?"

He shook his head. "No, I was kind of shangh—" Then he stopped, flushing. "I was asked if I would be okay with it."

"Which generally just means you're absolutely totally fine because that's what you were told you would do," she noted, with a laugh.

He nodded sheepishly. "I was pretty excited to hear I was coming here," he murmured.

"Good, then you can go. I'll stay here." She turned and looked back at Chef. "As long as you're okay with that?"

He gave her a big fat smile. "It's perfect."

She tried to explain her decision to Barret a little bit later.

He just shook his head and smiled at her. "Honey, you don't have to explain. After what you've been through, it's fine. I just worry about you so close to those damn doors."

She rolled her eyes at that and smiled. "Just think, now there's somebody else to keep an eye on me."

"Yet that's not what he's there for," Barret pointed out.

She glared at him. "He won't be needed for that either."

But it was obvious Barret wasn't terribly appeased.

"Would you rather I was out in the cold again?" she asked in a mocking tone.

"No, absolutely not," he stated. "So the kitchen is a good place, and I guess Chef will look after you." At that, she bristled, and he grinned. "I figured that would get a rise out of you."

"Sure, it would," she declared. "I really don't need looking after, you know?"

"I get it," he admitted, "but being protective just kind of goes with the territory."

"As long as you keep it in control," she noted, "we're

fine."

He flashed her big grin. "So, does that mean I still get cookies?"

"Maybe," she hedged, "as long as no more of those cracks come my way."

He laughed. "Nothing like cookies to keep somebody in line."

"Precisely what I thought."

As the day went on, she was happy with her decision, especially after a new storm rolled in, and everybody was pretty well benched.

Grumbling was heard all throughout lunch, and, when Joe walked in to get food, she looked up at him and smiled. "I guess the dogs are getting quite the holiday now, aren't they? I keep trying to get over there to see them. I'd love to bring more scraps but …"

He scowled at her and shook his head. "Don't. Or collect them and bring them to me. I'd rather have them out working rather than lazing around, getting fat," he muttered.

"Sorry, everybody gets benched in these conditions."

He shrugged. "I'll take them out for a run in a bit just to keep them active," he shared, "but, other than that, they're also pretty happy to be couch potatoes sometimes. When the weather turns this ugly, nobody really wants to be out. It takes a hardy group." He quickly loaded up with food and added, "I'm heading back over to the dogs."

At that, Chef stepped out from the back and asked, "You okay for supplies yet?"

He nodded. "I made sure I came up with enough for the three months," he replied. "I can shorten rations, if we have trouble getting in and out, but it's not what I want to do when the animals are busy and active. Plus they don't need as much when we're not working. However, when we are, well, that's a different story."

Chef nodded. "Let me know if you need any supplies. We got a bunch in today, so we'll have some fresh food back on the menu later."

"Good to know. I'll be looking forward to dinner."

She smiled. "You can always tell when we got supplies in."

"I know, right?" Joe laughed. "An awful lot of people are here to feed, so I don't know how you guys manage. It's all I can do to feed myself and the dogs."

"You look after the dogs," Chef suggested, with a big grin. "We'll take care of the rest."

She smiled as their work continued for the day, but Chef was right; they'd gotten in crates and crates of vegetables, salad fixings, and fruits.

Setting a bunch of fruit out into a big bowl, she turned to see Steven standing there, looking at her with an odd expression on his face. She frowned. "Problems?"

He shrugged. "I was just wondering what all the rumors are that I'm hearing."

"Ah, you didn't hear about any of that ahead of time?"

"Nope, sure didn't."

"It's just that we've had several accidents around the place during this session, and it's been tough on morale, you know?"

"I would think so," Steven acknowledged. "Nobody wants accidents to happen."

She smiled. "And we had a couple nastier incidents happen too. Murders."

He shook his head at that. "I don't get it."

"I know. Neither do I, and I lived through it," she

shared. "And yet not everybody was targeted. What are you hearing?"

He hesitated, then spoke. "Something about someone poisoning people around here."

She glared at that. "And that would be from Ralph."

He nodded. "I think that was his name. I've known the guy before, a bit of a mouthpiece."

"Yep, that's him," she replied, with a venomous tone. "Anything to set people off. He just wants to get moved out. However, because of his attitude, I'm pretty sure he'll be the last one out of here." She eyed Steven and stated, "Just ignore whatever he's got to say."

"I've known Chef for quite a while," he shared. "He usually travels with this CO, so I can't imagine poisoning being any concern."

She stopped, turned, and then looked at him. "Are you serious?"

He frowned. "What do you mean?"

"Why would you even bring that up? Of course it's not an issue. No way anybody here would poison people. That would leave thirty of us dead. That's the opposite of getting out of here."

He just nodded but continued to watch her. She let out her breath, wondering if she'd made a mistake staying around, but, if Steven wanted to worry about her abilities, did she suddenly have to be worried about him?

WHEN THE NEXT day dawned, no break came in the weather, but the tensions between Avalon and Steven didn't ease. It was so awkward that Chef asked her what the problem was.

She shrugged. "He heard rumors about poisoning, and now he's looking at me sideways because you would never do such a thing. Therefore, it must be me who made mistakes." Chef stared at her, and she nodded. "So, don't expect us to be best buds anytime soon. Believe me. I'm rethinking my strategy about being in the kitchen."

"Of course you are." Chef groaned. "That's really not what we want around here. The thought that he even brought it up to you is a little upsetting."

"You think?" she snapped, rounding on him. "I didn't do anything. I didn't even have a clue what they were talking about when Ralph brought up poisoning in the first place," she stated. "So it's pretty damn irritating to have some new guy start listening to Ralph."

"It was Ralph again, was it?"

"Yes, that guy is beyond irritating."

"I know," Chef agreed. "I always wonder why nobody fixed him before."

"Because nobody wants to get caught doing that."

"Maybe so," Chef said, "but there's also an awful lot of

shit flying around right now. It's all too possible that accidents are happening because people are short-tempered."

"Maybe."

DAY 9 MIDMORNING

WHEN THE WEATHER finally eased several hours after post-breakfast cleanup, Avalon was happy to see everybody heading out on missions and training exercises. When they came back in, cold and tired, but with a completely different attitude, she smiled. "It's good to have the weather shift, isn't it?"

"It sure is," one of the men replied, with a bright smile. "Any chance of a visit with you later and coffee?" he asked her, with a cheeky grin.

She shook her head. "Nope, not likely," she replied, with a smile.

Behind him, a guy spoke up. "That's because she's got a guy, and we're all too low-class for her."

She stiffened, hearing Ralph's voice. "Seriously? That's the angle you want to take?"

The other guy looked uncomfortable and added, "Hey, I didn't mean anything."

She shrugged. "You're fine. It's Ralph who doesn't like taking no for an answer."

"It's not as if I ever asked you," he snapped, glaring at her.

"You asked Barret instead. So it doesn't matter, does it?" she muttered, not liking the way the conversation was going. "Either way, you're out of line, so ..."

Ralph gave her a hard, ugly look and slammed down his dishes without cleaning them, then turned and marched out. She let out her breath slowly. The guy behind her winced uneasily. "Hey, sorry. I didn't mean to cause you any trouble."

She shrugged. "It's not your fault. It's been brewing for a while."

He just nodded and quickly made his escape.

Steven muttered, "Seems having females in the kitchen isn't such a great idea."

She stiffened and turned very slowly and looked at him. "What was that?"

He held up his hands in mock horror.

"Look. I don't give a shit what you think. I don't give a shit who you are. I certainly don't give a shit if you've known Chef before or not," she snapped, "but I've been here helping out, and I'm perfectly capable of taking my leave, if that's what the two of you want. Either way, I will not tolerate that kind of behavior. So keep your shitty little comments to yourself." And, with that, she slammed down the dishes and headed into the back.

Chef looked at her in concern. She shrugged. "Just two assholes."

His lips twitched. "I'm too old to be an asshole anymore."

She looked at him and then started to laugh in delight. "Thanks, I needed that."

He shrugged. "You know, when the young bucks get too big for their britches, we used to just send them to do more work outside."

"Sure, and that would work great, if there was more work to be done out there," she noted, "but there isn't, and

Ralph's got an attitude problem."

"You did turn him away, right?" Chef asked cheerfully.

"Yeah, I did, and I would do so again."

"And he apparently didn't take no for an answer that well."

"No, he didn't. I didn't think it was a big deal, but he keeps stirring the shit, trying to make my life miserable."

"Which just means that it's still irritating the hell out of him."

"But why is that my problem?"

"It's your problem because he's *stirring the shit*, as you said," Chef pointed out. "Therefore, it's something you have to take care of before it becomes a bigger problem."

She looked at him. "I think it's already a bigger problem."

He winced. "Sorry. Tell me if you want to transfer out of here, and I'll bring the other guy back."

She thought about the new guy's excitement to get into the survival training and sighed. "And yet I hate to steal that enthusiasm from him. … I know he really wanted to be here, not for kitchen duty."

Chef laughed. "Lots of people are dying to get away, and he wants to be here."

"Exactly." Avalon smiled. "Kind of feels bad to take it from him."

Chef shrugged. "Your choice. But if you can find a way to diffuse all the resentment coming from Ralph," he suggested thoughtfully, "it might help."

"Yeah, you got any way to do that?" she asked, turning to face him. "Since when does rejection come with any kind of release valve?"

"Oh, that's a good way to put it," Chef noted. "In my

world I just make cookies."

She burst out laughing. "You know, that's one of the reasons I like working back here. You're very real."

"Life's too short not to be," Chef declared in that same comfortable tone that she was well accustomed to by now. "If you can't make him go away, maybe you'll have to tell one of the others."

"Oh, I don't want to cause any kind of headache. There's enough hard feelings already."

"Yeah? But we don't need any more issues either."

"Oh God, I hope there aren't any."

By the time she was done, and Barret stood there, waiting for her, she gave him a half smile. "I'm glad to see you today."

"What's going on?" he asked. "I heard some pissed-off people were around."

She explained about Ralph and her snapping back at him once again.

Barret asked her, "Did he ever approach you, asking you out?"

"No, he never asked me out. He asked *you* if asking me out would step on anybody's toes," she reminded him, "and that seems to have hit him the wrong way."

"Interesting." Barret gave a light laugh. "Do you want me to have a word with him?"

"No, I don't." She waved her hand. "I don't think it'll make anything better and will probably just make things worse."

"You're right. It could go either way," Barret claimed, "but we do have to get through our time here."

He was right about that, so she didn't say anything more.

The moment passed quickly, and a sudden outcry came down the hall, somebody screaming for help. Barret took off, racing toward the sounds, as she followed at a slower pace. When she came around the corner in the hallway, Sydney was already on the scene, with Ralph vomiting violently all over the floor.

He glared at her as he upchucked more, then whispered, "It was her. It was her." Then he dropped to the floor.

Sydney quickly had two men pick him up and carry him to her clinic. She looked at Avalon and said, "Stay close."

Avalon just stared around at the others, who were all looking at her with hard gazes. Making a strangled noise of frustration, Avalon took off to her room. She hadn't done anything, absolutely nothing, but it seemed Ralph was bound and determined to blame her for something. Once she was settled in her room, she stopped and thought for a moment, then headed back toward Chef.

As soon as she saw him, she said, "Ralph is down, and he's been violently vomiting. When he saw me, he called out that it was me, that I had done something," she explained. "So just be aware that we'll have a hell of a headache to deal with."

Chef shook his head. "If anybody in this kitchen is to blame, it's me, not you."

"They won't believe that, and they won't believe that we didn't do something to him," she replied bitterly.

At that, Steven raced up. "They're saying we poisoned him."

"And how the hell did we manage to poison just him?" Chef asked, with a tone of disgust. "Nobody else is sick, right?"

At that, Steven looked a little confused, and then he

turned to her. "I think he's saying you did it."

"Yeah, he's saying I did it all right," she confirmed, her voice hard. "But, outside of the scene you saw today, I haven't seen him."

"But you did serve him."

She stopped, turned slowly, and looked at Steven too hard. "No, I didn't. He served himself."

"But you knew he wanted to be getting the next load of food."

"And what? I dumped poison into the serving pan where anybody could have gotten their meals?" she asked, staring at him in shock. "Seriously, is that what you think?"

He shifted uncomfortably, his gaze going from one to the other.

She swallowed her fury, almost shaking in an effort to control herself. "Chef, I'm going back to my room, so if you need me, … you know where I am." And, with that, she tossed down the towel in her hand and marched out.

In her room, she curled up in a ball, wondering just what the hell had happened. When Barret found her in her room a few minutes later, she stared up at him, willing the tears not to fall.

Barret sat down, wrapped his arms around her, and pulled her into a hug. "He'll be fine," he said warmly.

She nodded. "Any idea why or what's going on?"

"No, but Doc's given him something to empty his stomach, and he's still vomiting pretty good. But he swears that you poisoned him. So, yeah, we'll be looking down the barrel of an inquiry."

"More sideways looks, more judgment, more all kinds of things."

"Yeah, and I'm sorry because that's the last thing you

need."

"But apparently it's exactly what he needs. He needed to point the finger at me for some damn reason," she murmured, as she shook her head. "I swear to you that I didn't do anything."

"I know that," he declared. "Sydney knows that. Everybody else does too, if they stop to think about it."

"But a lot of people won't," she cried out. "And that'll be the hardest thing. And, now with him sick, after accusing me all this time, those people will still think that I did something. But where could he have gotten poisoned from?" she asked, shaking her head. "Everybody ate the same food."

"What we have to wonder is whether anybody else will get sick." Just then his phone went off. He looked down and grimaced. "His roommate is sick now too apparently." Barret got up. "I'll be back in a bit." And, with that, he took off.

She stared around the room, wondering just what the hell had happened. She hadn't done anything, at least as far as she knew, and now there was this new guy in the kitchen, and he had been there, but that didn't necessarily mean that he'd done anything wrong either. She stayed curled up on her bed, until a knock came on the door. She called out, thinking it was Barret. However, when Magnus came through the door, she looked up at him with a frown. "So, apparently now I'm in trouble for having done something I didn't do," she stated bitterly.

He gave her a half smile. "Not necessarily but his accusations have triggered a complaint investigation."

She nodded numbly. "Sure, it has, though it doesn't matter if I'm guilty or not. It's just because the guy hates me and that's what he's saying."

He sat down beside her. "You want to tell me what happened?"

"Nothing, absolutely nothing at all. I went through my day working in the kitchen, the same as I do every day. I make food. It's what I do. The same food you ate. The same food everybody ate. I was working the serving line for maybe ten minutes, but Ralph was getting ugly. I snapped at him, then I turned and left the rest of the serving over to Chef and to Steven, the new guy in the kitchen."

"And this new guy, do you know anything about him?"

"No, but he knew Chef before though," she replied. "So, they're already best friends, and I'm the one who's in trouble."

"So, it wouldn't have been you, yet that's what he's accusing you of."

"He wanted to ask me out, but Barret shot him down. So Ralph seems to think I rejected him, so he's all about payback, I presume."

His eyebrows shot up. "Is that what you think it is?"

"I don't know if that's what it is or not. I didn't even really realize that Ralph was going to ask me out."

He snorted at that. "You're not here to appease him by going out with him if you don't want to."

"Thanks for that because I'm pretty-damn sure that's not what Ralph's take is." She groaned. "I honestly have been sitting here thinking about it, and I don't know where any poison would have come from," She was almost on the verge of tears. "He had food out of the same pans as everybody else. When Barret took off not too long ago, he said Ralph's roommate had also gotten sick."

"Yes, apparently he finished off a cookie Ralph had eaten."

"A cookie? Not again with the poison cookies, Jesus,"

she declared, looking at him. "I baked cookies earlier today, but, as far as I know, nobody else got sick off them, and you can bet they didn't last long. So, if he even had a cookie, … that's still quite a surprise."

"Well, Sydney grabbed the cookie, or rather the little bit that was left of it. She wanted to run some tests on it. But again, her abilities to run any tests are pretty limited."

Avalon nodded slowly. "Sure, but to think that one cookie would have done that, it just doesn't sound right."

"Maybe not, but we have to do a full investigation."

She nodded. "So, am I allowed to stay here or do you want me to go down to the jail?" she asked, her tone bitter.

"You're fine right here," he said. "I just wanted you to tell me what happened. Everything counts, so be generous with the details."

She quickly went over the events occurring while she baked the cookies. The cookies were out the entire time, and Ralph was well known for taking a cookie after dinner every day, usually one. However, if anybody had deliberately poisoned a cookie, it would be a hard-pressed deal to determine which person would get it. She had no idea what the purpose would be and why anybody would give a damn.

"He's always just been noise," she shared, staring up at Magnus. "I mean, that irritating background noise that makes all the rest of this a pain in the ass too."

He nodded. "There's always that guy in a camp. I'm sorry you're going through this."

"Yeah, me too," she muttered.

When he got up to leave, she asked him, "Will you stop Barret from spending time with me?"

He frowned at her. "Why would I do that?"

She shrugged. "Maybe I'll poison him to death."

"Oh, I think you've had plenty of opportunity to do that by now if you were so inclined," Magnus suggested gently. "So just stand strong and expect that we'll get to the bottom of this, though it might take a little longer than you would want it to."

"It's not solved right now, so it's already taken a little longer than I wanted." Then she stopped, looked at him. "Is Ralph really sick-sick? Will he be okay?"

"He'll be okay. I've already talked to him once, but I'll be going back and talking to him again."

"Good, I hope you know I would never do anything to hurt him."

"I know that. And honestly, everybody else who knows you well also knows that. The problem is, a lot of people here don't know you that well." And, with that, he was gone.

Sitting alone in her room, she was scared to venture out. She knew there would be an awful lot of judgment coming her way from everybody around her, even if she didn't deserve it. The mood was just ugly enough that she wouldn't be surprised if people even came to her door. Groaning, she rocked back and forth, and then decided no way she would just sit here and take it. She got up and prepped for bed, then headed down to the washroom to clean up for the night. As soon as she stepped out, a group of people in the hallway froze, then turned and looked at her, their glares speaking volumes.

As Avalon brushed past them, one of the women, some of the newest to land in the base, called out, "How could you?"

"I didn't do anything," Avalon snapped right back in a hard voice. "Maybe you should get the facts first."

One of the guys snorted. "Jesus, the guy was just sweet

on you, nothing else, so you didn't have to try to kill him."

At that, she stiffened, then turned around. "Seriously? *Just sweet on me, so I didn't have to try to kill him*? Did you put those in the same sentence?"

One of the girls tried to pull him back, saying, "Come on. Let's not get into a fight."

"Why not? Will she try to poison us next?" he snapped.

An immediate silence came, as their gazes shifted to someone behind her. She knew instinctively that it would be Barret. She put her hands on her hips and glared at the four people in front of her.

"You all ate dinner. It didn't kill you, did it?" she snapped.

"Yeah, well, the night's young yet," he snarled. "For all we know, we'll have symptoms later."

"Nope, you won't," she declared. "But, hey, that's all right. You guys keep on thinking that I did it. I mean, if it makes you feel better to think it was me, then you don't have to consider that there is a real poisoner around here."

At that, one of the girls gasped and stared at Avalon.

Avalon shrugged. "Most of you guys and gals are newbies here. You don't have all the facts. If Ralph was poisoned, and I didn't do it, who did?" She looked back at the guy who had been accusing her and pointed a finger. "Maybe it was you." And, with that, Avalon walked into the ladies' room, without even acknowledging Barret. She quickly finished, and, when she stepped back out, he was leaning against the wall, waiting for her. She glared at him.

"I don't blame you. I mean, once people start blaming you for that shit, it won't go well, will it?"

"Why should it?" she asked. "I haven't done anything."

"No, but Ralph is still saying that you poisoned him. He

said he ate a cookie, and it was off."

"That wouldn't even be a poisoning, would it?" she snapped. "Maybe food poisoning, not *me* poisoning. Plus, if it *was* food poisoning, then everybody else would have got it. Maybe he has an allergy he hasn't been telling anybody about." Avalon now glared at Barret.

He held up a hand.

She realized she was verbally attacking him because of her frustration. "I'm sorry." She walked back to her room. "It's been a pretty upsetting evening."

"Sounds like a pretty upsetting day. What happened?"

She explained about deciding to stay with Chef, and then the new guy making accusations already. He stared at her. She nodded. "So, you know it didn't exactly go down well when Ralph started stirring shit about me poisoning the food." She shook her head. "I shouldn't be in the kitchen apparently, but I don't think anybody'll want me anywhere else either."

"It's Chef's decision if you should be in the kitchen or not," Barret noted, "and the cookies were out on the sideboard. So, if somebody had planned on poisoning Ralph, it's not as if there wasn't opportunity for everybody to do so."

She looked at him and smiled. "Thank you for believing that I didn't try to kill him."

"I know you better than that," Barret said. "You just have to give the truth a chance to work its way out."

"For all I know, he did it to himself." At that, Barret stopped and frowned at her. "I know. That would be foolish, but he's that kind of guy."

Barret didn't say anything, just waited until she was tucked up into bed. "I don't get to go to bed yet," he murmured, "but I'll check up on you later."

"Don't worry about it. I'll be asleep."

He left soon afterward. She got up, locked the door then curled up under the covers, knowing sleep would be the furthest thing from her mind, yet also the one thing she desperately needed. She didn't even know if she was supposed to report to the kitchen in the morning. All she wanted to do was go home. Resolutely she closed her eyes and drifted off to sleep.

BARRET TRACKED DOWN Egan in the medical clinic. Barret stepped forward and asked, "Any news?"

Egan shook his head. "Rooms are being searched for poison right now, but that's not being well received."

"Didn't you tell them it was just a matter of form?"

"Yes," Egan confirmed. "Of course there were lots of protests though. And they all know who to blame for that. Is she getting much flak?"

He nodded. "She's handling it though. There just isn't an easy answer right now."

"No, of course not," Egan agreed.

"Any particularly over-the-top reactions?"

Egan shook his head. "No, mostly fear, I think. And fear that we'd find something," he added. "I'm not terribly impressed with the atmosphere going on here."

"You can't blame them." Barret shrugged, as he looked back over at Sydney. "Do you have anything to enlighten us?"

She shook her head. "Whatever it was upset his system enough to induce vomiting, and that's the good thing."

Looking back over the room, Barret asked, "And you've released him?"

"Yeah, he's back in his room now. Theoretically he should be fine overnight."

"You didn't want to keep him here? Under watch?"

"No, and he didn't want to, which is understandable, I guess." She shrugged.

"But is it really though?" he asked.

"I don't know." She hesitated. "There is one other option here, and I feel terrible even mentioning it."

Both men automatically leaned in. "No, but you need to," Egan stated.

At that, Magnus opened the door, stepped in, then frowned when he saw them all. "What's up?"

She motioned at the two men and said, "I was just about to suggest something that I really don't want to say, but, in all fairness, I feel as if I need to."

"Speak up then," Magnus said.

She shrugged. "He could have taken something himself."

They settled back and nodded.

Barret added, "I wondered that myself." The other two looked at him, and he shrugged. "He's really got it in for Avalon, and this poison talk has been a theme for a while, dating back even to the trouble with the burner in the kitchen. It makes it really difficult for her if everybody thinks she's out to poison them. Even the new guy Steven in the kitchen was asking her about it, and it's only his first day. So, how does Ralph make it look as if she's out to poison them? He gets sick from something he ate, then publicly accuses her."

"And yet how could he have gotten sick from something that she made? That is my question."

"I don't know, but the implication is that she doctored his cookie somehow, sleight-of-hand or something. I don't know," Barret admitted in frustration. "I do know that she's feeling pretty rough over the whole thing, and I don't believe for a moment she had anything to do with it."

"No, I don't either," Egan agreed. "You're right, and this is not anything I want to be said out of this room, but Ralph's been a bit of a problem since he's been here. Several people have complained about his attitude, including Cherry, before she left."

"Cherry did?" Magnus asked, eyeing him.

Egan nodded. "He didn't want to take no for an answer, and she wasn't interested. However, because she was interested in other men, it caused a problem."

"Right. Of course," Barret said, with an eye roll. "Ralph is the kind of guy who figures, if someone's putting out, and Cherry was known for that, then she should be putting out to him."

"Jesus," Sydney muttered, sitting back and looking at him. "I hate to say that is an attitude prevalent in all forms of military, but honestly, here in these circumstances, it is a problem."

"And do we know for sure that Avalon said no to Ralph?" Magnus asked everyone.

"She didn't," Barret replied. "Ralph never asked her out directly. Ralph spoke to me, asking if it would step on anybody's toes if Ralph asked her out. Ever since then, he's given her trouble with this poisoning theme. Plus at dinnertime, it kind of came up again when someone else asked her to have coffee or something right in front of Ralph, who then had to put in his two bits," Barret explained. "I heard about it from a couple people, and they figured that's why she would have poisoned him."

"They figured that's why she would have poisoned him, but what if that's why he went and took something himself?"

"Do you have any idea what he took?" Barret asked Sydney.

She shook her head. "I don't know, but it had a pretty-fast reaction. Several things on the market that you can buy will produce that result, but I don't think he would have had anything on hand though. I mean, that would show a level of premeditation that we have no evidence to support."

"No, of course not," Barret replied. "Anyway, thanks for that."

She nodded. "Now, can you guys clear out so I can clean up this room and maybe get some sleep tonight?" she said, with a smile. "You're all keeping me very busy."

"Not trying to," Magnus noted gently.

"No, but, at the same time, it's best if we do keep on top of it," Sydney stated, "and that means keeping an eye on him and on her."

At that, both men turned to look at Barret. "I'll be looking after her, and I'm hoping to persuade her to let me stay in her room to that end. Yet I don't know that she'll go for it, though she's feeling pretty vulnerable at the moment."

"If you explain to her that it would give her an alibi overnight, reducing the opportunity for things to be blamed on her, it might help your case."

"Maybe," he admitted. "I'll have to see." He got up and looked at the others. "Now, what about Ralph? Any chance that whatever happened will rebound and that he'll be dead in the morning?"

Sydney winced at that. "That would not make me happy. … There's no reason for it. His vitals were stable.

Whatever was in his system appears to be out, and he was walking around just fine. Could something sneak back in? I don't know," she admitted, "but I guess it's possible. The real question is what hit him."

"If we knew that," Barret stated, "we would be a whole lot closer to having some of the bigger answers."

She smiled. "So, go chase them down," she muttered. "That's for you guys to do. My job is to try to keep them alive. Right about now, you're making that very difficult."

With that, Barret headed to his room, where he quickly packed up his few belongings and then walked down to her quarters quite boldly, without trying to hide where he was going.

When she answered the door, he slipped inside and just smiled at her. "Hey."

"Hey," she murmured in a sleepy tone.

He sat down on the side of the bed. "Whether you like if it or not, we've all determined that you should have somebody here with you. So, your choices are either room with me, or you get to go room with one of the new girls."

She looked at him, blinking several times, and she shrugged. "I guess in that case, you're the lesser of two evils."

"You haven't slept with me yet," he murmured. "I do tend to hog the bed."

"That's okay. So do I." She flung back the covers on the other side. "Also I get up early."

When he hesitated, it struck her as odd. She looked at him and asked, "Or do I not have a job?"

"Nobody has mentioned anything about that. As long as Chef is okay, then I presume your job is intact. Assuming that's what you want."

"I won't let somebody like Ralph stop me. However, if

everybody else decides that I'm too dangerous to be in the kitchen"—she gave him an eye roll—"then of course I'm out. But somebody needs to tell me so I can either get some sleep or not."

"I can walk down and talk to Chef about it, if you want."

"Isn't he in bed?"

"I'm not sure that man ever sleeps," Barret teased, with half a smile.

"Good point. Fine, go talk to him and let me know. I'm going back to sleep." And, with that, she rolled over and closed her eyes.

Barret quickly got up and made his way to the kitchen.

Chef was just prepping for bed, checking the stove, which she had been the victim of. As he was doing so, Barret looked at him and asked, "Is she to report here in the morning, or do you not want her in the kitchen?"

Chef frowned at Barret. "Absolutely she is to report here in the morning. That kid Ralph's a piece of shit," he spat, "and she didn't try to poison him. I need her."

"And yet you have somebody new and could get more if you needed it."

He shrugged. "Don't really like all those people messing around my kitchen," he muttered. "It's not big enough for that. I'd be happy to just have her honestly."

Barret studied him for a moment. "Do you think you'll get much flak from everybody else?"

"Don't care if I do." Chef faced Barret full-on, a glare on his face. "You better not be thinking she did something here."

"No, not at all," he protested. "I'm just trying to see what's best to keep the peace."

"The best is that we go forward," Chef stated. "Personally I wouldn't put it past that piece of shit Ralph to have taken something himself."

"That is a topic of concern. We just don't know what it might have been."

"He's allergic to vanilla, so that could be a place to start."

Barret stopped and stared. "Sorry? He's allergic to vanilla?"

"Yeah. Sorta common knowledge for me."

"So why is he eating cookies then?"

"We don't put vanilla in a lot of things to begin with, and the stuff that we generally cook here is something that everybody can have," Chef explained. "Once I realized we had someone here with an allergy to vanilla, I locked it up. It's an unusual thing," he added, with a shrug. "Yet I didn't want any mistakes made, so it's locked up in the cupboard over there." Chef pointed to the corner.

"You want to check for me that it's still there?"

At that, he got to his feet, lumbered over to the cupboard, quickly unlocked it, then spun around. In a hoarse voice, he said, "Damn. It's gone."

"Well, hell." Barret stared at him. "I guess now we know what it was that made him sick."

"And now we also have a bottle of vanilla on the loose," Chef added.

Barret said, "I never thought vanilla could be the culprit."

"Generally it isn't," Chef explained, "but a few people become quite ill from it, and I wouldn't have thought of it. I mean, he's not deathly allergic to it, but it does make him sick," Chef explained. "So that would make sense. Yet I wasn't thinking about anything along those lines, just because I know we haven't used it," Chef shared.

"So, just for the sake of form and not because I'm saying she did this, is there any chance that somebody could have just grabbed a bottle of vanilla and dropped something onto his cookie without him knowing?"

"I suppose. But somebody must have known that he was allergic to it, and somebody would need access to it." He stared at the cupboard and shrugged. "It's not that it would be all that difficult. I mean, I'm not here all the time, and neither is she, and it would only take a drop. It's already very, very concentrated. So, for baking, we wouldn't use much. Plus, as I mentioned, we're not using it with Ralph here. However, if we were, I would expect that bottle to last for maybe six months or more," he explained.

"And the fact that it's missing now …"

"It's a concern, but it's not that big of a concern in terms of cooking because I don't use it anyway," he repeated, "and that's because of Ralph. So now I'm not sure what you want me to do about it." Chef stared at the cupboard, as if that bottle would materialize out of thin air.

"But she would have had access?"

"Sure, as would everybody else." Chef nodded. "So really, what you're looking for is somebody who knew that he was allergic and had a motive for making him sick."

"That definitely changes things," Barret noted, as he moved about the rest of the kitchen. "Anything else missing?"

"No, I don't think so." Chef groaned. "At least not that I can see."

"You still feeding the dogs out back?"

He winced, then snapped, "Did she tell you about that?"

"I noticed it before she even told me." He grinned. "I see the pup Ratchet is one of them. I saw him racing back into his quarters, still swallowing, but he had a joyful kick to his stride."

Chef shrugged. "Back to the real issue—vanilla. It's small, concentrated. Because of the lack of space here," he motioned around, "I just have a very small bottle. It's not exactly something anybody will be looking for, and honestly it could have just been mixed up around here." He looked around. "I thought I'd locked it up, but maybe, with all the other changes we've been making and the mess with no staff, it's possible we didn't get it locked up," he muttered, as he frowned. "And it never would have been an issue until …"

"Nothing's ever an issue until it is," Barret murmured.

At that, Chef stopped and asked him, "How is she doing?"

"Outside of the accusations flying her way and people talking in the hallways and making her feel as if she's done something wrong," he shared, with a half smile, "she's wondering if she's supposed to show up in the morning."

He stared in astonishment. "Absolutely. I would be screwed if she doesn't."

"But you have one new person."

"Yeah, but he's not up to speed, and I'm not sure he'll ever be as good as she is," Chef admitted. "But, hey, if the brass doesn't want her here, that's a different story. I can't go against that."

"Nobody has said anything to her, so we're wondering if this is what you want."

"I'm very happy to have her here," he declared, his tone firm. "I have absolutely no qualms about keeping her in my kitchen."

"I'll tell her that then because I know she was quite concerned."

"She doesn't need to be. I mean, if that idiot Ralph is causing trouble, well, he doesn't have to come here. He can get moved out. Apparently it's *too dangerous* for him," Chef noted, with a derisive tone of disgust. "Keep an eye on him too."

"That's the plan. We're just not sure what it all means."

"It means you have to keep him away from her. Maybe somebody needs to keep an eye on her too," he muttered. "I wouldn't put it past that asshole."

"Put what past him?"

"Wouldn't put it past Ralph to do something stupid and to hurt her, if he doesn't get the desired results out of this."

"You make it sound as if you really think it was him."

"Don't know if it was or not, but he's the kind of asshole where anything goes."

"Plus we also have his friends to consider," Barret added.

"Yeah, but I wouldn't necessarily consider anybody here his friends. They hang around together, and everybody's kind of got this joking bet going on about girls, but I'm not sure *friends* is the term I'd use."

"Joking bet?"

Chef looked at him and nodded. "You know? The numbers game, notches on the bedpost type thing. Berry caught on early, and I remember her telling him to take his little problem away from her. He didn't take it very kindly, but things blew up pretty fast for her, so he didn't become an issue for her."

"They sure did," Barret said. "I hadn't heard about these guys doing that."

"No, and that's what happens when you get a bunch of

guys together who aren't happy about being here," Chef pointed out. "With all the problems we've got, you know perfectly well that it's always a challenge to keep people occupied. If you fail, they come up with something themselves."

"It shouldn't be like that though," Barret groused.

"Shouldn't be, but, if you can find a way to stop it, good on you," Chef muttered. "Now get lost, and tell her I expect to see her first thing in the morning."

"Will do." And, with a smile on his face, Barret headed down to her room.

DAY 10 EARLY MORNING

AVALON WOKE WITH a start, feeling something very off. When arms tightened around her reassuringly, she sagged back and looked up at him. "I half remember a conversation about you moving in."

"Yes," Barret confirmed, "and sometimes half a conversation is all you'll get, but it's early, and you're expected in the kitchen."

She groaned as she curled deeper into his arms and whispered, "Don't want to."

He chuckled. "Of course you don't want to, but Chef's counting on you."

"Are you sure about that?" she asked, opening her eyes and looking at him.

"Yep, I talked to him last night. As far as he's concerned, none of this had anything to do with you."

"Oh, I know it didn't have anything to do with me. I just can't figure out what made Ralph sick."

"It's quite possible that he ended up with vanilla in his stomach."

"Vanilla?" she repeated, raising up and looking down on him, as he propped himself up on one arm. "Vanilla? How is that—"

"Apparently he's allergic to vanilla. He doesn't get deathly ill, just violently sick to his stomach."

"Jesus, I didn't put it in anything. Chef told me early on that we couldn't use it, so I didn't."

"You didn't make anything with it?"

"No, not unless somebody switched it out for a different bottle or something. In that case, I wouldn't have known."

"Who would have done that?"

"I don't know." She raised both hands. "Nobody would have, unless they knew and were up to no good. But I still can't imagine someone taking the chance of Ralph getting seriously ill." She groaned as she lay flat again. "While you get to stay in bed, I on the other hand, really need to get up."

"I'll come down for coffee in a bit," he replied.

She looked down at him and saw an image that just took her breath away. "I don't know if you realize just how good you look right now," she whispered, "and I'd be more than willing to take the day off and just spend it in bed."

He opened one eye and gave her a lazy smile. "If I thought you were serious, I'd take you up on that offer," he declared. "However, I happen to know you're expected in the kitchen, and I know you're not the type to shirk your duties."

She rolled her eyes at that, as she pulled on her extra layer of clothes. "*Great.* I'm not in any hurry for this day to happen. Can you tell?"

"Listen. You didn't do anything wrong," he declared, "so don't let anybody push your buttons."

"Too late." As she looked back at him, stretched out in her bed, she sighed. "Damn, what a waste." As she stepped through the door, she heard him chuckling behind her.

"I'll be down in a bit."

She poked her head back in. "You don't have to."

"Doesn't matter if I have to or not, I'll be there."

"Oh, so you're just making sure I know you're coming so I have time to get some cookies or something made up ahead for you, is that how it is?"

He smiled. "I never say no to cookies, but, no, I certainly don't expect that. However, you're right. I will be keeping track of what's going on." When she frowned, he shook his head. "Don't bother arguing."

"You'll get all *guardy* on me?" she asked.

"*Guardy?*" He rolled the word around in his mouth. "Yeah, maybe."

"You don't need to, you know? Nobody'll come attack me."

"They might," he cautioned, "but they won't do it twice."

Such a warning filled his tone that she smiled, her heart filling with warmth. "You really do believe I didn't have anything to do with it, right?" she asked.

He waved his hand. "Go on and get to work. You don't need to ask such a silly question."

"Thank you, that means a lot to me." He opened his eyes and glared at her. She threw up her hands. "It's true."

"Fine. I'm glad it means something to you. However, it shouldn't because none of us have any doubts about you. So go. Go check in with Chef, and get the coffee on."

"Will do." And she headed down to the kitchen.

One of the nice things about working at this hour of the morning was that nobody else was ever up, and she could walk the hallways free and clear of prying eyes and suspicious gazes. When she walked into the kitchen to see Chef, he was already huddled over a cup of coffee. She smiled at him, as she poured herself a cup and sat down across from him.

He looked at her with relief. "Glad to see you're here,"

he muttered.

"Hey, I wouldn't have been, except apparently you told Barret that I was expected."

"Exactly," he said.

"You need to realize a lot of people may not be that happy to see me here."

"I don't give a crap if they're happy or not," Chef spat. "They better not say anything to me."

She frowned. "If they can prove that I was responsible …"

His gaze searched her keenly. "Were you?'

"No," she protested.

"Then shut up."

She slapped her mouth closed and stared at him.

He grinned. "Glad to see you can still take orders." Then he laughed openly. "Jesus, I know you didn't have anything to do with it. It's all just straight-up bullshit, so forget about it. That kid is talking shit through his mouth."

"Where else would he talk through?" she asked in a cheeky tone.

"His ass, of course. And, for guys like Ralph, it's exactly what they do. What else did Barret tell you?"

"I was pretty sleepy last night when he showed up"—she stifled a yawn even now—"but this morning, there was some talk about vanilla."

"Yep, vanilla," Chef confirmed, "and that's something for you to keep in mind."

"And yet we aren't using vanilla. You told me that we had some but weren't to use it, so I didn't," she replied, with a shrug.

"Good, But the fact of the matter is, somebody may have."

"Right, but as long as it wasn't me, then I really don't care. Although I guess that sounds wrong, doesn't it?" she asked. "I should care."

"No, you have enough to worry about without dealing with that."

"Seriously though, you have to expect that there'll be some complaints."

"They can complain all they want, but it's my kitchen. If they don't like it, … they can take it to the CO." At that, he gave her a feral grin. "And he and I have been together for a very long time, so that ain't going to make a damn bit of difference."

"Is the colonel a good guy?" she asked.

"He is. He's done some shit that kind of backfired on him, but, hey, that's true for all of us. I stand by him."

"You must have known him a long time."

"Decades. He tried to save my boy way back when, … and, for that, I'll always be on his side."

"Of course," she murmured. "I didn't realize you went that far back."

"Yeah, we do, and I know he's trying to retire and get the hell out, but he doesn't want to do it with disgrace on his head."

"No, of course not. Nobody would want their whole career tainted like that."

"You should know because the same thing is happening to you."

She winced. "I don't have the kind of accolades he does, and I don't think anybody really gives a shit about me. Not like they do about him."

"I haven't heard a whole lot of good since he got here, and it's definitely weighing on him."

"He hasn't had an easy run of it either," Avalon noted. "I mean, for all intents and purposes, it seems everybody's against him."

"Yes, and that's because of the way shit's going down here," Chef said. "Hopefully that'll be straightened up soon too."

She looked at him questioningly, but he didn't elaborate any further. "You do know that Steven implied that I might have poisoned somebody through negligence, right? That's when you caught us not getting along."

He nodded. "And that's bullshit too. I've seen you in action. Remember? You clearly know what you're doing, and negligence implies that you either didn't know or were too sloppy and didn't care enough to make sure what you were doing was correct. I haven't seen any sign of that at all."

"Thank you," she said, surprised at his defense. "It's nice to know that I get a passing grade from the chef."

"And, if I wanted to be a sexist asshole, I could tell you that it's preparing you for marriage when you get out of here, but I wouldn't do that to you."

"I appreciate that," she replied, with a smile. "Hate to think of that as the only thing ahead of me in life."

He gave a headshake. "You need to do whatever you want to do, but I can tell you that, when you find the right person and the babies start coming, chances are good that you'll want to stay home and raise them."

"Maybe so," she agreed because she had been thinking the same thing herself. "Still, a lot of women keep their careers these days, and I do want that for myself."

"Of course," he noted. "That doesn't mean you don't want to take a year or two and just spend it with them. But if you do, I really don't mind either way."

"Did you just have the one son?" she asked.

"I did," he replied, with a gentle smile. "Would have had more, but the missus and I couldn't seem to make that happen. And it wasn't really in us to go through all these newfangled technological routes that apparently are out there these days." He gave her a headshake. "Didn't seem quite right for us somehow."

"I've heard that from a couple people, but I imagine, if you're desperate for kids, for some, that may be the only answer."

"Maybe so," he conceded, "but we did have the one, and that was good enough for us. He was sent off on a mission, and the boss got him shifted to a safer area, so he put a stop to it. Yet something went wrong, and he ended up dying anyway," Chef shared. "He died protecting another family, so it's one of those sad cases where he went out with honor, but I wish to hell that he hadn't had to go at all."

"Yeah," Avalon agreed. "We hear of so many tragic situations in the kind of work we do."

"Absolutely," he murmured. "So, for that reason alone, I can smile when I think about him, instead of just feeling the pain of knowing I've lost him, but it's been a while. So, as they say, … time heals all wounds."

"I think that saying is a lie," she stated bluntly.

He looked at her and nodded sagely. "You're right. It doesn't heal anything. It just blunts the pain maybe, until something happens and stirs it all back up again," he replied, his tone dark.

"What about your wife?"

"What about her?" he asked, with another pained look. "Lost her to breast cancer a couple years back. And again, the boss gave me time off to go deal with it, and then I came back to work for him. We've been together ever since."

"And his wife?"

"He doesn't have one anymore. Both of our wives ended up dying from breast cancer, just decades apart."

"I'm sorry. You don't realize how prevalent that disease is until it touches your life."

"Cancer is a mean and ugly bitch, and, when it touches your life, it does it in the darkest, most heinous way possible." Chef shook his head. "I know the boss, and what matters the most to him is that he leaves with full honors. For him, it's all about his reputation, so, no, he won't do anything to screw that up."

"Good, so that means then he should be acting with full honor in all situations."

"And he is—unless you've heard something different."

"No. I just hear a lot of rumblings from some of the people about how he's not doing enough, … you know, to keep everybody safe."

"To be honest, I've heard those rumblings too. But you know that those things are usually coming from people who don't understand what's going on, who don't know what can and can't be done, and who want solutions and answers when really none of it's that simple. They are also the ones who balk and complain when actions are taken in their own best interests."

"I know," she acknowledged, analyzing her own situation.

"Now, you need to get moving. We got potatoes to scrub."

She groaned. "Not if you stopped ordering them."

"I could," Chef noted, "but then there wouldn't be anything for you to do."

"Oh, wow, look at that. I wouldn't have to peel potatoes for two hours."

"It's not that bad." Chef chuckled. "And we might just do roasted potatoes today too," he muttered, looking around the kitchen. "We got lots of spuds and lots of people needing carbs for this cold."

"Yeah, it's supposed to get pretty ugly, and I don't know if they'll get back out again for another day or two."

He nodded. "Happy food is what we all need right now. It keeps people content and tempers at bay, so remember that."

"I'll try," she replied, "that is, if I ever have those kids that I don't have yet."

"It'll happen one day," Chef proclaimed, "and you'll be damn good in the kitchen when it does. You've taken to this pretty-darn quickly."

"Thank you," she said. He wasn't given to compliments much, so she appreciated when they did come, particularly after the last few days.

He just snorted. "That's the last compliment you'll get out of me." He sent a hard look in her direction, and then he completely failed the tough guy look and gave her a big fat grin. "Still doesn't get you out of potato duty though."

Rolling her eyes, she got up and got to work, as she looked back over at him. "Is Steven not coming in?"

"He is. He's just coming in a little later."

"Okay. Won't matter." Ignoring that, she got to work. By the time breakfast was served, she was so busy that she forgot about everything else, until it was time to step out in front, with the crowd gathered. She shrugged as she looked over at Chef and said, "Here goes nothing."

As she stepped up to the plates to start serving food,

right there in front of her was Barret, first in line, and behind him was Magnus, followed by Egan and Rogan.

She gave them a ghost of a smile. "Thanks for the support, guys."

They nodded. "No need. We have the utmost confidence."

And, with that, she started serving the morning meal. At some point, she realized Steven had arrived and was aware of a harsh discussion going on behind her, but she ignored it, trusting that whatever happened would happen regardless. If she ended up having to leave the kitchen? Well, so be it. But, as it was, the issue appeared to be solved before breakfast was even over.

Nobody said a word to her, although several people cast worried glances around. However, seeing everybody else eating, they had a choice of eating or going without. Waiting for the next person in line, she looked up to see Ralph glaring at her.

She nodded. "Glad to hear you're feeling better."

"Nothing to do with you though," he retorted in a snippy tone.

She studied him. "I understand from Chef that you're allergic to vanilla, but, since that isn't something we use back here, I'm not sure how that would have happened."

"Maybe," he muttered. "But then again, you do keep it around, don't you?" he asked in a snide tone.

"I haven't seen any because Chef put it away," she stated, tilting her head to the side. "Have you seen any?"

He just glared at her, quickly snatched some food, and declared, "If you poison me this time, we'll definitely know where it's coming from."

"Not at all," she argued, "because I don't cook alone

back here. Therefore, it's the same scenario as every other meal here. And the cookies you ate didn't have any vanilla in them."

He stopped, looked at her. "What?"

She nodded. "The cookies that you ate? Remember? Yes, I baked them, but they didn't have vanilla in them."

He shook his head. "Vanilla's the only thing I'm allergic to."

"The only thing *you know of*," she pointed out gently. "Perhaps you're allergic to something else that you didn't know about, but the same thing applies. We didn't put vanilla in those cookies."

"Somebody sure as hell put vanilla into something," he snapped.

"I don't know anything about that," she stated calmly, then smiled up at the person behind him. "Good morning, what can I get you?"

As it was, it looked to be the same guy who had been so apologetic the other day. He smiled, … his gaze going from one to the other. "I mean, I don't want to intrude."

"You're not." She quickly served him sausage and eggs. By the time everybody was seated, she turned around to see Steven glaring at her, but Chef had been in and out, keeping an eye on things, as he had promised, not stepping in unless it was necessary. So far, it hadn't been, and she appreciated that too. She quickly set about refilling the serving tubs, before the next group came through, and finished just in time to see the colonel in front of her.

He took one look at her, nodded, gave her a half smile. "I hope there's a lot. Everybody'll be hungry today."

"There's always plenty," she said cheerfully, as she served him a big portion.

Chef stepped up beside her and took over serving up the food for the CO's plate and handed it off quickly. But the CO took the same food as everyone else, and she smiled at him. "Enjoy your breakfast, sir."

He nodded and headed right back to his own quarters. She was surprised at that. She turned to look at Chef and asked, "Is he okay?"

"He is. He just hasn't been feeling that great lately," Chef shared in a whisper.

"Then all this stress isn't helping either."

He didn't respond to that but turned and headed back to the kitchen and started cleaning up. She felt the tension emanating off Steven's shoulders. Every time she glanced in his direction, he wasn't looking at her though, which was probably a good thing.

By the time the dishes were done, and she turned and looked at Chef, and he nodded.

"You're good to go. Take a couple hours."

She asked, "What about lunch?"

He replied, "I've got a really big stew on, and some roast in the oven already. We've got it in hand, and you already did the spuds, so we're all good."

She nodded, then smiled. "In that case, I'll go grab a plate and eat."

"Didn't you eat earlier?" Chef asked, stopping and looking at her.

She shook her head. "No, I decided to wait." He glared at her, but she shrugged. "Hey, everybody was eating and happy enough. So I didn't want to go out there and disturb things," she added, with an eye roll.

He shook his head. "No need for you to feel bad. You didn't do anything. Remember?"

"I know. I know," she said, "but you also know that some people don't agree with you."

He shrugged. "That's their problem." Hearing half a snort from Steven behind him, Chef turned and asked, "Did you have something to say?"

Steven shook his head. "No, I didn't, but other people will."

"They're welcome to say whatever they want, as long as they say it to me. This is my kitchen. If you don't like it, you can go find some other place."

Steven flushed and shook his head. "No, sir, I'm happy to be here."

"Yeah, you'd damn-well better be," he muttered. "But, if you don't get over yourself real fast and accept the reality that she didn't have anything to do with this and behave accordingly, then you'll find yourself in a spot of trouble really quick."

And, with that, Chef turned his back on her and told Steven to work on the dishes. She quickly grabbed the food she'd set off to the side, warmed it up, and took her plate to her room. As soon as she stepped into her room, she felt everything sagging away in relief. Thank God. Some time for herself, for a few minutes to relax, except she didn't get a few minutes. When a knock came on the door, she called out. and Sydney replied. Opening the door, Avalon let her in. "Hey, come on in. I was just trying to grab a few minutes and eat."

"You don't eat with us?"

She shrugged. "This morning was a little dicey, and I didn't want to set anybody off."

Sydney gave her a lopsided grin and nodded. "Understood."

"So, what's up? Did you need something from me?" she asked curiously.

"I've talked to Chef, and I've talked to Steven about the vanilla in the kitchen," she explained. "I just wanted to hear your side of it."

"Sure, but there's not much to tell. I've never seen vanilla in the kitchen here. Of course I've used it myself many times but never here. Chef told me that we don't use it here, when I asked about it the first time I made cookies. I didn't have any reason to not follow his directions, and I've never worked in a commercial kitchen before, so I didn't give it a thought." She paused for a moment, then added, "I never went looking for it, so I didn't see it, but I understood from Chef that it was up in the locked cupboard, which really doesn't lock."

"A locked cupboard that doesn't lock?" Sydney asked curiously.

"Yeah, it's kind of a joke, like every other lock around here. I mean, it's not as if we have any strong precautions here that could keep anybody out who's interested. All these trainees are well equipped to pick any lock around here."

Sydney laughed. "Everybody here is pretty capable of popping a lock, aren't they?"

"Exactly." Avalon smiled. "So, it's not exactly something that'll keep anybody out. Just calling it the 'locked cabinet' is kind of a joke."

"But this isn't a joking matter. The vanilla in this case was more than a prank," Sydney said, "but, with everything else going on, it was a prank on the scary side, and we want to make sure that it doesn't happen again."

"Oh, I agree with you there," Avalon stated, "particularly since everybody's looking at me over it."

"No, not everybody," Sydney stated. "We firmly believe that you didn't have anything to do with this, but it is possible that somebody is doing it on purpose to discredit you."

She stared at her. "That's possible. I wondered if Ralph had done it to himself."

Sydney nodded. "I did ask him that, point-blank, and he got quite irate. I have to admit I believed him."

"Good enough. All I know is that I didn't do it. … I know that my room was searched while I was at work and that other people had their places searched. Did the vanilla ever show up?"

Sydney shook her head. "No, but it's not as if it would be hard to dispose of."

"Not hard to dispose of, but, if you were to pour it out somewhere, you would think it would leave enough of an odor to make someone notice."

"Maybe," she agreed, looking at her, "but not outside."

"Oh, now that's true," Avalon said, "and a small bottle would be easy to get rid of."

"That's assuming," Sydney noted, her tone hardening, "that whoever was only playing a prank and not wanting this as a prelude to something much darker."

Avalon stared at the doc and winced. "And that would imply that there could be a second attempt."

"Exactly. So Ralph has been told to keep to a very strict diet and to only eat in the kitchen. So, at the first sign of any illness, to come to me, so I can get his stomach emptied," Sydney shared. "However, I'm really hoping that this is a one-off incident."

"Jesus, I would sure as hell hope so." Avalon frowned at her, stumped. "I mean, does somebody have it in for Ralph, or does somebody have it in for me?"

"Or is somebody out to get both of you?" Sydney asked.

"Oh, *great*," she murmured, "because I really, … I don't know what to think." She was completely dumbfounded that anybody would even consider making a joke out of this. But the alternative of it being deliberate and enough to cause more than a passing moment of illness was too much to even think about. "So, in Ralph's case," Avalon asked cautiously, "could it kill him?"

"Could it? If he didn't have immediate access to medical aid? Possibly. In this case, it just made him very sick, but I also don't know how much he ate."

"But it would only be in a cookie, right?"

"The cookie didn't smell like it had any vanilla to me, but he ate the whole thing, except for one bite to give to his buddy."

"Oh, yeah. How is it his buddy got sick? Surely he's not allergic to vanilla?"

"Honestly," Sydney shared, with half a smile, "I think seeing how violently ill Ralph was then combined with the realization that he'd eaten the same thing and made him feel quite nauseous. so he panicked."

"Oh, so it's not as if he got sick himself."

"No."

Feeling better about that, she nodded. "That makes more sense. It's amazing how quickly those ideas can fly through this place, isn't it?"

"It can happen pretty fast, so, yes. We just want to nip those things in the bud."

"I wouldn't want it to be something people think about either," she murmured. "Anyway, I don't know what else to tell you. I don't know where the vanilla is. As far as I know, it's supposed to have been in that cupboard, but, because we don't use it, I can't say I've ever seen it."

"Right. That's what I came to check on, so thanks." At that, Sydney stood. "We'll get to the bottom of it. Don't you worry."

"It's hard not to," Avalon admitted. "Especially now that you've put an even more ominous thought in my mind."

Sydney smiled. "I didn't tell you just to worry you," she pointed out. "However, if you do sense anything or find or smell or in any way suspect the presence of vanilla, let me know."

"Again, it still shouldn't kill him, right?" she questioned.

"No, it shouldn't, but I can't say what a larger dose would do."

"Right, and I guess that's the point, isn't it?"

"It absolutely is. A little bit can make him very sick, but a lot could be far worse. Plus we don't have facilities for that here," Sydney explained. "So, it's the circumstances here and the fact that it could happen while he's out on a training mission. … It's all too possible."

"*Great*," Avalon muttered. "Thanks for that."

And, with that, Sydney was gone.

BARRET WALKED DOWN the hallway toward Avalon's room, when he saw Sydney step out. He waited for her to approach, then asked in whisper, "Is she okay?"

"She is. I had already spoken to Chef and Steven, so felt that I needed to speak to her personally as well. She's on her break and trying to get some food down right now." Sydney smiled. "So good timing on your part."

"I do worry about her," he said. "She's quite distressed that anybody would even think she had something to do with it."

"Of course she is. Nobody wants to be accused of something like this. However, I'm more concerned that we don't have the vanilla bottle, and I don't know what a stronger dose would do to Ralph."

"And you're thinking that's a problem?"

She gave him a lopsided look. "Have you gotten any indication that life here is normal and that it's not something we should worry about?"

"No," he admitted, "not at all."

"Exactly, so, until we find that bottle, we can't put the issue to rest. Once we find it, I'll still have to figure out if some has been emptied into some other container for another purpose too."

"*Great*," Barret replied. "I can see why Avalon's not feeling terribly good about any of this."

"Nobody can feel good about it," the doc said, "especially Ralph."

"And you don't think he did it himself?"

"I don't know." She shrugged. "He seemed pretty credible when I asked him, and I don't think he would have intentionally made himself quite that sick on purpose. Maybe enough to start puking, but this went well beyond that scenario."

"That could have been exactly it though," Barret pointed out. "Like Ralph thought he'd do it to make himself sick, so he'd have something to back up his ongoing accusations and could get other people looking at her sideways again—only it went too far."

"And that's possible," Sydney agreed. "It absolutely is

possible. I just don't know for sure, and so we'll keep an open mind." And, with that, she was gone.

When he reached Avalon's door, he knocked. When he pushed his head in, she asked, "What's the point of living here if you still have to knock to see if you can come in?"

He laughed and stepped inside. "I didn't want to overstep my boundaries."

"Okay, good to know," she replied sarcastically. "I'm not exactly sure what the boundary is, but, hey, it's nice to know you didn't want to overstep it."

He rolled his eyes at her mood. "I take it the talk with Sydney didn't go well."

"She just pointed out that, until the vanilla is found, it'll be suspect in any other accident involving Ralph," she shared in a curt tone. "I wouldn't wish that on anybody. I guess he's taking it easy today because his stomach is sore from all the puking. And, of course, he's feeling pretty rough and hard done by, and she doesn't really believe that he would have done this to himself. She believed him when he told her that he didn't have anything to do with it."

"Which is also why we did a full search of his room and grilled both him and his buddy to make sure that his buddy didn't give it to him, just to cement whatever joke they were planning."

"Oh, that's great," she muttered. "Can't say I would want to see that happen either."

"Nope, and yet it's possible. It's all possible," Barret claimed, "so we'll err on the side of being safe."

"Sounds good to me," she muttered. "Of course Steven's been an absolute ass too, though Chef shut him down pretty fast. I'm really glad to have Chef in my corner."

DAY 10 AFTER DINNER

D INNER WAS OVER. Avalon was tired, but it had been a good day, although she wasn't sure that Steven's presence had helped much with the workload. She wanted to mention it to Chef, yet, at the same time, she wasn't sure it would be prudent. As she looked around to see what else needed to be done, Chef pointed at the doorway.

"Go," Chef said. "You've done a ton of work today. Get lost." She glared at him. He sighed. "Look. You can't just work away your troubles."

"Are you sure?" she asked, with an eye roll. "I thought I was doing a good job of it."

"No, it's called avoidance," Chef clarified, "and you still have to spend some of your evening with other people. They need to see you out there, being one of them."

"Not if I stay in here and keep working," she noted cheerfully.

"Nope, not allowed."

She glared at him and shrugged. "Fine. I have to get up early in the morning anyway."

"I wanted to suggest that Steven can do the early morning shift, and you can come in a bit later. You've already done a ton of work."

"I won't say no to sleeping in for a change," she admitted. "It's been a long time since I've had a chance to do that."

He nodded. "Good. So, sleep in tomorrow," Chef ordered, "and I'll see you sometime after breakfast is served. Show up on the other side of the counter and eat first. Then we'll talk and see where we're at for the day."

"Good enough," she said, then unexpectedly gave him a hug, then quickly dashed away. She heard him chuckling behind her, so she figured that at least she hadn't insulted him in any way.

With that, she walked away, feeling a sense of joy. Several other people caught the smile on her face, but, instead of waiting for her to explain, they quickly dodged out of her way, as if to avoid her, and her smile disappeared.

She mentally shrugged, knowing that she couldn't really blame them, not when everybody was thinking the same thing, but it still hurt. It hurt in ways that she hadn't really expected. She headed to her room, determined to have some time to herself and to forget everybody else's ugly behavior. As she came down the hallway, she found herself face-to-face with Ralph.

He glared at her.

She shrugged. "I'm sorry about what happened, but I had nothing to do with it."

He didn't say anything and just continued to glare and didn't get out of her way.

She sighed. "Look. I've said all I have to say. So, if you can just let me get by, we can both go about our business." She stepped to the left, but he stepped up in front of her, blocking her path. She took a deep breath, stared at him. "Seriously?"

He nodded. "You're the bitch who tried to poison me," he snapped.

"And what if I'm not the person who tried to poison you?" she asked, looking at him.

"What do you mean? Of course you are."

"What if I'm not? Just consider the possibility for the moment. What if I'm not the one who tried to poison you? For all I know, you did it yourself to make me look bad. I mean, you've been on this campaign to shit on me all along, and this is just more of the same damn thing."

"You really think I poisoned myself?" he asked in shock.

"Why not? Somebody poisoned you, but it sure as hell wasn't me. And let's not forget the fact that this was not poison. This was vanilla."

"Yeah, and I'm allergic to it. It makes me really sick."

"I understand that, but it's not as if it was arsenic or something," she said.

"Who's to say that you won't do that next time?" he spat back at her.

"Look. As I already told you, I didn't do it the first time," she stated, determined not to lose her temper. "And it would be really nice if you would stop making such innuendos in my face. Or behind my back for that matter because I didn't do anything to you."

He glared at her.

Avalon added, "I sure hope they searched your room for vanilla, just as they searched mine."

He stared at her, incredulous. "I didn't poison myself. That is ridiculous."

"I didn't do it either. So, it looks as if we're back to the same problem. If I didn't do it, and you didn't do it, you might want to spend some of that energy considering who else might have."

He shook his head. "Nobody else gives a damn enough

to try to do that to me."

"Maybe not," she agreed, "but what if you had a conversation with somebody and implied that maybe things would be better if I was out of here, if only there was some way that you could make that happen?"

He stared at her, and, if she hadn't been watching so closely, she might not have seen the jolt in his eyes.

But he shook his head. "Now you're just making shit up."

"Or maybe not," she stated, with a feral grin. "Just keep it in mind because, if whoever it was thinks that you might figure it out, they might just try it again. I don't know whether using more would hurt you or even worse," she shared, with a shrug. "But, while you're busy telling everyone it's me, whoever did it is still out there. So, if you didn't do it, you might want to give that some thought."

"That's ridiculous," he muttered, but his tone had lost its edge. He inched past her, as if trying to get as far away from her as possible.

She gave him as much room as she could and then quickly disappeared down the hallway to her quarters. Once inside, she quickly opened up her phone and called Barret. When he answered, she told him, "Hey, I'm back in my room, but I ran into Ralph on my way here."

"Did he say something to you?" he asked, his tone sharp.

"Yeah, he did, but I don't really blame him because it seems as if he seriously thinks I did it. I did suggest that maybe he'd spoken to someone or had bitched about me to someone and that maybe they had taken it upon themselves to make it look as if I was guilty. He got an odd look on his face, as if I had hit home with something I said. So, did you check his room?"

"I didn't personally, but one of us did. I can check into it though."

"And his roommate's belongings too?" she asked.

"You really think somebody would have done it for that reason?"

"I don't know what reason people do shit around here," she admitted, "but I haven't been exactly very popular since Scott died and since I started to work in the kitchen. So I don't know what to say to that. I just know that Ralph had an odd reaction when I suggested that."

"Good enough. I'll follow up. Stay in your room, okay?"

She laughed. "Believe me. I'm exhausted, so that won't be a problem, but I do get to sleep in tomorrow."

"Oh, do you now?" he noted, his voice purring gently.

"Yes," she replied, "but that doesn't mean you do." With that, she quickly hung up, laughing to herself. She did have a book that she'd been rather desperately trying to get to and hadn't really found the time, so she curled up in bed with the book in hand.

When a knock came on the door, it took her a minute to get her head out of the book, and she called out, "Who is it?"

And, with that, the door opened, and Ralph poked his head around the corner. "Hey. … You know what you said earlier?"

She nodded. "Yeah, what about it?"

"I just … I did mention it to somebody. I was kind of … I was kind of upset," he admitted sheepishly. There was just something about his tone that was off.

"Yes and? And what?"

"Just … do you really think somebody would do that?"

"Sure. The bottom line is, if you didn't do it, and I didn't do it, then somebody else did." He nodded absentmindedly. "If you have any idea who might have done it, you need to go talk to somebody about it."

"That's why I'm asking you because I don't know where they would have got the vanilla from."

"I don't know either, but it was in the kitchen. I just don't know if they would necessarily know much about it."

He nodded at that. "Anyway, sorry to bother you."

"Hey, wait, wait, wait," she said, bolting from her bed. "Why did you come?"

"I just … I wanted to make sure you didn't do it," he said, his tone apologetic, as he looked at her. "I just needed to hear it from you again."

"I did not do it," she stated firmly, looking at him square in the face. "Honestly, I was thinking that you did."

"I didn't," he said, backing up, "but you're right. That means somebody else did."

And, with that, he hurriedly strode down the hallway.

BARRET ANSWERED HIS phone to hear Avalon on the other end, explaining what had just happened. "Okay, that's strange," he said. "I'll go talk to him."

"Yeah, you do that and maybe now."

Hearing the worry in her tone, he replied, "I'm already heading toward his room."

"Good, because I don't like the way he was acting. He was, I don't know, I can't really put my finger on it."

"Maybe try."

"Sad maybe, betrayed certainly, … like he had a good idea who might have done it but didn't want to think it was true."

"And yet it's quite possible that whoever did it also didn't know what Ralph's reaction would be."

"Right, allergies can cause all sorts of different reactions."

"In this case, it just made him sick."

"Right. I don't want to say it didn't *hurt him*-hurt him because of course it made him quite sick, but I am worried about the rest of the bottle."

"Yeah, you and Sydney both."

BARRET RACED DOWN the hallway toward Ralph's room.

When he got to the assigned room, he knocked but got no answer. He popped open the door and checked inside, but nobody was there. Swearing, Barret looked around, trying to figure out where Ralph would have gone. Barret headed toward the kitchen area, pulling out his phone, and called Magnus. Barret quickly explained a little bit, knowing that he couldn't give too many details, not when he was racing around and people could be listening.

But Magnus related that he was already in the kitchen and for Barret to meet him there. As soon as Barret stepped into the dining room, he saw Ralph off to the side, sitting all alone.

Bypassing Magnus, Barret walked over, sat down in front of Ralph, and said, "We need to talk." He looked up at him. She was right; there was a haunted look on his face.

Ralph shook his head. "It was just an accident. ... I'm sure it was just an accident."

"I'm not," Barret disagreed. "You need to tell me what the hell's going on here."

He hesitated. "Look. I went and talked to her. I guess because I needed to hear from her again that she really hadn't done it."

"And?"

"And I believe her," Ralph replied. "The crazy bitch thought I might have done it," he said, with a return of some of his spirit. "But she's also right that, if she didn't do it, and I didn't do it, therefore, somebody else did," he stated in a whisper, looking around.

Barret nodded. "Who do you think that somebody else would be?"

He shook his head. "I just didn't want to think about it, and I'll put it down to the fact that he didn't know it would have this kind of a reaction."

"That's quite true. Nobody suspected it would be as severe as it was, but the fact is that you're doing okay."

He nodded. "That's the thing. The fact that I'm doing okay is really … it's good, but that was pretty nasty, and it also shows me that this allergy that I've kind of ignored most of my life is now becoming a bigger problem than I had ever realized because somebody could use it against me."

"You still haven't told me who it is that you think would have done this."

"And I'm not going to," he said, "because I don't think it was intended to hurt me. I think it was more intended to—" And then he stopped, looking uncomfortable.

"To hurt her."

He nodded, wincing. "Yeah, I think that's exactly what it was. And, for that, I'm sorry. I wouldn't want everybody looking at her like I have been."

"They already have been because of you, … because of the finger that was pointed at her. You've been laying the negative foundation around here for quite some time. Then, when you got sick, you very publicly accused her yourself."

"And that was wrong," he said. "I didn't mean it."

"You did mean it, but now that you're not so sure that she did it, you don't know how to backtrack."

"No, I don't. I need to think about it a little more."

"Don't spend too much time on that because remember. The bottle is still missing."

"Yes, but I don't think the intention was to hurt me, so finding the rest of the bottle is more just a loose end. You want to locate it, so it's not a problem."

"But it's a problem no matter what," Barret repeated. "So, if you find it, I suggest you let me know and don't touch it and let me know."

"I think it only hurts me if I ingest it," Ralph explained. "Honestly I don't really know. When I found out I was allergic, I just avoided it, though I never really understood. It's one of those stupid ingredients that's in everything."

"In everything and nothing," Barret said, "and Chef knows perfectly well enough that it's not in his cooking because he's kept it away, knowing you were allergic."

"I suppose he deals with all kinds of different diets, doesn't he?"

"Absolutely he does, and his job would be on the line, not to mention potential criminal consequences, if he had deliberately missed something like that. Plus, it's not just you with allergies here. Helen was one, and he makes special food for her, and now you. That was another time when you deliberately pointed the finger at Avalon for no reason."

"I know." Ralph gave a headshake. "I'm sorry. I didn't mean to mess up her life."

"You did, and all that talk beforehand just got somebody

else to do this to mess up her life further," Barret stated bluntly. "So, I don't quite understand why you're apologizing for that now, except that I don't think you intended it to go this far."

"No, I didn't. I really didn't."

"Good, then you still need to tell me who it is that you're thinking might have done this."

He shook his head again, refusing. "No, I won't do that. It's a friend."

"Some friend," Barret stated bluntly.

"Yes, I know, but again I don't think the intention was to hurt me."

"Okay then. Go talk to that friend of yours, if you think that's what you want to do, but do it quick. Find that damn bottle and make sure that it's safely handed over to somebody, not empty, just to make sure that we get it, so it can be put away safely."

He nodded and stood up. "I will."

Barret let him walk down the hallway, as Magnus walked over and muttered, "I heard part of that."

Barret quickly filled him in and motioned at Ralph. "Come on. I want to follow him and find out who this friend is. We can't let it go."

"Why not?" Magnus asked.

"Because I'm pretty sure it was a little more than that, and, now that he has been caught out, I don't know if he'll be quite so quick to hand over the bottle because that would imply guilt."

Together, the two men followed Ralph just out of sight, until they got to his room. When they heard the door *click* at the room, they nodded. "Did we check every room?"

"I thought so," Magnus noted. "I know Sydney went

looking into his stuff, but I don't know if she went into the best friend's stuff."

"That's the thing because I suspect it may be the best friend who has the bottle."

When the sound of an argument interrupted their discussion, they both raced over and knocked on the door. When there was no answer, only sounds of a scuffle starting on the other side, they opened the door.

"Stop!" Barret yelled, as he stepped inside.

There was silence, and both men turned to look at him.

Barret fisted hands on his hips. "Now I want that bottle, and I want it now." Then he held out his hand to the roommate.

The friend, whose name he thought was Thomas, looked from Ralph to Barret and back, then wailed, "You told them that I did it?" he cried out.

"No, I didn't," Ralph declared, his tone hard. "But, just as if I figured it out, they did too."

Thomas shook his head. "I don't have the damn bottle, so whatever."

"Are you sure?" Barret asked.

"I don't have it. I never did."

But something in his tone Barret didn't believe. "If you don't have it now, where did you put it?"

Thomas turned and glared at him.

"Look. I can smell vanilla in here," Barret declared. "And obviously we now have to move Ralph out of here just to keep him safe."

At that, his friend looked at Ralph, an almost sorrowful look on his face. "It's probably too late for that."

"What the hell do you mean?" Ralph asked, then his expression changed, and he looked over at Barret, reaching for his throat, before he collapsed to the floor.

Magnus and Barret picked him up and raced him to the medical unit, calling for Sydney.

As she quickly went to work on Ralph, Barret stepped back and looked at Thomas who'd followed them down. "You put it in that damn tea of his, didn't you?"

He turned pale and nodded slowly. "I didn't mean to hurt him though. Everybody said it wouldn't hurt him."

"So then what? You did it a second time? The violent vomiting wasn't enough for you?"

"No, because I figured that …" He stopped, shook his head. "It doesn't matter what I figured."

Barret looked over at him. "Why did you do it a second time?"

He swallowed. "I didn't mean to. I was trying to get rid of the last of the vanilla, and I dumped it into my glass, and I wanted to toss it."

"What glass?" Barret asked.

"I had a licorice tea mix," he explained, "and it had vanilla pods in it. Not like real vanilla. It's just that flavor. And he took it, and he drank it."

"Ah, Jesus." Thomas turned toward Barret.

Barret shook his head. "I don't know if anybody'll believe that."

"I swear to God, I didn't." But there was just that look in his eye, one of fear.

And Barret shook his head again. "You could have just handed the bottle back."

"No, I couldn't have," Thomas argued. "Nobody would have believed me."

"So now we're supposed to believe that it was an accident. You have some brains on you, genius. Use them. Did you think that would save you?"

"It wasn't a full bottle. I just dumped it because I was afraid he wanted to see it, and then he saw the cup and thought I had brought the drink for him, I guess. Before I knew what was happening, he'd grabbed it and tossed it back. He was so furious, so upset and irate. He did it just now, and I didn't know what to do."

"That explains the look on your face when I walked in."

He nodded. "Jesus, I don't want anything to happen to him."

"Neither do I," Barret agreed, "but this is no longer your issue."

And, with that, he turned to see Magnus standing there, waiting.

Magnus motioned at Thomas. "You're coming with me, Thomas. Some investigators need to talk to you."

"Just one now. The other investigator, he's dead, isn't he?"

"Yeah, he is."

"I wouldn't mind getting out of here anyway," he muttered. "I feel like shit now that Ralph drank my tea."

With that, Magnus led him away.

Barret looked over at Sydney and her nurse, as they started pumping Ralph's stomach.

Sydney met his gaze and shook her head, looking concerned. "He's alive, and hopefully I can keep him that way. I did hear what Thomas said. The fact that it was in a tea should be easier on Ralph. He's breathing, and I've got him started on the meds. Thank God you were right there. I think we got him in time." She smiled at Barret. "Now go relax, Barret. You can't do anything here. This is my department now. You did what you could, and you saved him tonight. So, good timing on your part."

He shook his head. "What if I hadn't gone there?" he asked, turning this head and looking at Ralph. "I mean, such a simple thing."

"I know, but, in this case, it all turned out for the better. Now go," she said, pushing him out. "Maybe let Avalon know she's off the hook."

"Right," he said, brightening up.

At that, he turned and raced toward Avalon's room.

DAY 10 NIGHTTIME

AVALON OPENED HER eyes to see Barret squatting down in front of her. "I heard a bunch of commotion," she said, "and I didn't even want to go out and see what was going on. It was cowardly of me, I know, but I was afraid somehow it would be my fault."

"I understand," he said, "and, in this case, it was probably best that you stayed inside."

He explained what had happened, and she just stared at him. "So, his friend did it in order to make me look guilty?"

Barret nodded. "They'd been talking about doing something to get you in trouble, but what Ralph didn't realize was that his friend had gone ahead and taken what they were joking about and made it a reality."

"Jesus."

"He had just poured the rest of the vanilla into his cup of tea to hide it, right before they were having this argument, and Ralph picked it up and chugged it, in anger, I suppose."

She gasped. "Will he be okay?"

"I think so, but he will be pretty sick for a while."

"What about Thomas?" she murmured.

"You know his name?"

"Yeah, sure," she replied. "He's been here for a while, and so have I."

"I know, but it didn't stop him from trying to set you

up."

She shook her head. "I don't even know what to say to that. I mean, was it a practical joke? Was it deliberately to get rid of me? I don't know what to think. I never did anything to hurt either one of them."

"No, but I guess they were just sitting around one day, trying to figure out how to make you pay for not having gone out with them."

"Or for putting their stupid game to an end," she muttered. "I heard from Berry that they had this stupid little notch-post game going. I didn't want to say anything to them, but it's so juvenile and so wrong, particularly in this situation. I, for sure, didn't give Thomas or Ralph the time of day after that."

"Apparently that rejection really hurt," he noted.

"Apparently enough that he wanted to do something to hurt me and get back at me or whatever. So that explains all the snide comments and the poisoning accusations that started from the time I began helping out in the kitchen."

"I think he had demonized you in his mind so much that he believed it was you. Then today, after the two of you spoke, he realized it was Thomas. Afterward, in the chaos and the emotions of their argument, Ralph ended up drinking tainted tea, laced with vanilla."

She nodded. "I don't even know what to say."

"Well," he said, as he started pulling off his clothes, "the good news is you get to sleep in, and the better news is that now I'm off for the night." She sat up and looked at him, and he grinned. "Of course maybe that means you don't want me here anymore."

She opened her arms. "It's been really nice to have you here," she murmured.

"Only nice?" he asked in a teasing tone.

"Oh, I don't want to be too eager," she stated, with an eye roll. "But you are taking a damn long time getting out of those clothes."

He burst out laughing, quickly stripped down to the skin, and winced at the cold. "Will you share any of that heat?"

"Absolutely, as long as you'll share some of yours," she said, with a chuckle.

And, with the two of them quickly wrapped up under the covers, she smiled. "There is something to be said for body heat."

"There's a lot to be said for body heat," he repeated, with a smile, as he wrapped her up in his arms and pulled her close.

She tilted her head back and asked, "Is it really over? At least the poisoning gossip?"

"It is really over," Barret confirmed, with a smile. "Absolutely over."

"Thank God for that. Maybe now, when people find out what really happened, they'll stop looking at me sideways."

"I'm pretty sure they will." Barret grinned.

"So, these poisoning events were what? Just another unfortunate incident to go along with all the others in this very unfortunate scenario going on here?" she asked.

"It is, and it's not a reflection on you. It's not a reflection on the CO. It just is what it is," Barret said. "So, let's take some time to relax and to let it go. When you get up in the morning, you may still have to deal with Steven, but, when he finds out the truth, he'll likely back off too."

"I hope so," she muttered. "I can't say the two of us are getting along very well, and it made me question whether I really wanted to stay in the kitchen."

"Of course," Barret agreed. "Nothing quite like having an asshole on your back all the time."

She laughed. "Isn't that the truth. Did you know that Chef and the CO go way back?"

He nodded. "Yep, I sure did."

"I don't know the whole story, something to do with the brass trying to help Chef keep his son alive. Unfortunately it didn't work in the end, but the CO did everything he could to help Chef's son."

"That kind of devotion is amazing, isn't it?"

"He was there for him when Chef's wife died too," she added, "which was a few years ago now."

"Right, breast cancer, wasn't it?"

"Yeah, it sounds as if both of their wives died of breast cancer," she added.

"It's sad enough that one went that way, but for both of them? That's brutal."

"But it's also a bonding experience, I guess. Not exactly a bond I want to have."

"Nope, I wouldn't think so," he muttered, as his hand drifted up her belly to cup her breast. "Besides, these things are beautiful."

She murmured something indistinguishable, as his hand gently cupped and squeezed, before stroking up above and then down to her ribs and under her shoulder to pull her a little closer into his arms.

She mumbled again, and he whispered, "You don't need to talk."

"I wasn't planning on talking," she said. "I just can't stop making sounds when you do those things. It feels so damn good. It's been a while," she muttered. "I just hadn't realized how much of a while."

"We're not in a rush," he told her. "We've got all night."

"Yeah, but is it only for the night?" she asked, looking at him. "Not that I'm pushing, you know?"

"I figure we're still here for quite a few more weeks, so we should work out any kinks in our relationship by then, don't you think?"

She laughed. "Oh, no doubt, but I tell you what. If you say you want to go for a holiday, and you choose Iceland or something, I'll tell you to go alone."

He burst out laughing. "What? You want to go down to the Caribbean or something like that?"

"No, but I could go for kayaking in Alaska. That would be cool."

"Oh, I like that idea," Barret agreed, looking at her with a smile.

She nodded. "I love kayaking. I love kayak adventure tours too."

He leaned over and kissed her gently. "A woman after my own heart."

"Maybe not so much," she said, with a smile, "but still we've got some things in common."

"We have a lot in common," he stated firmly. "Honesty, morals, ethics, all kinds of things, the stuff that you don't think really matters, until it matters."

She wrapped her arms around his neck, pulled him down for a cuddle, and said, "I think you're talking too much."

He let out a bark of laughter, lowered his head, and kissed her until her toes curled, sending her belly in flight with butterflies.

When he finally lifted his head, she whispered, "Dear

God, you can do that anytime."

"I will. I promise."

He lowered his head again, and, by the time she was more than ready for him, he was still teasing her, until she was crying out in frustration. He slowly entered her body, stretching her wide to accommodate his girth. When he finally started to move, she almost screamed with joy, coming apart in his arms time and time again. He collapsed beside her, exhausted and yet replete.

She murmured something, as she curled up against him.

He whispered, "I didn't hear you."

She smiled. "That's okay. There's time for talking later."

"I just wanted to know what you said," he told her, with a laugh.

"I said it was perfect, absolutely perfect."

He leaned over, gave her a hard kiss. "I don't know about perfect," he hedged. "I think we need to practice a little more. A couple things we could do a little differently."

She placed a finger against his lips and whispered, "We can repeat it as often as you want, but it doesn't change one fact. It was perfect."

EPILOGUE

W HEN WHALEN BROWN woke up the next morning, it was almost noon, but he'd been up half the night, dealing with generator issues. He was now in the kitchen, and he smiled to see both Barret and Avalon come in together. "There they are. The sleepyheads finally decided to show up."

She flushed as she walked over. "Hey. How're you doing?"

"I'm doing fine. Maybe not as good as you two are though."

She laughed. "Nothing quite like finding out what the hell happened to make all the rest of it go away."

"And to make you guys take another step in your personal world."

She flushed and nodded. "Still, it was a good choice."

"It was, indeed. Barret's a good man," Whalen stated.

She smiled and grabbed two cups of coffee and came back. "I got to sleep in for the first time since ... God only knows how long."

"And you won't get it again," Chef announced from the counter. "I told Steven to shift out of the kitchen."

She stared at him in dismay. "But then it's just the two of us again."

He nodded. "Rather have you in my corner any day," he

declared, with a big fat smile. "But somebody new is coming in, and I might shanghai them too."

"Who's that?" Avalon asked.

"Her name is Chrissy, and she's a baker. Although I'm not sure that she wants to be doing any of that work here. Let me just say she was a baker before she signed up."

"So, you'll shanghai her into the kitchen, will you?" Avalon repeated in a teasing manner.

"Absolutely. At least if I can." Chef looked over at Whalen and frowned.

Whalen frowned right back.

Chef laughed. "Do you know her?" Chef asked. "You know her from somewhere?"

Whalen shook his head. "Don't think so. Don't think I know anyone named Chrissy."

"That's because it's Crystal," Chef clarified.

At that, Whalen stiffened, and he nodded. "Yeah."

"I figured you knew her, but I can't remember why."

"That's because we were an item a while back," Whalen shared. "If it's even the same person, which I don't know for sure that it is."

But then a bright and cheerful woman walked into the room. She stopped when she saw Whalen, and the smile fell away. "*You*," she said, almost a bit venomously.

He groaned. "Hi, Crystal."

"It's Chrissy," she stated. "You're the only one who ever called me that."

"Because it's your legal name."

"Doesn't matter. I always preferred Chrissy."

He nodded. "Point taken." He looked over at Chef. "Yeah, I know her." Whalen stood and looked over at her. "How you been?"

"I've been fine. How about you? I mean, after all, the last thing I heard from you was, *I'll see you after work*."

He winced. "Yeah, that was a while ago."

"Five years," she declared, as she crossed her arms over her chest. "I joined up because of you."

He stared at her. "Really?"

She nodded. "I wanted to understand the draw that made you choose this life over me." And, with that, she gave him a fat smile and added, "And now I get to find out for myself."

This concludes Book 4 of Shadow Recon: Barret.
Read about Whalen: Shadow Recon, Book 5

Shadow Recon: Whalen (Book #5)

Deep in the permafrost of the Arctic, a joint task force, comprised of over one dozen countries, comes together to level up their winter skills. A mix of personalities, nationalities, and egos bring out the best—and the worst—as these globally elite men and women work and play together. They rub elbows with hardy locals and a group of scientists gathered close by …

One fatality is almost expected with this training. A second is tough but not a surprise. However, when a third goes missing? It's hard to not be suspicious. When the missing man is connected to one of the elite Maverick team members and is a special friend of Lieutenant Commander Mason Callister? All hell breaks loose …

The last thing Whalen expected when he was called in to investigate the strange events at the arctic training camp was to find his old girlfriend, Chrissy. And as the first meeting showed, she was still angry at him. Not exactly the type of under cover existence he'd been hoping for.

Chrissy joined the military because of Whalen. Not to chase after him but to understand why he did what he did – or more to the point why he'd chosen this life over her. Now older and wiser, but still as in love with him as ever, she finds herself in the kitchen of the camp from hell. She only wants to finish her tour and head back home to open a bakery with her best friend.

Too bad some one at the camp has other ideas. And it's going to take everything the two of them can do to keep both of them safe… Even as others show up dead.

Find Book 5 here!

To find out more visit Dale Mayer's website.

https://geni.us/DMSSRWhalen

Author's Note

Thank you for reading Barret: Shadow Recon, Book 4! If you enjoyed the book, please take a moment and leave a short review.

Dear reader,

I love to hear from readers, and you can contact me at my website: www.dalemayer.com or at my Facebook author page. To be informed of new releases and special offers, sign up for my newsletter or follow me on BookBub. And if you are interested in joining Dale Mayer's Reader Group, here is the Facebook sign up page.
http://geni.us/DaleMayerFBGroup

Cheers,
Dale Mayer

About the Author

Dale Mayer is a *USA Today* best-selling author, best known for her SEALs military romances, her Psychic Visions series, and her Lovely Lethal Garden cozy series. Her contemporary romances are raw and full of passion and emotion (Broken But … Mending, Hathaway House series). Her thrillers will keep you guessing (Kate Morgan, By Death series), and her romantic comedies will keep you giggling (*It's a Dog's Life*, a stand-alone novella; and the Broken Protocols series, starring Charming Marvin, the cat).

Dale honors the stories that come to her—and some of them are crazy, break all the rules and cross multiple genres!

To go with her fiction, she also writes nonfiction in many different fields, with books available on résumé writing, companion gardening, and the US mortgage system. All her books are available in print and ebook format.

Connect with Dale Mayer Online

Dale's Website – www.dalemayer.com
Twitter – @DaleMayer
Facebook Page – geni.us/DaleMayerFBFanPage
Facebook Group – geni.us/DaleMayerFBGroup
BookBub – geni.us/DaleMayerBookbub
Instagram – geni.us/DaleMayerInstagram
Goodreads – geni.us/DaleMayerGoodreads
Newsletter – geni.us/DaleNews

Also by Dale Mayer

Published Adult Books:

Shadow Recon

Magnus, Book 1
Rogan, Book 2
Egan, Book 3
Barret, Book 4
Whalen, Book 5
Nikolai, Book 6

Bullard's Battle

Ryland's Reach, Book 1
Cain's Cross, Book 2
Eton's Escape, Book 3
Garret's Gambit, Book 4
Kano's Keep, Book 5
Fallon's Flaw, Book 6
Quinn's Quest, Book 7
Bullard's Beauty, Book 8
Bullard's Best, Book 9
Bullard's Battle, Books 1–2
Bullard's Battle, Books 3–4
Bullard's Battle, Books 5–6
Bullard's Battle, Books 7–8

Terkel's Team

Damon's Deal, Book 1
Wade's War, Book 2
Gage's Goal, Book 3
Calum's Contact, Book 4
Rick's Road, Book 5
Scott's Summit, Book 6
Brody's Beast, Book 7
Terkel's Twist, Book 8
Terkel's Triumph, Book 9

Terk's Guardians

Radar, Book 1
Legend, Book 2

Kate Morgan

Simon Says... Hide, Book 1
Simon Says... Jump, Book 2
Simon Says... Ride, Book 3
Simon Says... Scream, Book 4
Simon Says... Run, Book 5
Simon Says... Walk, Book 6
Simon Says... Forgive, Book 7

Hathaway House

Aaron, Book 1
Brock, Book 2
Cole, Book 3
Denton, Book 4
Elliot, Book 5
Finn, Book 6
Gregory, Book 7

Heath, Book 8
Iain, Book 9
Jaden, Book 10
Keith, Book 11
Lance, Book 12
Melissa, Book 13
Nash, Book 14
Owen, Book 15
Percy, Book 16
Quinton, Book 17
Ryatt, Book 18
Spencer, Book 19
Timothy, Book 20
Urban, Book 21
Hathaway House, Books 1–3
Hathaway House, Books 4–6
Hathaway House, Books 7–9

The K9 Files

Ethan, Book 1
Pierce, Book 2
Zane, Book 3
Blaze, Book 4
Lucas, Book 5
Parker, Book 6
Carter, Book 7
Weston, Book 8
Greyson, Book 9
Rowan, Book 10
Caleb, Book 11
Kurt, Book 12
Tucker, Book 13

Harley, Book 14
Kyron, Book 15
Jenner, Book 16
Rhys, Book 17
Landon, Book 18
Harper, Book 19
Kascius, Book 20
Declan, Book 21
The K9 Files, Books 1–2
The K9 Files, Books 3–4
The K9 Files, Books 5–6
The K9 Files, Books 7–8
The K9 Files, Books 9–10
The K9 Files, Books 11–12

Lovely Lethal Gardens
Arsenic in the Azaleas, Book 1
Bones in the Begonias, Book 2
Corpse in the Carnations, Book 3
Daggers in the Dahlias, Book 4
Evidence in the Echinacea, Book 5
Footprints in the Ferns, Book 6
Gun in the Gardenias, Book 7
Handcuffs in the Heather, Book 8
Ice Pick in the Ivy, Book 9
Jewels in the Juniper, Book 10
Killer in the Kiwis, Book 11
Lifeless in the Lilies, Book 12
Murder in the Marigolds, Book 13
Nabbed in the Nasturtiums, Book 14
Offed in the Orchids, Book 15
Poison in the Pansies, Book 16

Psychic Visions Series

What If…
Talking Bones
String of Tears
Inked Forever
Insanity
Psychic Visions Books 1–3
Psychic Visions Books 4–6
Psychic Visions Books 7–9

By Death Series
Touched by Death
Haunted by Death
Chilled by Death
By Death Books 1–3

Broken Protocols – Romantic Comedy Series
Cat's Meow
Cat's Pajamas
Cat's Cradle
Cat's Claus
Broken Protocols 1-4

Broken and… Mending
Skin
Scars
Scales (of Justice)
Broken but… Mending 1-3

Glory
Genesis
Tori
Celeste
Glory Trilogy

Biker Blues

Morgan: Biker Blues, Volume 1
Cash: Biker Blues, Volume 2

SEALs of Honor

Mason: SEALs of Honor, Book 1
Hawk: SEALs of Honor, Book 2
Dane: SEALs of Honor, Book 3
Swede: SEALs of Honor, Book 4
Shadow: SEALs of Honor, Book 5
Cooper: SEALs of Honor, Book 6
Markus: SEALs of Honor, Book 7
Evan: SEALs of Honor, Book 8
Mason's Wish: SEALs of Honor, Book 9
Chase: SEALs of Honor, Book 10
Brett: SEALs of Honor, Book 11
Devlin: SEALs of Honor, Book 12
Easton: SEALs of Honor, Book 13
Ryder: SEALs of Honor, Book 14
Macklin: SEALs of Honor, Book 15
Corey: SEALs of Honor, Book 16
Warrick: SEALs of Honor, Book 17
Tanner: SEALs of Honor, Book 18
Jackson: SEALs of Honor, Book 19
Kanen: SEALs of Honor, Book 20
Nelson: SEALs of Honor, Book 21
Taylor: SEALs of Honor, Book 22
Colton: SEALs of Honor, Book 23
Troy: SEALs of Honor, Book 24
Axel: SEALs of Honor, Book 25
Baylor: SEALs of Honor, Book 26
Hudson: SEALs of Honor, Book 27

Lachlan: SEALs of Honor, Book 28

Paxton: SEALs of Honor, Book 29

Bronson: SEALs of Honor, Book 30

Hale: SEALs of Honor, Book 31

SEALs of Honor, Books 1–3

SEALs of Honor, Books 4–6

SEALs of Honor, Books 7–10

SEALs of Honor, Books 11–13

SEALs of Honor, Books 14–16

SEALs of Honor, Books 17–19

SEALs of Honor, Books 20–22

SEALs of Honor, Books 23–25

Heroes for Hire

Levi's Legend: Heroes for Hire, Book 1

Stone's Surrender: Heroes for Hire, Book 2

Merk's Mistake: Heroes for Hire, Book 3

Rhodes's Reward: Heroes for Hire, Book 4

Flynn's Firecracker: Heroes for Hire, Book 5

Logan's Light: Heroes for Hire, Book 6

Harrison's Heart: Heroes for Hire, Book 7

Saul's Sweetheart: Heroes for Hire, Book 8

Dakota's Delight: Heroes for Hire, Book 9

Tyson's Treasure: Heroes for Hire, Book 10

Jace's Jewel: Heroes for Hire, Book 11

Rory's Rose: Heroes for Hire, Book 12

Brandon's Bliss: Heroes for Hire, Book 13

Liam's Lily: Heroes for Hire, Book 14

North's Nikki: Heroes for Hire, Book 15

Anders's Angel: Heroes for Hire, Book 16

Reyes's Raina: Heroes for Hire, Book 17

Dezi's Diamond: Heroes for Hire, Book 18

SEALs of Steel

The Mavericks

Kerrick, Book 1
Griffin, Book 2
Jax, Book 3
Beau, Book 4
Asher, Book 5
Ryker, Book 6
Miles, Book 7
Nico, Book 8
Keane, Book 9
Lennox, Book 10
Gavin, Book 11
Shane, Book 12
Diesel, Book 13
Jerricho, Book 14
Killian, Book 15
Hatch, Book 16
Corbin, Book 17
Aiden, Book 18
The Mavericks, Books 1–2
The Mavericks, Books 3–4
The Mavericks, Books 5–6
The Mavericks, Books 7–8
The Mavericks, Books 9–10
The Mavericks, Books 11–12

Standalone Novellas

It's a Dog's Life
Riana's Revenge
Second Chances

Published Young Adult Books:

Family Blood Ties Series

Vampire in Denial
Vampire in Distress
Vampire in Design
Vampire in Deceit
Vampire in Defiance
Vampire in Conflict
Vampire in Chaos
Vampire in Crisis
Vampire in Control
Vampire in Charge
Family Blood Ties Set 1–3
Family Blood Ties Set 1–5
Family Blood Ties Set 4–6
Family Blood Ties Set 7–9
Sian's Solution, A Family Blood Ties Series Prequel
    Novelette

Design series

Dangerous Designs
Deadly Designs
Darkest Designs
Design Series Trilogy

Standalone

In Cassie's Corner
Gem Stone (a Gemma Stone Mystery)
Time Thieves

Published Non-Fiction Books:

Career Essentials

Career Essentials: The Résumé
Career Essentials: The Cover Letter
Career Essentials: The Interview
Career Essentials: 3 in 1